Two Doors Down

TWO DOORS DOWN

MARY HARGREAVES

JOFFE BOOKS

Joffe Books, London
www.joffebooks.com

First published in Great Britain in 2024

Cover art by Jarmila Takač

ISBN: 978-1-83526-730-1

*For Nora, whom I would allow to distract me from my writing
for ever and ever and ever*

CHAPTER 1

Eve

'She was a total psycho, I promise you,' Robert leans over the table conspiratorially. 'It was a trip to Marbella, for fuck's sake. *Marbella.* You'd have thought I'd said I was going to Bangkok, the way she reacted.'

He laughs and kicks me lightly under the table, as though we're in this together.

'How weird.' I prop my chin up with my hand, because otherwise my head will fall off from boredom. 'It almost sounds like she didn't trust you.'

'Exactly!' Robert roars and sloshes his pint in the general direction of his mouth. 'Was it my fault that her ex-boyfriend cheated on her? No, but she did a brilliant job of making me feel like it was. It really gets on my tits when women blame every man on the planet for something that *one* of us did, you know?' He pouts.

'It's a real burden for you all, I'm sure.'

'I mean, look,' he looks left, and then right, and then directly into my soul, 'Everyone's done it once or twice, right? We're all human.'

I lean forward and grab his wrist. 'But never in *Marbella*,' I gasp.

He blinks, then frowns and leans back. 'No. Well, I mean . . . wait, are you joking?'

I sigh quietly. 'Remind me again what you do?' I swirl the dregs of gin around my glass as Robert begins the speech I've heard three times already but haven't yet actually listened to. It's something to do with investment banking, I think; that or civil engineering. Or was that Danny, from last week? Who cares, really.

Robert is an online dating conquest; one I found on the Tryst app precisely eight hours ago. His main picture was one of him on a donkey at Blackpool beach, wearing a sombrero, some speedos and nothing else. He had a can of Red Stripe in his hand. More than eight hours between discovery and meeting would have allowed for too much of a reality-check on my part, and I haven't got the time for second guessing. I'd just like to get the formalities over with and skip to the good part.

I inspect his biceps as he talks. Robert's biceps are his personality, which is fine by me. He catches me looking and tenses, his voice squeaking slightly with the effort of speaking and peacocking at the same time. I tune back in. '. . . brought in over a million for the company last year, actually. Management presented me with a plaque and everything.' He laughs, as if this is all very embarrassing, but something tells me he's got it hung above the mantelpiece at home. 'Got promoted off the back of that one big deal, actually . . .'

We're getting into it now, I can feel it. 'Congratulations.'

'Thanks.' He smiles self-deprecatingly.

Leave it there, Robert.

'Thirty-two to fifty k, just like that.' He snaps his fingers.

Aaaaand there it is: Robert's annual salary. Like a slightly less socially-unacceptable dick pic, I did not ask for it, but it has been bestowed upon me regardless.

My phone starts ringing and I swoop into my bag to retrieve it. Robert's chest deflates; he's shown his top card at the wrong moment.

It's Jess. 9 p.m. on the dot, regular as clockwork.

'I'm sorry, I have to get this.' I flash Robert my most apologetic face and swipe across to answer. 'Hello?'

'My nan's dead, my dog's run away or my boyfriend's left me. Pick one.' Jess drawls, and then giggles as she scuffles with something in the background. '*Stop* it, Johnny!'

I weigh up my options in my head. I'm presenting first thing tomorrow morning, and there are still a few figures I need to double-check. Also, I'm having a genuine car crash of an evening, and personality-wise, Robert is a horror of a man. It's a no-brainer.

'Glad everything's OK, you had me worried there for a second!' I chirp back to Jess.

She cackles. 'You tart.'

'Speak soon, bye!' I put the phone down and turn back to Robert, who is not-so-subtly tugging his shirt a little lower to reveal the top of a rather firm pec. The moment for small-talk pretence is over. It's time for us to both get what we came here for. 'Shall we go back to yours, then?'

CHAPTER 2

Eve

I wake up as the light filters through Robert's standard-is-sue-IKEA bachelor blinds. I am far too hot. The heatwave we've been promised is finally taking root, and Robert's naked chest is stuck to my back like cling film. His hand is clasped around my boob, like it's a port in a storm.

I prise his fingers off me and peel myself away, sliding quietly from under the duvet. My clothes are in a pile in the corner, and I bundle them up, hunting for my handbag. I dig through the shadows of unwashed socks and damp towels before I find it, tossed atop a half-folded exercise mat.

I fumble with the door to Robert's ensuite and step inside, curling my hand back through the gap to turn the light on so I don't wake him up. The shower is big and completely filthy, with conditioner-matted hairs — blonde, I note, and clearly not belonging to Robert and his chestnut short-back-and-sides — clinging to the glass screen. I step inside gingerly, scrubbing myself, and then use last night's clothes to pat myself dry. In the zipped area of my work bag is a fresh top, skirt and a pair of knickers and tights. I dress quickly, slick my hair into a tidy bun and then deftly swipe on some mascara and concealer. A quick spray of Robert's deodorant and I'm ready.

I'm about to step back into the bedroom when I hear the mattress creak. I freeze. The sound stops, but I can't take any chances, so I sit down on the toilet lid and pull out my laptop, spending twenty minutes going over this morning's numbers. When the silence has dragged on long enough, and my presentation is up to date, I unlock the door, tiptoe past Robert's bare arse, and leave.

* * *

'Really glad the sunflower thing worked so well, Eve.' One of the marketing assistants says after I've wrapped up my briefing. I step aside to let people pass.

'Me too.' I smile. 'It was a great idea, keep them coming.'

She nods and I leave, emerging into the open-plan office area and checking my watch. Three hours, that meeting took. We could have done it in two had Brenda spent less time talking about her broken drainpipe and more time chairing like she was supposed to. All in all, though, it was a success.

I let myself into my office and scan through my Outlook calendar, checking for any gaps. There's one between 8 p.m. and 9 p.m. this evening, so I enter 'Exercise bike' and 'Review expo visuals' to fill up the slot. I pull out my paper calendar and copy the entries in there, too, using yellow pen for 'extracurricular'.

A shriek from beyond my office door catches my attention, and I look through the glass wall to see Jess launching herself at Kirsty, who is trying to direct a weekly briefing. I count to three before there's a knock on the door.

'Eve?' Brenda slinks in, her boggling eyes trained on the wall behind me. 'I don't want to be a party pooper, but this is the third time now.'

'I know, Brenda. I'll have a word.'

'I love the open culture of this office as much as the next person, but if your friend wants to keep visiting she really is going to have to tone it down a bit.'

'I'll talk to her, don't worry.'

'It'd be a shame for everybody to lose their privileges because of one person.'

I stand up and walk around my desk, sticking my head out of the door. 'Jess, Kirsty's in the middle of something. Come in here.'

Jess releases Kirsty, who returns to her meeting, and bumbles over to the door, her dreadlocks swinging. 'Hey! How was last night, you minx?'

Brenda's eyes bulge.

'Good chat, Brenda, thank you. I'll deal with it.' I begin shutting the door and she shuffles backwards until she is officially out of the room, and the conversation.

'Jess, you're making everyone hate me.' I sink into my chair. 'Can you tone the screeching down a bit?'

'Shit, sorry.' She covers her mouth with her hand. 'Was I really loud?'

'A bit. Just come straight in here next time.'

'Alright.' She rustles around in her tote bag and produces two steaming boxes of noodles. 'How *was* last night, anyway?'

I glance at the door; Brenda is still silhouetted behind it. 'I'll tell you in a bit. How's Johnny?'

Johnny is Jess's latest 'boyfriend'. About six months ago, she attended a yoga convention with work and met a throuple who made such an impression on her that she decided to go polyamorous. It's been a tumultuous time.

'OK, I think . . .' She tucks one leg underneath her and her Birkenstock leaves a brown skid across the white leather of the chair. 'He's been seeing *her* a lot.'

'His girlfriend?'

She rips the lid of her noodles off with force. '*I'm* his girlfriend, Eve.'

'Wasn't she his girlfriend first?'

'If you want to get technical about it, then yes, I suppose so.' She pouts into her lunch and I ready myself. Jess can only do anger for about eight seconds before she implodes.

Her eyes fill. 'It's just like, am I not enough? What am I missing?'

'Nothing, there's *nothing* wrong with you.' I fork a piece of broccoli and blow on it. 'You're totally fine.'

'Then why does he keep running back to her?'

I chew slowly, taking my time before I reply. 'It's not for you, Jess.'

'What isn't? Johnny?'

'Polyamory.'

'Yes it is!' She swipes a tear from her cheek. 'Sharing love is the like, essence of who I am. It's the most spiritual thing you can imagine.'

I'm saved from responding by the arrival of Kirsty, who perches on the edge of my desk and starts demolishing a salad. 'What are we talking about?'

Kirsty is my second-in-command and work bestie. Since Jess visits for lunch a few days a week, they've become quite close, and with my office serving as a multi-function oasis for bitchy catch-ups and solitary desk lunches, I haven't seen the inside of the staff canteen for over a year now.

'Jess is having some issues with Johnny.' I raise my eyebrows.

'It's not *me* who's having issues, it's him and that weasel he keeps running back to.'

'Weasel?' Kirsty splutters. 'Aren't you guys supposed to all be in a relationship together?'

'And how would that work when I'm straight?' Jess looks at Kirsty like she's lost the plot.

'But you said that *sharing love* was what—'

'I know what I said!' Jess slaps her fork down, tears forming in her eyes again. 'It's very complicated.'

Kirsty widens her eyes at me, and I shrug. There is no getting through to Jess. My phone vibrates on the table.

Robert: *Did u just leave????*

I sigh, and tap back a response.

Me: *I left four hours ago*

Robert: *Nice of u 2 say bye*

Me: *Didn't want to wake you*

Robert: *Y u being cold??*

Me: *Look, I had a nice time, but I think we should leave it here*

Robert: *WTF? Why?*

Me: *I'm not in the market for a relationship*

Me: *Plus, we don't have much in common*

Me: *Also, I hate Marbella*

Robert: *U said you'd never been 2 Marbella??*

Me: *I haven't*

Robert: *WTF????*

'Who is it? Is it the guy from last night?' Jess leans over the desk and peers at my screen. Kirsty reaches across and plucks the phone from my hand, her fork wedged in her mouth. She scans through our conversation.

'I'd give you my usual speech about being picky, but this one really does seem quite dry.'

'Yeah, but you never know!' Jess yanks the phone from her hand and scrolls through. 'He could just be shy? Or maybe you just need to get to know him more, see what he's really like under the bravado.'

'Am I losing my mind?' I ask. 'We literally have this conversation every week. I'm not looking for a boyfriend, so what does it matter?'

'But what if you're binning off someone really incredible?!' Jess gawps at me.

'I don't care if I'm binning off Tom fucking Hardy, Jess, I'm not interested,' I snap.

'He seems to really like you.' Kirsty sticks her bottom lip out at me. 'Meanie.'

My phone vibrates in Jess's hand. 'Oh, he's messaged again!' She reads it. It vibrates again. '*Oh.*'

'What? What does it say?' Kirsty takes the phone back. It vibrates once more. I eat my noodles. 'Oh, Jesus. What a complete arsehole.'

I snatch the phone out of her hand and read what he's written.

Robert: *Giving me the silent treatment now??*

Robert: *Gud luck getting anyone else 2 shag u*

Robert: *U look like a cauliflower anyway wouldn't touch u with a bargepole*

I smile sweetly. 'You're right, guys. I should *definitely* give him a chance.'

CHAPTER 3

Eve

'What about Jared, the new guy?' Kirsty waves her champagne flute in the direction of the bar, where a huddle of developers are talking and picking at a bowl of wasabi peanuts.

'What about more champagne?' I reach out to grab a full glass from a passing waiter's tray and lift it to my lips.

'You're impossible.' Kirsty smiles. 'But fine, I get it. No men unless they're precisely picked by you and your crappy Tryst metrics.'

'Thank you.' I tap my glass against hers. 'Look, here comes the man of the hour.'

Kirsty turns as Dev Kalhora strides into the room, a charming grin plastered across his face. Dev is Head of Marketing at our company, Florina, the biggest floristry retailer in the UK.

'I see Eleanor's ready to pop,' Kirsty comments, her eyes drifting towards Dev's wife, who sits prettily on a velvet chair, her gigantic bump at odds with her tiny frame.

'Still another month to go yet,' I say. 'Twins show more, apparently.'

'Well, they would, being literally two times the size.' Kirsty steps back as Graham, the IT manager, worms his way into our huddle.

'Evening, girls.' He's wearing old-fashioned braces and has his hair slicked back behind his ears. There's something vaguely attractive about Graham, until he opens his mouth.

'We're not twelve, Graham.' I take another sip of my champagne.

'Stop flirting with me, Eve, it's unprofessional.' He winks at me and I roll my eyes.

'What's the news on our new friend Jared?' Kirsty nods towards the bar again.

'Why, are you interested?' Graham asks.

'I'm married, Graham.'

'Well, it can't be our Evie here. Eyes for no man unless they're made of protein powder.'

I roll my eyes again. 'Fuck off, Graham.'

Kirsty interrupts our usual back and forth, pointing over our shoulders. 'Oh look, Brenda's been at the strawberry daiquiris again.'

We turn around. Brenda is wearing a floor-length, skin-tight pink dress, covered in black roses. She's got one leg up on the chair of Florina's CEO, Michael Peters, and is looming over him provocatively.

'God, poor Michael. It's always him, isn't it?' My hand hangs by my side, and I feel Graham brush my wrist with his fingers as he speaks. I pull away, annoyed at myself for the small pang of desire I feel.

I carry on watching Brenda. She's worked at Florina since before I was born, and is a walking contradiction. She's married to a vicar, reads dirty novels in the canteen, has yet to make eye contact with a single one of her colleagues and hits on our CEO at every function. He's actually stopped coming to as many, it's become that predictable.

A chafing screech comes from the microphone at the front of the room, and I reluctantly turn away from the bi-annual

Brenda show. Dev has mounted the stage, and is now beaming down at us, his perfect, eye-wateringly expensive teeth fluorescent under the artificial lights.

'Hello, everyone.' He raises his hand, and a cheer goes around the room. 'Thank you all for coming. I'm aware that this seems rather grandiose for a twelve-month paternity leave send-off, but after six years at Florina you guys feel like family, and it didn't feel right to leave for so long without having some kind of celebration.'

'Wonder what I'd get if I got myself knocked up,' Kirsty mutters beside me. 'A Papa John's spread in Meeting Room One?'

We both glance over to Eleanor, who is staring at Dev adoringly. Then my eye is caught by Brenda again, who is still draped over Michael's lap, holding the stem of a maraschino cherry between two sticky fingers.

'Do you think he's going to announce his cover?' Graham murmurs in my ear, and the smell of him makes my legs ache.

'No,' I say, but I'm not sure. My heart picks up pace a little. Would he? Surely not. Not here, in front of everybody?

'Are you excited?' Kirsty whispers, joining in our conversation.

'He won't do it here!' I nudge them both. 'Shut up.'

'We've got an exciting year ahead of us,' Dev continues, 'and I'm sad that I won't be able to share it with you all. But rest assured that the person filling in for me will bring just as much brilliance and originality to the table as I do.' He winks, and laughter ripples around the room. I brace myself. If he does do it here, what will I do? I rehearse a quick speech in my head, in case he asks me up onto the stage. I pat my hair down.

'So he *is* going to announce it.' Graham looks at me from the corner of his eye, smirking.

'No! I don't know,' I hiss.

'Right, I think I've bored you all enough now,' Dev blesses us with one of his crinkle-eyed smiles, a poster boy for sexy, laid-back fathers-to-be. 'I'll let you get back to your evenings; enjoy the free bar!'

He steps down from the stage, and my heart sinks.

Kirsty turns to me. 'Not today, then.'

'Not today.' I shake my head. 'He'll probably do it in private, one-on-one.'

'Yeah.' She smiles and nudges me softly. 'A preliminary congratulations, anyway.'

I smile back. There'll be plenty of time for celebrating later. It's only four weeks until Dev leaves, so it can't be that long until I find out. I run through his roles and responsibilities in my mind; as Head of Digital Marketing, and with an impressive advertising background, it's been obvious from the start that I'd be taking over for him once he went off on paternity leave. I've waited five months for the formal announcement; I can wait a few more weeks.

'Ladies!' Brenda has somehow broken into our circle and is leaning on Graham for support. 'What a night, eh?'

'It's been a wild one, Brenda.' Graham glances at the clock above the bar. It's only nine o'clock.

'Don't suppose I'll see as much of you once you're running ship,' she slurs, her eyes drifting towards me.

'Of course you will; I'll only be next door.'

Her eyes almost meet mine for a second, and then she sinks into one of the chairs behind us and lets her head hit the table with a soft thud.

'Night night.' Graham picks up a napkin and places it uselessly across her shoulders. 'Let's leave her to sleep it off a bit, eh?'

He gives me a look, a slight arch of his eyebrow, and I turn to Kirsty quickly. 'I need the bathroom, you coming?'

'Sure.'

We make our way through the tables of people, laughing and nudging each other as long-awaited romances and arguments play out in front of us, brought to light by free alcohol. Jim and Molly from accounting are finally having it out over her habit of scrambling eggs in the office microwave; Chris and Pete from sales are necking by the kitchen door. We're sharing the room with another office party — the space half-heartedly partitioned with flimsy poster boards — and people are filtering through to cross-pollinate, inspecting the wares on the other side. Through the gap I see a table in disarray with bags and coats and empty glasses, most of its occupants dancing a few metres away, save a bearded guy and a red-faced man leaning drunkenly towards him to shout above the music.

'Look at those two.' Kirsty points towards the front, where Dev is stroking Eleanor's stomach lovingly. We skirt into the ladies' toilets and she jumps up onto the sink. 'He's really got it all, hasn't he?'

'Well, he worked hard for it.' I reapply my lipstick in the mirror.

'We're all working hard.'

I snap the cap back onto my lipstick and look at her. 'Of course we are. I guess some of us just work even harder than others.' I was thinking of some of the newer marketing staff, who vie for promotions but don't put in the work that merits them. But the way Kirsty's looking at me, I can tell she's taken it the wrong way.

'I'm in the office 'til seven most nights,' she says forcefully.

'God, no, Kirst, I didn't mean *you*. You're a total powerhouse.'

'Mmm.'

'What's up?' I meet her eye through the reflection in the mirror.

'Nothing.' She looks away and starts turning the tap on and off. 'I can't believe you'll be my boss soon.'

I laugh. 'I'm already your boss.'

This isn't ground we usually cover — Kirsty and I were a dual hire, coming in at the same level on the same day. She'd always seemed content to do her job while also enjoying everything outside of it. When I got promoted a couple of years ago, there was no bad blood between us; I'd forced my way onto the next rung, while she'd lived a varied, jam-packed life and stayed where she was. A steady, healthy relationship, several sports-club memberships and a fierce closeness with her family are testament to where her priorities lie. Since I

14

took over as manager, she's really knuckled down and the department is doing better than it ever has. I know it's mostly because of how brilliantly we work together, how good our rapport is. How well I manage her, if I'm being completely honest.

'Yeah, yeah, I know, but I mean *really* my boss. Do you think things will change?'

'What do you mean?'

'The shift in the power dynamic. Do you reckon we'll still be as close?'

I stop inspecting my fringe and turn to face her. 'Of course we will. Why wouldn't we be?'

She shrugs. 'I don't know. When one of you gets higher than the other . . .'

'I'm already higher than you,' I say again, and then realise how pretentious it sounds. 'I mean, we're already at different levels, and we're totally fine.'

'Yeah.' She gives me a funny smile, but before I can decode it she's leaning in for a hug. 'I hope you remember that.'

I pull away, laughing. 'Where has this come from?'

She shakes her head, throwing her hands in the air. 'Oh, god, ignore me. It's the champagne. Shall we go back out?'

We emerge back into the function room, and my eyes immediately seek Graham. I shouldn't, I shouldn't. Work and pleasure should not be combined, I know that. I tell myself every time. But it's easy, familiar. We've done this dance a thousand times.

'Whoops,' Kirsty cackles, and I follow her eyeline. 'Looks like we've got some serious mixing going on.'

Graham is wrapped around someone I don't recognise: a pretty, blonde girl in her early twenties. She must be from the party next door. Frustration blooms in my chest. 'Typical.' I flash Kirsty a smile. Graham pulls away from the girl, before leaning back down to whisper in her ear. As he brushes her hair to the side, he looks up, and his eyes lock with mine.

I pull my bag up higher on my shoulder. 'Shall we head off? I've got some work to do.'

CHAPTER 4

Adam

Whoever decided that sharing function rooms was a good idea must be raking it in.

It only took an hour of the free bar for people to start mingling, and now the tab's used up, nobody wants to go home. Janie, Katie's ward manager, would usually have left by now, but she's deep in conversation with a smart-looking middle-aged guy, one of the first to slide through the partition before it became a gaping walkway, and is hammering the bar like her life depends on it.

I turn away from people-watching and back to my table. Conversation is excited and screechy over the music; everyone is hyped up after the awards and gossip is floating on the air. Most people have abandoned their seats and are dancing, grabbing each other's hands and throwing their heads back to scream choruses at the panelled ceiling. I love working for myself, but if there's one thing I miss, it's the social life.

I catch Katie's eye across the makeshift dance floor and smile. She looks beautiful tonight in a long, black dress and bright red lipstick. Post-box colour, I'd say, but I'd probably get an eye-roll for it. It's most likely called 'vixen' or 'vampire' or 'blood of twenty virgins', or something. Katie meets my gaze and looks away quickly.

'How long have you two been together?' The red-faced guy sitting next to me leans over and shouts into my ear. Jeremy? Dominic? God, what's his name?

'Six years!' I hold up my fingers in case he can't hear me.

He leans back in his chair and puffs out his cheeks. 'Jesus, that's a stretch, isn't it? Probably get less for mugging someone.'

'Yeah, probably, but then you'd be a mugger,' I reply.

'You're single, then?'

'Nah, got a missus.'

'Ah, how long?'

'Six months, and she's already reining me in.' He raises his eyebrows at me, as if I know what he means. I don't.

'What do you mean?'

'You know, telling me I can't go here, can't go there, got to stay home and watch films and all that bollocks.' He's beyond pissed, and he takes another slurp of his beer.

'Why don't you break up with her, then?' I ask.

He looks at me. 'You're funny, you are.' His gaze travels across the room and lands on a couple just beyond the partition; a guy in his early thirties from the company next door, and one of Katie's colleagues, another nurse whose name I can't remember. 'Look at them, there. Don't you miss it?'

I look at them. They're all over each other, close whispers and stroking arms. 'I think if you're missing that, you're probably in the wrong relationship.'

My phone starts buzzing across the table, so I reach for it. *Chloe*. I reject the call, switch my phone to silent and bury it in my pocket.

When I look up, the man is staring at me, his eyes bloodshot. 'We *were* like that, at the start.'

It takes me a second to remember what we were talking about. 'We all are. You can be like that with anybody, in the beginning.' I look around for Katie, to see if she'll save me, but she's disappeared.

'What's the general expiry date, do you reckon?'

I turn back to him. 'What, on a relationship?'

'No, on that fun bit before it all turns shit.'

'Depends.' I look over at the couple again. 'If it's the right person, it'll morph into a different kind of fun.'

The kind of fun Katie and I have, I think. Easy Sunday mornings and walks into town. No second guessing, just knowing. Closeness. Sixth senses. Showering together replaced with showering while the other person brushes their teeth. Never going to bed alone. Favourite films and surprise discoveries.

Dominic-or-maybe-Jeremy snorts. 'Yeah, alright, mate.'

Katie appears by my side and I wrap my arm around her waist.

'Shall we go?' She riffles through her handbag, turning her body, and my hand slips from her side.

'Sure.'

Katie nods at Dominic-not-Jeremy. 'See you on Monday, Dom.'

'See you.' He goes back to staring into his pint, and we shout our goodbyes to the rest of the table before heading for the exit.

'God, he was a total nightmare,' I say, skirting around two girls leaving at the same time as us.

'Who, Dom? He's alright.'

'I feel sorry for his girlfriend.'

'Oh, it's fine, she's a bit of a slut anyway.'

'Wow.' I stop walking and laugh, looking at her. 'When did you get so judgy?'

She won't meet my gaze. 'It's not *judgy*, Adam, they both cheat on each other all the time.'

We keep walking out onto Oxford Road, and I wave my arm for a taxi. One rolls up but one of the girls we overtook a moment ago strides purposefully to the door and gets inside before I can even open my mouth. I turn back to Katie. 'Did you have a good night?'

'Yeah, it was nice.' She smiles. 'You?'

'It was good to be out at a work event.' I grin at her, feeling a sudden pang of gratitude for just having her here, with me, asking about my evening. 'I never thought I'd say it, but I do miss them.'

'Hmm.' She checks her phone. 'Should I get an Uber?'

I let the knowledge that she isn't listening to me slip away. She's had a long week, and it's been a long evening. 'Are there any? It's busy.'

She's tapping on her phone, presumably sourcing a taxi, so I move back to the street, flagging black cabs as they approach from the distance and letting my hand drop as they near with their lights off.

'Have you found one?' I call over my shoulder, but she doesn't reply, so I pull my phone out and check the Uber app. There are six cars hovering around the building, each a one-minute drive away. 'There are loads, shall I order one?'

Katie still isn't listening, so I walk back and reach out my hand to touch her shoulder. She jumps and locks her phone, slipping it into her bag. 'Sorry, I was just telling Janie that we left. Didn't manage to catch her.'

'Shall I order one of these?' I tilt my screen towards her and she nods.

Three minutes later we are sitting in the back of an unnecessarily large minivan, weaving through the heavy Manchester traffic towards home. I gaze out of the window at the city lights and drunk Saturday nighters, feeling a light warmth spreading through me. Aside from being collared by Dom, it was a good night. Katie won the Improving Personal Care Award for her trust, and seeing her up there collecting her trophy filled me with so much pride I thought I might cry. She works ridiculously long shifts, and having a rare night out together punctuated with her being rewarded for her efforts felt significant.

I undo my seatbelt and shift over to her, wrapping my arm around her shoulder. 'Congratulations,' I murmur into her hair.

'Stop it, Adam.' She bats me away, turning to look out of the window. 'I'm tired.'

I pull back. 'Everything OK?'

'I'm fine. I've just had a long day, and you're drunk.'

'I'm not drunk.' I had three beers over the course of the evening, and if anything, I just feel a bit wiped.

'Just leave it.'

The car pulls up outside our front door and Katie gets out. I thank the driver and follow her, through the hallway where she kicks off her shoes and into the kitchen.

'Do you want tea?' I ask, as she pours a glass of water from the tap and glugs it thirstily.

'I'm going to bed.' She puts the glass down on the side heavily and brushes past me, kissing me lightly on the cheek. 'Night.'

I watch her leave, her dress trailing on the floor without the added height of her heels, and wonder what I've done.

CHAPTER 5

Eve

It's the morning after Dev's party, and I am annoyed with myself for being annoyed about Graham.

In the cold, clear light of day, I feel nothing but aggravation towards him. Every single time we go out, he does this to me. In fact, he does it even when we're *not* out, just in the office. It's totally my fault, obviously; there's a weird dynamic between us and I encourage the flirting. It's not like he's shooting his shot in the wrong direction, either: nine times out of ten I end up back at his place after office drinks.

There are no feelings involved, just sexual attraction, which definitely isn't a good enough reason for me to have been pissed off that he tried it on with someone else. Plus, I told myself I'd stop this after last time, and I gave him the cold shoulder all evening, so what did I expect?

I'm on my exercise bike, simultaneously pedalling and filling in my diary for next week. I've got back-to-back meetings on Monday, which is good, and then the rest of the week is filled with admin, client briefs and preparation for the annual florists' expo. I've purposefully kept things flexible, ready for when Dev comes by to break the news.

'Sweat harder, pump faster!' My bike screams at me, and I mute the sound. If I sweat any harder, I will die. It's only 8 a.m. and already the temperature is nearing 30 degrees. I've got the back door wide open, but there isn't even a hint of a breeze.

I take a slug of my water and reply to a message from Will, who asks if red wine is OK for this evening. I tell him I'll bring a bottle, and he sends back a thumbs-up emoji.

Alongside Jess, Will is my best friend. He's a clinical psychologist with a wife and a newborn baby, and he has his shit together. Will is one of those people who never seems to work hard or put any effort in, but somehow always ends up on top. He's so laid back he's practically horizontal.

A noise from behind me startles me, and I turn around, but there's nothing there. My online exercise class is almost up, so I hop off the bike and walk towards the back door, peering outside.

'Huh.' One of my dead potted plants has fallen over, its crispy foliage scattered on the patio. The air is so still that even the leaves on the trees aren't moving. I push the casualty to one side with the toe of my trainer and go back indoors, pulling out the Pledge and starting my Saturday morning cleaning routine.

I dust the whole house from top to bottom before going over the kitchen and bathroom and then hoovering with my three different cordless vacuum cleaners. Finally, I mop the tiled floors and then jump in the shower.

As I do my seven-step skincare routine, I plot my succession plan. Florina has done well under Dev's leadership, but I know I could make improvements. Our digital marketing is outstanding (thanks almost entirely to me) but our in-store materials are holding us back. We recently scored a slot in ASDA's gardening aisle, and we could be making more of it. I'm thinking of a limited-edition brand makeover, switching our colours from deep and romantic to light and pastel, to appeal to Gen Zs buying their first potted plants as they go to university at the end of the summer.

With the shape of something forming in my head, I hurry out of the bathroom and to my study, where I grab a piece of paper and sketch out some basic designs for new plant pots. Greys and sandy beiges to house cacti and succulents, warm, matte terracotta for our flowers and shrubs. Wonky shapes with mismatched edges; maybe four different designs so they look homemade, like McDonald's chicken nuggets. I snap a photo and send it to Kirsty to gauge her opinion — she comes from an arts background and has a good eye for these things.

By the time six o'clock rolls around, I've booked in three social events for next week, subscribed to two boxing classes and organised one Tryst date with a personal trainer called Chris. I head off to Will's via the only bakery still open on Burton Road, where I buy a huge red velvet cake, and the Co-op, where I pick up a bottle of Malbec.

Nina, Will's wife, answers the door looking harassed. Their one-month-old baby, Benny, is screaming in her arms.

'Hey!' She gives me a one-armed hug and steps back to let me pass. 'What's all this?'

'Cake and wine. I didn't want you to feel left out.' I head into the kitchen, knowing this house as well as I know my own, and sit down on my favourite bar stool. Will steps in from the garden and stoops down to give me a hug.

'Nice.' He takes the wine and starts uncorking it.

'I'll have a small one, actually.' Nina pulls an extra glass out of the cupboard and sets it down next to the other two. 'I've expressed enough for the evening.'

Will pours out the wine while Nina wedges the teat of a bottle into Benny's mouth. He sucks hungrily, and Nina does the same. 'Jesus, that's good.'

'Is this the first time you've drank since getting pregnant?' I ask, taking a sip.

She nods. 'Socially, yeah. You've turned up at a brilliant time.'

'Cheers to that.' We clink glasses and Will leans against the counter.

'So, how are things?' he asks. 'Have you heard from the big boss yet?'

'Dev,' I clarify, 'and no, not yet. I thought he might announce it last night, but he didn't.'

'Do you think he'll come back?' Nina asks.

'Oh, yeah. It'll be twelve months on the dot, knowing Dev. But the experience will open a lot of doors.'

'Eve has plans to go solo.' Will winks at me.

'Wow,' Nina raises her eyebrows, 'ambitious.'

I detect something strange in her voice, but Will starts talking and I put it out of my mind. 'And how's Brenda? Still ogling?'

'Always. She almost looked me in the eye for a brief second last night, after drinking about a litre of vodka.'

'I wonder what it is. Repression?' He puts his therapist face on, his brow slightly creased, his lips pursed.

'God knows, get her on your couch and find out.'

He laughs. 'Oh, hi, Brenda, I've had a tip-off that you're a bit weird, do you fancy paying me £130 an hour to figure out what's wrong with you?'

Nina shrugs. 'Why not, drum up a bit of business.'

'You could have a go at couples' therapy?' I suggest. 'Get the vicar in as well.'

'Don't,' he sighs. 'That sounds like my idea of heaven.'

Nina drains her glass and goes to pour another. 'Go and pop the barbecue on, Will, it takes forever.'

He looks at her for a second too long, his eyes flitting to her glass, and then walks out onto the patio. Nina notices.

'If he says one word, I will scream.'

'Is he not a fan of you drinking?' I guess, slightly surprised by her tone.

'Not with Benny.'

'But you've expressed?'

'Yeah, but one of us has to stay alert. Makes sense that it'd be me considering it's my job the rest of the time.' Her voice is bitter, and I'm even more shocked. For as long as I've known them, Will and Nina have been a power couple — I've never seen even the slightest ripple on the surface.

'How's Benny doing, anyway?' I ask, steering us onto neutral ground. 'Is he . . . eating well?' What can you ask about a one-month-old? He's hardly been up to much.

She snorts, but doesn't answer. 'You want a squeeze?' He's fallen asleep now, so she detaches him from his bottle and places him in my arms.

Will pokes his head through the patio doors. 'Shall we sit outside? We can put Benny under the umbrella.'

We move out onto the patio, me still clutching the baby, and I position myself in the shade.

'How's Jess?' Will calls as he drops the burgers onto the barbecue.

'Heartbroken.'

'Not Johnny again?' Nina shakes her head. 'It's not for her.'

'No, it really isn't. I can see how it appeals to her — the people who introduced her to it are all really happy with each other — but she's just not built that way. She's a complete monogamist, I just don't think she knows it.'

'Is she still not coping with Johnny seeing his other girl-friend?' Will asks, tapping the barbecue tongs against the grill.

'No. But I think she sort of sees it as the price she has to pay to be with him.'

'Hmm.' Nina frowns. 'We should have had her over tonight, Will. Offered her some support.'

Will shrugs helplessly. 'I did ask. She had a late class.'

My arm starts to ache, and I wonder how Nina carried this kind of weight around with her for months on end. I open my mouth to ask if she wants Benny back, but she stands up and goes inside, bringing another bottle of wine back out with her.

'Oh!' I exclaim, once she's back at the table, and lift Benny towards her. 'I think he wants Mummy.'

Nina blinks slowly. Benny is the picture of serenity. 'It's alright, he's still asleep.'

I lower him back into my lap. Sod it. 'Could we put him in a . . . basket, or something? My arm hurts.'

'Oh god, of course.' Nina rakes her hands down her face. 'Sorry, I bet you've been dying to put him down.' She stands up again and goes through into the kitchen, a little wobbly on her feet. She comes back with a carry seat and we settle him in.

'Does he always sleep this much?' I ask.

Nina sits back down opposite me and laughs loudly. 'Will! Will, did you hear that? Eve just asked if he always sleeps this much.'

Will chuckles. 'Don't go there, Eve. It's the only conversation we'll have all night.'

Nina flashes Will a look I haven't seen before. It's quick, and as soon as I notice it, it's gone. 'I'll refrain myself from boring you, but no. Not when we sleep, anyway.'

'So he's up all night?' I say, aghast. How does she get anything done?

She nods and smiles, but to my horror, there are tears forming in her eyes. 'Oh god, Nina, I'm sorry.' I reach forward to grab her hand, and she sniffs, the tears disappearing. 'Could you maybe keep him up during the day so he's tired at bedtime?'

Nina pulls her hand out of mine and slaps herself on the forehead. 'Why didn't I think of that?' She's not trying to be funny, and she isn't smiling.

I laugh off the awkwardness. 'I'm sorry, that was really unhelpful, wasn't it?'

Nina sniffs. 'No, I'm sorry. I'm all over the place.'

'You'll be fine.' I pat her arm. She's got a beautiful house, a gorgeous husband and a healthy, happy baby. 'Just keep going and keep your head up.'

'Classic Eve solution.' Will comes over with a steaming plate of burgers. 'Keep going, head up, don't stop.'

I shrug. 'It works.'

We eat and chat until the sky is dark, and Will and I realise that Nina hasn't spoken for a while. The bottle of wine is empty and her nose is almost touching her half-eaten burger.

26

'Nee,' Will puts his arm around her shoulder. 'Come on, let's get you to bed.'

By the time he returns, Benny is awake and screaming again, his mouth wide and gummy. Will heats up a bottle and settles in opposite me.

'He's so . . . *loud*,' I comment, raising my voice over the noise.

'Yup.' Will sighs. 'Sorry about . . . Nina's not been feeling great the past few days.'

'Must be hard,' I nod. 'But she really wanted this, didn't she?'

Will studies me for a moment. 'Just because you want something doesn't mean it's easy when you get there.'

I don't say anything. Three years of IVF and huge amounts of debt. I wouldn't have expected it to be a walk in the park, but nothing's ever easy is it?

'I know you don't get it,' Will says, meeting my gaze.

'Of course I do.'

'No, you don't.' He smiles. 'You're too single-minded to land your dream life and then dwell on the negatives.'

'I wouldn't say that.' And I wouldn't, really. I'd say that if you want something, and work hard to get it, once you're there you shouldn't look back. You should focus on the next goal and just get on with it. I try to put myself in Nina's shoes, knowing objectively that motherhood is not a one-size-fits-all experience, but I can't do it.

'You want to offer some advice.' Will is eyeing me, a smile creeping at his lips.

'No!' I protest. But I really, really do. I want to tell him to get Nina a meditation app and suggest she gets outside more. 'I mean, can she get on that Peanut thing? The mum social network? Meet some people?'

Will laughs softly. 'Not everyone is a problem-solver, Eve. Proactivity isn't a universal character trait.'

'But I want her to be happy! Doesn't she want to be happy?'

'Of course she does. But this is hard time, and a new time, and she hasn't found her rhythm yet. She doesn't see an obvious solution to everything like you do.'

I stay quiet, letting the point slide. 'I brought a cake.'

We open it up on the table between us and eat with our hands, all three of us scoffing noisily as Nina sleeps upstairs.

CHAPTER 6

Adam

There are times in life when you are drunker than you believe. Times when you sit in the back of a taxi and boldly declare, 'I honestly don't feel pissed at all', and the driver looks at you in the rear-view mirror like he'll be praying for you later that evening. These are the times when you wake up the next morning with a headache the size of your own shame and an unrelenting queasiness that follows you all the way to a greasy fry up and beyond.

This is not one of those times.

I am cycling to work and my head is clear. I had All Bran for breakfast, which may be a crime against tastebuds and joy, but is a pretty solid indicator of a non-hungover appetite. I remember the details of last night clearly and can reflect upon them with normal hindsight, not gut-clenching shame.

You're drunk.

That's what Katie said, isn't it? She pushed away from me because I was drunk. I told her I wasn't drunk, and I really wasn't.

I cast my mind back to the way she kissed me on the cheek as she went to bed. The way you'd kiss a distant uncle at a Christmas party. I clench the handlebars of my bike uneasily. She has never been this distant with me, not even when I let Fergus crash in our spare room after a night out and he vomited all over our new Laura Ashley bedding.

I pull up outside Okie's house and chain my bike to the fence surrounding his front garden. I put my thoughts about last night into a box for later, and ring the doorbell.

Mr Adeyemi answers the door wearing a crisp suit and a sage-green tie. 'Adam.' He holds his hand out and smiles.

'How are you?' I ask as I step inside and take off my shoes.

'I'm well. How are you?'

'I'm good, thank you.' I start to make my way towards the dining room, but I stop and turn around. 'I thought I might . . . broach the subject, today. If you think it's a good time.'

He nods. 'Today's a good day. Maybe he'll tell you what he wants.'

'I hope so.'

Mr Adeyemi gestures with his hand, and I enter the dining room. Okie, my top-performing student, is sitting at the table, his week's work laid out in front of him. As I close the door behind me, he keeps his eyes trained on the sheets of paper, each laid out precisely one centimetre away from the next.

'Good morning, Okie.'

'Hmm.' Okie looks up and fixes his gaze somewhere over my right shoulder. 'The lines weren't even this time.'

I move around the table and look down at the worksheets. He points to one in the middle. He's right; the lines I type for him to fill in his answers aren't consistent — one has an extra underscore.

'I'm sorry about that. Thank you for pointing it out. I'll make sure I amend it.' I pull a chair out and sit down. 'Shall we go through your answers?'

He nods and presents me with his workbook, where he has done his calculations before recording his final answers on the sheets. Everything is ordered immaculately and easy to follow, as usual. And, as usual, there isn't an error in sight.

'This all looks great, Okie.' I give him his book back and he places it on the table. 'I think you've got the logarithms sussed.'

Okie has everything sussed, that's the problem: I'm attempting to tutor someone who knows it all already. Okie's autism means that he struggles in classroom settings, and is far beyond the level expected from his age group. He attends the local SEN school when he can, but the large groups, lack of resources and unchallenging learning material mean that he gains very little but stress, unmanageable outbursts and setbacks. Noticing Okie's passions, and at a loss with what to do, his father has employed private tutors to coach him in Maths, Physics and Chemistry. He works fourteen-hour nights, seven days a week to pay for it.

'I wonder if maybe we could have a chat today, Okie.' I tread carefully, more than aware that one wrong step could set our rapport back weeks. 'About your future and what you'd like to do.'

Okie stares at the table.

'You'll be sixteen in a couple of weeks; I wondered if you'd considered the kind of career you'd like to have,' I continue.

'A chemical engineer,' he says, bluntly. I lean forward, glad to have something to work with.

'That sounds brilliant.' I nod. 'Do you know what you need to do to become a chemical engineer?'

'A Levels.'

'Yeah, exactly.' I weigh up my next statement in my mind carefully before I ask it. 'And then university.'

Okie stiffens, and begins tapping his fingers against the table. It's a sign, and I quickly try to dial things back. 'But that's something we can talk about another time.'

His tapping intensifies, and I resist the urge to place my hand on his shoulder; my idea of comfort-offering would be painful for him.

'How about we start with something small? Shall we start doing some past papers and think about booking you in for your A Levels?'

Okie doesn't respond, and his tapping continues.

'Maybe we could devise a plan together? Something that you'd be happy with?'

He nods and takes his hands off the table, clenching them in his lap.

I pull out a piece of paper and hand it to him. 'So, as we talk, do you want to write things down in a way that makes sense to you? I'll say what steps we need to take, and you can create a timeline? We can pay special attention to the parts you're specifically worried about.'

Okie takes a pen and holds it over the paper. I go through the process slowly: preparation, past papers, booking in for exams. Taking the tests, what the process will be like, waiting for the results. Applying to university, getting a conditional offer, accepting a place. Transport, living arrangements, options, choices. Throughout, Okie reacts when something breaches his comfort zone: large lectures, public transport, halls of residence. I have him put a star next to these areas, and tell him that I will research what's available and report what I find back to him each week. Then I ask him to circle our first step, and we break it down and make it our focus.

Precisely an hour after our session begins, and while I'm still talking, Okie methodically starts putting away his things, tucking our plan into the front page of his folder. Mr Adeyemi comes into the room, and Okie slips out, leaving us to talk.

'Shall we have a coffee?' Mr Adeyemi asks, and we go through into the kitchen.

I sit at the table. 'I think that went well.'

He nods, stirring Nescafe into two mugs and splashing in some milk. He places the coffees on the table and pulls out a chair. 'Chemical engineering?'

'Yes. He seemed pretty set on it.'

'He is.' He stares thoughtfully into his drink. 'Okie struggles to attend a school designed for people like him. Universities aren't so accommodating.'

'No.' I rub my hand through my beard; I've recently started growing it, and it's equal parts itchy and comforting. 'I have a proposition, though.'

My Adeyemi looks up. 'Go on.'

'You've known for a while that I . . . have my issues with tutoring Okie.' During our first session, Okie pointed out an error in a question I had set, and subsequently sped through an entire hour's worth of material in under ten minutes. I told his father to save his money; I could continue sitting with him for two hours each week, and take home my pay check, but it wasn't right. Okie didn't need coaching to achieve his potential, he needed a pathway that appreciated it. Mr Adeyemi asked me to stay, aware of his son's talents. He wanted Okie to engage in something he enjoyed with another human being, and didn't know where else to turn.

'I think this is an opportunity for you and Okie to see some kind of reward for the money and effort you're putting in,' I continue. 'I can go through past papers with him for half of our sessions, and the other half we can spend going through the application process and talking things through.'

'I can't ask you to do that.' Mr Adeyemi shakes his head. 'It's not your job.'

'I haven't done my job properly with Okie since I met him.' I lean forward, almost pleading. 'Honestly, if you're OK with it, I'd love to help. I can research the support and resources available to Okie in the time I'd usually be preparing for lessons.' I lean back. 'And anyway, it's good to be adaptable.'

Mr Adeyemi thinks for a second, blowing hot steam across his coffee cup. He takes a sip, nods, and then smiles. 'If you're happy then I'm more than happy.'

'Great.' I feel a rush of excitement. 'I think you should speak to his other tutors and ask them to switch to A Level past papers during his sessions. I'll sort out booking him in for his exams.'

'That sounds like a good idea.' He nods and stands up, but pauses for a second, his hand on the back of his chair. He looks at me. 'Do you think he can do it?'

I pull on my coat and swing my bag onto my shoulder. 'I *know* he can.'

* * *

I'm buzzing all the way to my next lesson, cycling twice as fast as I usually do. Halfway there, I pull over and put my earbuds in. I dial Katie's number before setting off again.

'Adam?' she answers, and I hear the noise of the TV in the background.

'Guess what!' I say breathlessly.

'Hang on, before I forget,' she cuts in and I clamp my mouth closed. 'Chloe called, said she's been trying to get hold of you for ages.'

My stomach drops. 'Oh, right.'

'She sounded a bit frantic. You ignoring her?'

'No, no.' I ease off the pedals slightly, my mood plummeting.

'Right.' She sounds nonplussed, but doesn't push it. 'Anyway, what did you want to tell me?'

'Oh.' It takes me a second to drag my mind back to the reason for my call. 'Erm, I'm going to tutor Okie into university.'

'Who? The one you always feel terrible about?'

'Yeah, the one whose father works himself to death to pay for tutoring he doesn't need.'

'That's good,' she says, but I can tell she's distracted.

'Yeah.' My bubble is burst, but I shake my head and press on. 'We're going to do past papers, and I'm going to see if I can get in touch with a few different universities to see what support they offer, and—'

'Oh, Adam, I've got to go — the window cleaner's here,' Katie says apologetically as the doorbell goes. 'Sorry, we'll speak when you get home this evening?'

'No problem, yeah, of course.' I say goodbye and ring off, all the excitement I felt a moment ago evaporated. I try to bring it back, but I am suddenly unsettled. I push it down and pedal harder, weaving my way through traffic towards my next student's house.

CHAPTER 7

Adam

'So yeah, I think I can do it.' I sit back in my seat and smile at Hugh, who is engrossed in the television. 'I mean, it's not like anything I've ever done before, but I'm up for the challenge.'

Hugh looks at me and grins, his mouth wide open.

'Knock knock!' A nurse slips in through the door. She's young and blonde and pretty. 'How are we today, Hugh?' She turns to me. 'Hi, I'm Becky. I'm new, so you won't have seen me before.'

'Hi Becky.' I hold out my hand and she shakes it. 'I'm Adam, Hugh's brother.'

'And are you a fan of *Moana*, too?' She winks at me conspiratorially.

'I don't think my opinion means anything, to be honest.' I laugh, and Hugh claps his hands, singing along delightedly as Moana sails across a choppy sea.

'I know all the words off by heart, and I've only been here three days.' She starts stripping the sheets off Hugh's bed, bundling them into a laundry basket. 'He's a very handsome man. You two aren't twins, are you?'

'No.' I laugh again, because it's a common question. We are remarkably similar. 'He's a year older than me.'

She brings a freshly pressed sheet out of the cupboard and billows it out, sending the smell of lavender detergent across the room. 'He certainly gets a lot of visitors, there's been someone here every day since I started.'

'Who was here yesterday?' I ask.

'Short guy, quite skinny? Had a bit of an accent. He brought this.' She holds up a stuffed toy of Hei Hei, the accident-prone rooster from Hugh's favourite film, and then passes it to Hugh, who clutches it gleefully.

'Piotr.' I grin. 'He's just encouraging the obsession.'

Piotr is one of my best friends; we've known each other since we were fourteen, and his love for Hugh almost matches mine. He's here every week, and the other members of our group, Fergus and Bil, often pop in, too. When everything happened — when Hugh and I lost everything — our friends rallied around us, forming a tight and impenetrable circle that now feels as encompassing to me as any traditional family unit.

'He was nice,' Becky finishes plumping a pillow and turns to me. Her eyes meet mine and she blushes, averting her gaze.

'He's married,' I say, laughing.

'Oh, no, I didn't mean that.' She shakes her head, her face bright red now. 'Never mind.' She picks the laundry basket up and moves towards the door, brushing against my shoulder unnecessarily as she goes. Wait, is she flirting with *me*? No, that's ridiculous. 'I've got to do the rest of the beds now, but I'll be somewhere on the corridor if you or Hugh need anything.'

She slips out, and I sink back into my chair. 'That was weird, wasn't it?' I ask Hugh.

Hugh bounces up and down in his chair, clapping excitedly.

I try to get into the film, but I've seen it so many times it doesn't capture my attention anymore. My eyes drift towards the window and I sigh.

'Everything feels a bit off at the moment,' I admit. I do this often, come and talk to Hugh when things aren't going too well. I'll tell him my good news and my bad news, and even though I don't know whether he truly understands what I'm saying, it helps.

My brother was born with the umbilical cord wrapped around his neck. He suffered oxygen deprivation, and as a result has cerebral palsy. He's bubbly and friendly and completely obsessed with *Moana*, and he's the most important person in my life.

'I mean, I'm really happy with work and everything. I've got loads of summer students booked in looking to get a head-start for next year. But things with Katie . . . I don't know. She's being really distant with me.'

Hugh squeals as Maui, Moana's nemesis-cum-ally, is thrown into the ocean.

'I wonder if it's work, or stress, or boredom, or just me?' I ponder out loud. 'Or maybe I'm imagining things; maybe everyone has a few off days.'

Even as I'm saying this, I know that Katie's attitude towards me recently is more than just a bad week. After six years together, I know her almost better than I know anyone, and she isn't being herself. We've always been one of *those* couples, blissfully happy and in sync and irritating to everyone around us. The boys used to pretend to gag when we sat with our arms around each other at the pub, but they were happy for us. Recently, it feels like a chasm has opened up between us, and I can't seem to cross it to get to her.

My phone beeps and I check it; it's a message on the group chat. I tap out a response as Hugh stares intently at the television, clutching poor Hei Hei by the throat and throwing him around in his lap.

> Piotr: *So are we all up for Dublin? Weekend of the 23rd?*
>
> Me: *Yes, holiday definitely needed!*
>
> Bil: *I'm in. What's up, Ad?*
>
> Me: *Nothing major, I'll FaceTime this week?*

Piotr: *Add us all to the call and we'll go through the plan. You at Hugh's?*

Fergus: *Only coming to Dublin if we can go to the Little Museum*

Me: *Will do, and yeah, here now. Thanks for the rooster — he's even more infatuated now*

Piotr: *That's not possible*

Bil: *You can go where you want Ferg, I'm not stepping foot in a place that stinks of soggy anoraks and doesn't serve alcohol*

I lock my phone, smiling. We all know we'll end up spending at least three hours wherever Ferg wants to go, just to stop him grumbling while we do the less highbrow stuff. And we all know that Ferg will secretly have a great time drinking pints on Temple Bar, but will never admit it.

Moana continues, and I see it through to its happy end before standing up to leave. Hugh reaches for me and I wrap him in a hug, letting him plant a wet kiss on my cheek. 'Ugh, slobber chops,' I tease, ruffling his hair, and he shrieks happily. 'I'll see you in a couple of days, OK?'

I put Moana on again from the beginning and leave him fixated on the TV. His therapists will be in later to play games with him, but Hugh would watch Disney on repeat for his entire life if he could. Before *Moana* came out, it was all about *Mulan*. Hugh likes a strong female lead, it seems, and I can't blame him. Both stories are great until you've seen them eight thousand times.

I go out into the corridor and close the door behind me. As I'm leaving, Becky comes out of one of the other residents' rooms.

'Nice to meet you, see you later.' I smile, and head towards the exit.

'You too, Adam.' She stops in the middle of the corridor. 'Hope to see you soon.'

I leave through the exit doors and jump back on my bike, suddenly feeling strange. I push off, heading home to talk to Katie.

CHAPTER 8

Eve

Tomorrow is the day.

I've just had a calendar invite from Dev, asking to meet in my office at 4 p.m.. It's Sunday, so my calendar is full of life admin, like calling my parents, and it's taking everything in me not to tell them the news before I've even asked how they are.

'How are you both?' I squint at the screen. Mum's finger is over the camera, and I can just make out the edge of my dad's bald head in the corner. 'Mum, I can't see you, move your hand.'

'What?' Dad bellows. 'Can you hear what she's saying, Carrie?'

'Go and get the whatsits, Mike. The thingamajigs! There!' Mum's finger moves away from the camera and I see her gesturing wildly towards the wardrobe. 'The things for your ears!'

'These?' Dad pulls out a pair of earphones.

'Yes! Bring them over here.'

There's a lot of muffled scratching and some tame swearing as Mum gets the earphones hooked up, and then she puts her glasses on, pulls the tiny microphone up to her mouth, and screams.

'CAN YOU HEAR ME, EVIE?'

'Oh my god, Mum.' I wince. 'You don't need to shout.'

'What's she saying?' Dad's voice is distant.

'Give him one of the earphones, Mum, then I can talk to you both.'

Another stressful five minutes pass as they set themselves up, and eventually, we're having an actual conversation.

'How is everything out there?' I ask, noting their tan. 'You both look very brown.'

'Oh, it's lovely. Just lovely, isn't it Mike?' Mum nudges Dad, and he nods. 'At the beach every day, aren't we?'

'We are. And how's our girlie? How's your job?'

I swallow down the annoyance at the tone in my dad's voice, as though he's asking a paperboy how his Saturday rounds are going, and try to focus on the fact that they've remembered to ask this time.

'It's good.' I can't help myself. 'I'm being promoted tomorrow.'

'That's wonderful!' Mum beams. 'Will you be the manager?'

'I already *am* the manager.' I take a deep breath. 'I'll be head of the whole marketing department.'

They nod, smiling. 'That sounds great, love.' Dad fiddles with his earphone.

'It's actually really important,' I press. 'You remember I work for Florina?'

'Of course!' Mum retorts. 'Of course we remember that.'

Before I worked my way up at Florina, I'd managed to quickly move my way up the ladder at an agency neither of them had ever heard of. When I moved onto something more recognisable, I assumed they'd take more interest — everything in Mum's garden back in the UK came from Florina's flagship store in Chorley — but they just don't seem to get it.

I take a deep breath and remind myself that I am thirty-three now, and my parents' stance on my career choices should not affect me.

'And will you get a little salary increase?' Dad asks.

I grind my teeth. 'Yes. There'll be quite a big jump in pay.'

'Well that's just brilliant news, isn't it, Mike?' Mum nudges Dad again. 'You'll have to come out and visit us so we can celebrate.'

'Sure,' I say, with absolutely no conviction. I can't foresee a time in the next decade when I'll have time for a holiday to the Costa del Sol. I haven't been away in years.

I shut up about work and listen to Dad grumble about a paella he had that tasted 'too Spanish' for half an hour before saying goodbye and ringing off.

I order a poké bowl on Deliveroo and then set about reorganising my kitchen cupboards, despite never using most of the stuff in there. I clean every plate and bowl, wipe down the tins and packets, and soak all of my cutlery in fairy liquid and Dettol before drying it all off and placing it back in the drawer, neatly stacked.

As I clean, I think about tomorrow. I imagine what I'll say, who I'll tell first. It will have to be Kirsty, because I have a surprise up my sleeve: as soon as my position is announced, I will put her forward for my old role for the next six months. I know that she knows this — why wouldn't she? She's my closest friend in the entire company, and she's really good at what she does. She'd be perfect for it.

My lunch arrives, and I eat standing up, swiping through our competition's Instagram pages as I lean against the kitchen counter. I'm making some notes on my phone — more yellow hues, yearly subscriptions, tongue-in-cheek captions — when it rings, and Jess's face consumes my screen.

I swipe to answer and a grainy image of her and Johnny appears. 'Hey.'

'Hello!' she cheers. 'Just thought we'd drop in to say hi and see how your Sunday was going.'

I wince at this. Since when was this a *we* situation? Johnny is wedged in next to Jess, looking down at his phone, confirming my suspicions that he's been forced into the video call against his will.

'I'm good, how are you guys?' I fork one last piece of avocado into my mouth and crumple the cardboard box into the recycling.

Jess squints at the camera. 'Are you eating standing up again?'

'Yes.'

She sighs and shakes her head, her dreadlocks bouncing. 'We're going to Bundobust tonight, aren't we, Johnny? Apparently the fried okra is incredible. They also have this mung bean dhal, which is apparently brilliant for your metabolism, and . . .'

I let Jess talk about her evening plans while I wipe down the kitchen surfaces and wash my fork. Every so often, I glance at Johnny, who still hasn't looked up from his phone.

'And how are you, Johnny?' I ask once I'm done, interrupting Jess's monologue about the benefits of lentils for the digestive system.

'I'm alright, yeah, cheers.' Johnny still doesn't look up from his phone.

Jess glances towards him, and I catch her eyeing his screen.

'Is it tomorrow you get the promotion announcement?' she asks, tearing her gaze away.

'Yep, four o'clock.' I smile. 'We'll have to celebrate this weekend.'

'Yes, let's!' She nudges Johnny in the ribs. 'Are you coming out with me and Eve this weekend?'

He looks up briefly. 'Can Polly come?'

Jess's jaw sets. 'No, she cannot.'

'Who's Polly?' I pry.

'Polly is Johnny's — I mean, our — erm . . .'

'She's my girlfriend,' Johnny drawls.

'Oh.' I raise my eyebrows. Jess hasn't put a name to her nemesis before.

43

'*Our* girlfriend, technically, Johnny!' Jess squeals, her face red. 'And she's not coming.'

'How can she be your girlfriend too when you won't even be in the same room as her?' Johnny slips his phone into his pocket now.

'Because we're a throuple!' Jess exclaims, her hair taking on a life of its own now. 'There are *three* of us!'

Johnny sighs. 'We've been over this.'

'I think I'll call back later?' I say, hovering my finger over the 'end call' button.

'No, Eve, stay!' Jess whips her head back towards the camera. 'I just want to be able to *understand* how it's fair that Johnny gets two girlfriends but I only get him.'

'You can go and get another boyfriend if you want.' Johnny frowns. 'I've told you that.'

'I don't *want* another boyfriend!' Jess shrieks. 'I want you!'

Johnny shrugs again.

Jess is about to cry, I can feel it in the air. 'I've got to go, Jess, I'll call you later,' I say quickly.

'I can't *believe* you've just said that, Johnny—'

I cut her off mid-sentence.

I put my phone on the side and go to empty the bin, but I freeze as a muffled squeak comes from the open back door to my left.

I tiptoe over and poke my head out, feeling the blistering heat of the sun on my face. I blink into the brightness, letting my eyes adjust. There doesn't seem to be anything there. I lean back, intending to return inside, but then I spot it. In the shadow by the fence is a malnourished-looking tortoiseshell cat, swishing its tail and staring at me.

Our gazes lock, and I narrow my eyes. I haven't seen this cat before; it must be one of the neighbours'. I've only spoken to a couple of them once or twice in the three years I've lived here; I'm rarely home for long enough to chat — weekends like this are a rarity I like to avoid — and when I am, I'm always busy.

The cat yawns, and I wonder whether it's had a drink recently. The temperature is reaching thirty-three degrees now. What if it's lost?

I nip back into the kitchen and pour some water into an old Tupperware box, before stepping back outside and leaving it on the patio. I look up to beckon the cat over, but it's gone.

I sigh and go inside, jumping on the exercise bike and asking Alexa for a news roundup, biding my time until the big day tomorrow.

CHAPTER 9

Adam

I am reading an article titled 'Top 5 UK Universities for Students with Autism'. It's jumping forward a few steps in our plan, but starting with the end goal and working backwards means I can have answers up my sleeve for any questions Okie might have.

I discount UCL immediately, because of the distance, even though it apparently has a brilliant disability support system. Sheffield *could* work, in theory, but again, it's not close enough to seem like an easy jump for Okie, who struggles to visit his grandparents in Cheshire. I keep scrolling, my fingers crossed tightly in my lap. Come on, come on, come on. If the University of Manchester has made it onto this list, we've hit the jackpot. It'll be a ten-minute car journey for Okie each day. He can remain living at home and take private transport to get each day off to the best start.

Sussex . . . Brighton . . . there! I stop, a whoosh of air leaving my body, as what I'm looking for appears on my screen. I scan through it quickly: *Designated disability advisor . . . broader supportive community . . . academic and social growth programmes . . .*

I click off the article and find the switchboard number for the university, jotting it down and circling it so I remember to call later. I head downstairs to make a coffee — frothy milk and finely ground Italian beans, the one hipster facet of my personality — and then make my way back up to the office to start researching A Level exam times. I'm halfway up the stairs when my phone pings.

Piotr: *Guys, I've got my finger over the 'book flight' button — confirm within next 5 secs or you'll be paying for a holiday you're not coming on*

Fergus: *25th? For how many nights?*

Piotr: *[Forwarded message] We've been over this a billion times — 2 nights*

Bil: *I'm down, time's the flight?*

Me: *Same*

Piotr: *Early, that's why it's cheap*

Fergus: *Yep I'll be there*

Piotr: *[GIF of dancing banana] Mint! Send me your passport details so I can check us all in and pick our seats — it's an extra fiver, Ferg, don't have an aneurysm*

Fergus: *I'll just sit wherever the system puts me, I'm not giving more money to Ryanair than necessary*

Bil: *Aw, come on Ferg*

Me: *I'm fine with that, thanks Piotr — I'll send you my details now*

Me: *Sit Ferg next to me, and order him the full English as well, it's only twelve quid*

Ferg: *DO NOT DO THAT*

I lock my phone and take a slurp of my coffee, climbing the last few stairs and going into the office. I open the top drawer of the desk, my passport is usually in here with all the other important things I always seem to lose. The drawer sticks and then opens forcefully, making my hand jerk and splashing coffee all over the carpet.

'Oops.' I rub at it with my sock. Katie will go mad. She's always been a bit of a perfectionist, making sure the house is as on-trend as possible, but it's like I've got a blind spot for these kinds of things. She once had the sofa reupholstered in a different colour while I was away with the boys and I didn't notice for two weeks.

I rifle through the drawer, but I can't see it. I pull out my crumpled paper driving license and smooth it out, and find my national insurance card gathering dust in the back corner, but no passport.

I go through the other drawers in the desk; it's not unlike me to forget where I've put something, so maybe I shoved it in one of these by mistake. When did we last go away? I rack my brains. Crete, last October. Katie and I did an all-inclusive thing for a week. She was looking after my passport, wasn't she? She usually does — she doesn't trust me not to leave it somewhere and get us stranded.

I leave my coffee on the desk and go into the bedroom, my mind taken back to our holiday. Katie was beautiful — she always is — with three different outfits for every day and a jam-packed itinerary of sunbathing planned. Was she being different with me even then? I cast about among my memories, trying to pinpoint specific events. I wanted to go and explore, and she didn't, saying we'd paid for all-inclusive and might as well enjoy it. I went to a few places on my own; the island with the abandoned leper colony, the old town, but I didn't mind. We holiday differently, we always have done.

She was on her phone a lot, I do remember that. Avoiding me? A memory takes shape in my mind: me, in the pool, splashing water onto her sunbed and asking her to join me. Her rolling her eyes and muttering something under her breath, not seeing the funny side, pulling her wide-brimmed hat down further over her face.

I remember the sting of the rejection; the feeling that something wasn't quite aligned with us for a second. I swam until I forgot, and by the time I got out, everything seemed fine.

I shake the memory from my mind; these past few months have been a blip. When I got home from Hugh's the other day, I asked Katie if everything was OK, and she said it was. She blamed her distance on work stress, and I believe her. You don't win an award without putting in the graft. I'm sure that once everything quietens down, things will start to look up.

My phone beeps again with a message from Piotr, urging us to send our passport details over before all the good seats get taken. I focus on what I'm doing. If Katie had my passport, it'd probably be in the drawer of her bedside table.

I pull out my phone again and send her a message.

Just looking for my passport — is it in your bedside table? Do you mind if I check?

She's at work, so won't reply for a while, but I know she'll be fine with it.

My phone squawks angrily as Piotr sends a string of SOS emojis, punctuated with Bil and Ferg handing over their details. I pull the drawer open.

I can't see it straight away — coils of jewellery and neatly stacked sentimental birthday cards cover the top of the drawer — so I lift some items onto the bed and look underneath.

There! I pull out a passport and open it, but it's Katie's. Surely they'd be together? If it's not here, it must be in my suitcase on top of the wardrobe. It's the only other place I can think of.

I go to close the drawer, but something catches my eye. Something burgundy, right at the back. I reach in and pull it out.

It's a pair of knickers. I feel a flush of guilt immediately; this is Katie's drawer — I shouldn't be looking at anything that isn't my passport. I lift a few more things out of the bottom of the drawer, intending to put the pants back where they were, but underneath is more underwear: cup-less bras, razor-thin thongs, lace and bows and trailing, delicate ribbons snaking across the bottom of the drawer.

There are no tags: my mind takes note of this immediately, subconsciously. I've never seen any of these things before.

Katie is completely entitled to her privacy. Perhaps she bought these, tried them on, and is waiting for the right time to show me? I put everything back quickly, my emotions battling with each other, and start piling the stuff on the bed on top, without looking. My hand finds something silky and smooth, and on instinct, I pull it onto my lap. It's a drawstring bag, black and shiny.

I shouldn't open it. I shouldn't.

My fingers find the knot of fabric at the top and I untie it, pulling the mouth of the bag open. I tip the contents onto the bed.

Three items. I force my eyes to take in one thing at a time.

A small vibrator. That's fine, that's OK. It's healthy, it's normal, it's not a sign of anything. I almost feel relief, but my eyes have already begun to process what else is now lying on the bed.

A pack of Kama Sutra cards. Also fine. They're used, the packet worn and the cards inside bent. Maybe she got them second-hand? Maybe she's saving them for a special occasion?

As my eyes land on the final object, the one I spotted at the start but didn't let myself process, my innocent explanations evaporate. XL condoms. A strip, with one torn off.

Katie has been on the pill since we met. We have never used any other form of contraception.

My stomach lurches, and I stuff everything back into the bag quickly, my hands shaking. I stack the drawer back up, piling on the jewellery I bought her and the childhood birth-day cards, trying my best to make it look like nothing's been touched.

My head reeling, I push the drawer shut, but as it goes, I spot it.

Slipped down the side, tucked in next to the black silk bag.

There it is.

My passport.

CHAPTER 10

Eve

I clock Kirsty as soon as I walk into the office. I'm here early because I couldn't sleep, and it's a relief to see her. I want company in my excitement.

'Coffee?' I sit on the edge of her desk. 'I need a triple shot.'

She grimaces, not taking her eyes off her screen. 'I'm totally swamped. Been here since five.'

'Oh.' I frown, running through the work I've assigned her. Perhaps Dev's given her some extra bits to do, clearing his desk before he steps down. 'Well, do you want me to grab you one?'

'It's alright, I'll make one in the kitchen in a bit.'

I lift myself up from the desk, pushing my bag back up onto my shoulder. 'No problem, text me if you change your mind.'

She flashes me a smile and I turn to leave, feeling off balance. 'Oh!' I turn back as I reach the door. 'Did you get those designs I sent you on Saturday? What did you think?' Kirsty didn't reply to my text, and I had to remind myself that some people practice work-life balance and don't engage on the weekend.

'Hmm?' She looks up from her screen. 'Oh, yes, sorry, I did. I . . . I'm not really sure, Eve. The colours are a bit . . .

I've got it in my diary to have a look at them properly later in the week.'

She goes back to her screen and I stare at her. What is wrong with her today? I feel wrong-footed, unsure of myself. We usually collaborate on things like this, there's no hierarchy involved. So why do I feel like a primary-school child whose work hasn't made it onto the wall?

'Right, sure, no problem.' I smile. 'I'll see you later then.'

I buy the strongest coffee Starbucks has and sip it throughout the morning, feeling unsettled. Every so often I glance through the glass wall of my office, watching Kirsty chat with our colleagues. At some point, she gets up and walks over to the lift, but Dev quick-marches over to her before she can get inside. They talk, and she laughs in a way that I can tell is exaggerated. Eventually, she disappears into the lift, and when she comes back she sits at her desk and doesn't move for another hour.

It's nothing, I'm sure. She must be tired, and if she didn't like my designs, that's fine. I can cope with critical feedback. I'm sure she'll have a proper chat with me about it later. Maybe she's nervous about stepping into my role? She's never really been one for the spotlight, and she knows it'll be announced as soon as I've had the go-ahead from Dev this afternoon.

I push the thoughts from my mind and throw myself into our new Instagram campaign for a few hours before Jess hurtles through my door at midday.

'Today's the day!' She throws herself at the chair across from me and spins around. 'Eve Slater, CEO.'

'I'm *not* going to be CEO, Jess.' I laugh, pulling the breakfast muffins I bought at Starbucks from my bag and switching off my screen.

'Well, whatever it is.' She slaps her hands onto the desk. 'Yay!'

Brenda slinks past the door and stops by the water cooler, leaning her back against it and shamelessly staring inside.

'You and Johnny made up?' I ask.

'What? Oh, that. We didn't *fall out*, Eve, it was a discussion.' She takes a huge bite of her muffin, crumbs spraying across the floor. 'It's good to have healthy dialogue in a relationship. When we were on the retreat, our zen master told us that conflict is actually the source of true connection . . .'

My phone vibrates and I pull it out as she continues speaking. It's Will.

Will: *You free for coffee this week? Could do with a chat.*

Me: *Let's do drinks, celebration time!*

Will: *Can't do evenings — got a baby, remember?*

Me: *Oh yeah, what a buzzkill. Joking. OK, Wednesday?*

Will: *Sure.*

'. . . and the alignment of tantric energy — Eve, are you listening to me?'

'Sorry, yes.' I lock my phone and click into my Outlook calendar, quickly typing in my coffee with Will. 'Fancy lunch at the café with Will on Wednesday instead of here?'

'Sure.' She crumples up her muffin wrapper and tosses it at the bin, missing. 'Oops. So anyway, how are you feeling? Are you excited?'

I shrug, trying to look nonchalant, but impatience is churning inside me. 'I just want it confirmed so I can start planning.'

'Oooh, planning.' Jess winks. Jess works as a freelance spiritual healer, and thinks that words like *planning* are very corporate and serious. 'And Tryst? Any news there?'

'Got one lined up this week.' I look towards my computer as it pings with a calendar reminder: *Paternity cover meeting. Dev Kalhora and Eve Slater in 3 hours.*

My stomach somersaults.

'Well, let me know how it goes.' Jess stands up and pushes her chair under the desk with her foot. 'I've got an appointment in ten, so I've got to run.'

'Alright.' I click into my PowerPoint as she heads for the door. 'See you later.'

I spend the afternoon buried in my expo presentation. In two weeks, the National Floristry Fair takes place in Dublin, and I'm presenting. It's the biggest event in the flower business calendar, and we have the largest stand. I've been asked to talk about marketing challenges in a data-conscious digital world, and I've spent weeks collating statistics and figures to present to some of the most important marketing people in the industry.

I try to focus, but my concentration is off. Every ten minutes my eyes flick towards the clock, watching the time edge towards my meeting with Dev. The expo takes place just before I'm due to take over, so it's important that I make an impact to get my name on the map.

Four o'clock rolls around, and my heart leaps as I see Dev striding towards my door. *This is it, this is it, this is it.* All of my hard work, everything I've pushed for since I left university, is about to finally come my way.

'Eve.' Dev pokes his head around the door, his smiling eyes crinkled just the right amount in the corners. 'May I?'

'Of course, come in!' I stand up and gesture towards the empty seat opposite me. It feels strange to have him on the lesser side of the desk and I briefly wonder why he scheduled this here, and not in his own office.

'I imagine the next few months will be markedly different to this.' He smiles calmly as he sinks into the chair, his eyes roaming around the tidiness of my office.

'I imagine so,' I reply easily, struggling to hide my impatience.

'Eleanor's wondering how we'll cope.' He rolls his eyes, as if sharing an in-joke with me. 'As if the baby has an unfair advantage over two adults.'

I laugh and lean back, comfortable in his confidence. 'I'm sure she'll get used to the new normal.' I spot Kirsty looking at me through the glass wall, and imagine telling her the news.

Dev nods. 'She'll be fine.' He slaps his knees. 'Right, let's get to it. I'm sure you know why I'm here.'

I smile. 'I have an inkling.'

'Ha. Always one step ahead.' He winks. 'Well, as you've rightly guessed, I'm putting you forward for my paternity cover.'

It feels like my heart is going to beat out of my chest. Excitement is bubbling in my throat. I cough. 'That's fantastic news, thank you.'

'No need to thank me.' He waves his hand. 'It's you who's put the hard work in.'

'You know I love working here.' I uncross my legs and then cross them again, trying to expel some energy. 'I'll give it everything I've got.'

'I'm sure you will.' He pushes himself up from his chair and moves towards the shelves in the corner. I'm practically vibrating, willing him to leave the room so I can get Kirsty in here and tell her the news. Dev moves towards the door.

'Shall I get Brenda to find some time in our schedules for handover?' I ask, clicking through my calendar. 'Thursday afternoons are looking good at the moment . . .'

Dev stops and turns around, a confused smile on his lips. 'Well, let's not be premature. I'll have a decision for you after the expo.'

My head is a blur of popping champagne bottles and updated CVs, so it takes me a moment to process what he's said. I freeze, looking up from my computer screen.

'Sorry, a decision?' I'm on the backfoot, suddenly, and I clutch the armrest of my chair. I thought he just made a decision?

'Yes, between you and the other candidate.' Dev studies me and cocks his head. 'I thought you knew there were two of you going forward for the role?'

I falter. 'I . . . yes, I did imagine that might be the case.' I nod. 'Who is it, if you don't mind me asking?'

Dev frowns, and a coldness seeps up through my feet and into my stomach.

'I'm sorry, I assumed this was something you were aware of. I was certainly under the impression that you'd discussed it among yourselves, given how close you are.' He clocks the look on my face, and I blink, trying my hardest to seem unfazed. *No.* No, it can't be. 'It's Kirsty, Eve. She threw her hat in the ring a few weeks back.'

I am rooted to my chair for a moment, my jaw clenched shut. I can't compute the words he's saying, it doesn't make sense. Dev stares at me, and I come to. I nod, standing up, my hands in fists by my side.

'Of course, of course, I remember now.' I smile, my mouth dry. 'Well, thank you so much for coming in. I look forward to hearing your decision.' I reach out to shake his hand.

'I am sorry.' He takes my hand, looking unsure now, and know my face is giving me away again. 'I assumed . . . well, in any case, we'll know the outcome soon enough.'

'We will.' I flash him my most professional smile.

He looks at me for a second longer, and then makes his way out of the door. I look past him as he leaves, my eyes seeking Kirsty, but she's nowhere to be seen.

CHAPTER 11

Adam

'Ferg, do you only answer the phone the third time you're called as a lifestyle choice, or do you just enjoy being annoying?' Bil raises his eyebrows into the camera as Ferg's face joins ours on the screen.

'I don't like having it on loud; it's distracting.' Ferg shrugs. 'I was watering my tomatoes.'

'You know the police are going to raid you one of these days,' Piotr chips in. 'They'll see all the pigeons on your roof and know that you're hotboxing the place.'

'Well, they'll be sorely disappointed once they get inside.' Ferg has been attempting to grow every variety of tomato in his spare room for the last three years. He keeps the radiator on extra high to create a greenhouse effect, and his insulation is so shocking that the local birds use his roof as a roosting spot. He notices us laughing and tuts. 'Say what you want, you won't be complaining when I come to the Christmas buffet with a fresh panzanella.'

'What in shit's name is a panzanella?' Bil cries.

Ferg rolls his eyes. 'You're all philistines.'

'Anyway!' I force my way into the conversation before it kicks off. 'Let's talk Dublin.'

'No, wait,' Ferg says. "Before Bil gets his laddish itinerary out and bores us all to death, tell us what's up.'

'Everything OK with Hugh?' Piotr asks.

'Hugh's fine — his new home is brilliant.' I smile, and I watch as the slight crease of worry smooths itself from Piotr's forehead. They all experienced with me what happened at Hugh's last residential care, and have been checking in more regularly than usual at this new one. 'It's nothing, really . . . well, OK, some good news, first. Remember that student I told you about? Okie, the really gifted kid?' They nod. 'Well I'm tutoring him into university.'

'Wow, that's amazing news!' Bil cheers. 'So he's actually going to go and get his degree?'

'He's actually going to go and challenge himself, like he needs to.' I grin. '*If* I can pull it off.'

'You will, mate.' Piotr smiles. 'Well done.'

'We'll see.'

'So what's up, then?' Ferg asks, his black-and-white cat, Milo, snaking across his lap.

'Honestly, it's nothing. I'm probably overreacting.'

'Maybe, but a problem shared is a problem halved and all that bollocks,' Bil says.

'Agh, I don't know. It's Katie.' I feel disloyal even saying it. I have never spoken negatively about her behind her back.

'What?' Piotr leans in. 'Katie? Is she OK?'

If there was ever a sign that me and Katie have been smooth sailing from the word go, it's this. I bring up her name and they assume something's wrong with her, not that our relationship might have hit a bump. My heart swells a little. We're fine, everything's fine — nothing could break this.

'She's OK.' I take a breath. 'She's just been . . . she's been off, really, recently. Not talking to me as much, not wanting to go near me, being a bit . . . secretive?' Now I'm saying it out loud, it feels more real, and I realise that her behaviour can't be swept under the rug. 'And I found some stuff, in her bedside drawer.'

'Oh, god.' Ferg stares into the camera, his hand paused over Milo's back. 'What . . . kind of stuff?'

I shake my head. 'Stuff I can't really find an excuse for.' I tell them what I found, laying out my reasons for looking and the guilt I felt. When I finish speaking, there's a silence, and Bil coughs uncomfortably.

'Well, look, maybe there's a rational explanation,' Piotr tries. 'Maybe she's bought it all for your next holiday, or—'

'One of the condoms was missing and the cards look pretty well-used.' I sigh, feeling defeated. 'None of the under-wear had any tags on it.'

There's another silence, and I feel a headache coming on. Saying all of this, vocalising it, almost makes me feel stupid. Last night, when Katie got home, we sat and watched TV and I turned it all over in my head, trying to find a reason, an explanation that wouldn't incriminate her but now that I've laid it out for the boys, I realise I was kidding myself.

'This is really shit, Adam. I'm sorry,' Ferg says eventually.

'Well . . .' Bil says.

'What?'

'No, nothing, it doesn't matter.' Bil shakes his head. 'Maybe there's an explanation.'

He says it half-heartedly, and I look closely at the screen. None of them seem as shocked as I'd expected. Piotr is looking down, away from the camera, and Ferg is shuffling awkwardly in his seat.

'I texted her before I went into the drawer, asking if she minded me looking,' I push on, ignoring their reaction. They know how good Katie and I were. They just don't know what to say. 'I'd already looked by the time she answered.'

There's a pause, and I know what question is coming next. 'What did she say when she replied?'

'She said my passport wasn't in there so there was no point in me looking.' I rub my hand through my beard. 'I told her I hadn't looked, and she ran upstairs to get it when she got home, told me it was in the office drawer. I'd put it back where I'd found it, so I know that was a lie.'

Bil sighs. 'You need to talk to her.'

'But whatever explanation she comes out with, would he believe it?' Piotr asks, a hint of anger in his voice. 'Whatever she says, the seed of doubt has been planted.' He looks at me and winces. 'Sorry, Ad. I'm not trying to make you feel worse, I just can't see an innocent explanation.'

'Just because we can't think of one, doesn't mean there isn't one, does it?' I sit up in my chair. 'This isn't like her, is it? She wouldn't do something like this?'

The silence is longer this time, and panic grips at my throat. Eventually, Bil leans towards the camera. 'Whatever happens, Ad, we're here — you know that, right?'

I shake my head. 'Thank you, I know that, but—'

'Have you heard from Chloe?' Ferg blurts. 'If she knew about all of this—'

Piotr talks loudly over him, and I swallow down a sick feeling at the sound of Chloe's name. 'No matter how it turns out, we've always got Dublin!' he cheers, his voice too bright. 'Come on, let's take your mind off things. Ferg, we'll get your museum requests out of the way first, and then we can get onto the fun stuff.'

'I've got some brilliant distraction techniques,' Bil pipes up. 'You'll forget all about this in no time.'

For the next half an hour Bil goes through his stag-weekend-esque plans for our trip to Dublin, and Fergus and Piotr rein his ideas into a manageable itinerary. I only half-listen to what's being said. I can't concentrate, the twinge of a headache I felt earlier is intensifying, and I feel dazed, confused, unable to make sense of things.

By the time we're done, my head is somewhere else entirely. I end the phone call and pace the room, replaying their reactions in my mind. I'd expected shock, outrage, complete denial that anything could possibly be happening, but instead they seemed . . . unsurprised. Awkward. Pitying.

Chloe.

I shake my head and pull myself up, pushing everything out of my mind. I'm going to have to speak to Katie. Confrontation is not my strong suit. I hate feeling uncomfortable, and making other people feel awkward makes my skin crawl. I try to rally myself — this isn't cut-and-dry, is it? There are a million potential explanations, and Katie deserves the chance to explain before my imagination runs away with me. I owe her that . . . but a large part of me wants to pretend it isn't happening, close my eyes and wait for it to go away.

To distract myself, I call the University of Manchester switchboard and ask to be put through to disability support services. The woman at the end of the phone lists off the support available, and I jot it all down, the good news a pleasant distraction. Assistive software, human support, learning skills, library assistance . . . there's so much potential. As she talks, I imagine how I'll relay it all to Okie. Too much at once will make him retreat, but I want it to be clear that he won't be doing this alone.

For brief moments, I am excited and absorbed in the information I'm getting, but every time Katie is out of my head, a noise outside makes my eyes dart to the window, bringing me back to reality, checking whether she's home.

The woman at the end of the phone transfers me over to the admissions team, and I go to the kitchen to make a coffee while I listen to the hold music. As I'm filling the cafetière, I unwillingly practice what I'm going to say to Katie. Will I be direct? Present her with the evidence straight off the bat? Or will I sit her down, ask if she has anything to tell me, give her the opportunity to explain herself more civilly?

There must be an innocent reason behind what I found, I think as I push the plunger down, Pharell Williams' *Happy* blasting in my ear for the second time, no matter how convinced the boys seemed to be. Could those objects be from a previous relationship? Katie had several boyfriends before we met, and while she's not a sentimental person, it wouldn't be completely beyond the realms of possibility that she'd keep things from her past. I've got a keyring from Mexico that I bought while on holiday with my ex-girlfriend. It's similar, isn't it?

On autopilot, I begin walking up the stairs as the pre-recorded voice on the phone apologises for my wait. My hand is in the drawer before I even know what I'm doing. I dig around; the bag was at the back, near the bottom . . . where is it?

I shift the phone to my other ear, using my shoulder to prop it up as I move things around carefully. If I can just check the date on the condoms . . .

'Hello, University of Manchester admissions, how can I help you?'

It takes me a second to remember what I'm supposed to be doing.

'Oh, hi.' I keep riffling, pulling things out onto the bed and pushing papers from side to side. 'I'm enquiring on behalf of one of my students; he's hoping to apply this year, and—'

A noise downstairs makes me pause.

'Hello?' The man on the phone chirps.

It's a key in the door. Katie's home.

'I have to go.' I stab the 'end call' button and throw everything back into the drawer, kicking it shut with my foot once, twice before it finally closes.

'Adam?' Katie's coming up the stairs quickly, her feet heavy on the carpet. 'What's that banging?'

I throw myself backwards onto the bed, rolling over to my side and holding my phone in front of my face. I try to slow my breathing as she enters the room.

'What's going on?' She glances around, and I notice her eyes pause on her bedside cabinet. 'Is everything OK?'

'Yeah,' I say automatically, feigning distraction from my screen. 'Everything's fine.'

CHAPTER 12

Adam

I still haven't said anything.

It's not that I'm certain nothing's going on, although I'm pretty sure it isn't . . . but there's a part of me — a big part, a hopeful part — that's sure this must be a big misunderstanding.

An even bigger part of me knows that once I open the box, there'll be no going back. Accusing Katie is like throwing a grenade into a room full of balloons.

It's three hours since she got home, and I'm half watching *The Repair Shop* while I do this week's marking. Katie's in the kitchen, making pasta and humming happily.

'Linguine or spaghetti?' she calls, and I look up.

'I don't mind.' I smile, but it feels wobbly. What if this is our last evening together? *No, it couldn't be.* It's inconceivable.

I drag my eyes back to my marking, trying to concentrate on the equations in front of me. She couldn't have, could she? And if she has, what does that mean for us? I try to imagine a world without Katie in it, but I can't. Maybe I should let this slide; whether she's been with someone else or not, our relationship might stand a better chance if she's got it out of her system.

I sit back in my chair, shocked at myself. *What am I thinking?* Let her cheat on me so she doesn't realise how bored she is? I grip my pen tighter in my hand.

'Tea's ready!' she calls through again, and I stand up and make my way into the kitchen.

'It's just a basic tomato thing from a jar, sorry,' she says, sitting down. 'I couldn't be bothered chopping onions.'

'It looks great.' I twirl some pasta around my fork but my stomach churns.

There's silence as we eat, but as I force another mouthful down I realise she's staring at me.

'What?' I try to laugh.

'We haven't spent much time together lately.' She's holding her fork in mid-air, her dark eyes trained on mine. A droplet of pasta sauce hits the table and splatters onto the side of her bowl.

I swallow. 'I know. I've missed you.'

Is it over? Is whatever she's been doing finished?

She hasn't been doing *anything*. There's nothing going on.

'Let's go somewhere this weekend. The beach. We could get a hotel, maybe? Go for a big walk and a nice dinner?' She's looking at me, pleading, as if she knows I know. Or am I imagining things?

'That sounds good.' I can't help it; the idea is intoxicating. A night away together, a meal out, fresh air. We could talk things through and put it all behind us.

'Great.' She smiles and sits back in her chair, looking relieved. 'What do you reckon, St. Anne's?'

'Or Blackpool,' I tease. She hates Blackpool; every summer of her childhood was spent at Pontins and she doesn't have fond memories.

'Shut up.' She laughs, reaching over and swiping me on the arm.

Impulse makes me grab her hand. 'I love you.'

Her eyes widen, then she shakes her head and laughs, tugging her hand back. 'Where's that come from?'

I shrug, trying to ignore the sting from her reaction. 'We don't say it as much anymore.'

She picks up her fork and moves the remaining spaghetti around her plate, not meeting my eyes. 'That's just the nature of relationships, isn't it? The longer you're together the less sugar-sweet everything is.'

I think back to Dominic and his 'everything turns to shit' attitude. 'Well, maybe I liked it when things were sweeter.'

A flush creeps up her neck, as if she's embarrassed for me. 'Adam,' she laughs again, her eyebrows furrowed, 'what's going on?'

'Nothing.' I smile. 'Just a thought.'

I stand up from the table and clear the plates, taking them to the sink, rinsing the cutlery and stacking the dishwasher, my back turned. When I glance over my shoulder she's gone into the living room, and I can hear the TV.

She didn't say it back.

But she wants a weekend with me.

I clear the sides and wipe down the table, putting my phone on charge next to the toaster. I make two cups of tea and take them into the living room, placing them on the table and sitting next to Katie on the sofa.

'What are we watching?' I ask.

She shuffles forwards and cups her tea in her hands. 'I might go and run a bath, actually.'

'Oh, OK.' I watch her as she stands up and makes her way towards the door, leaving behind the TV programme she just put on.

She stops as she reaches the door. 'Have a think about where you want to go this weekend. I think there's a new spa hotel in Lytham we could try?'

Despite everything, my heart lifts again. 'I'll have a look.'

She disappears upstairs and I sink back into the sofa. My impulse to bury my head in the sand is almost overwhelming. I could watch *Selling Sunset*, drink my tea, go to bed and then wake up tomorrow pretending none of this is happening.

I pull my feet up onto the sofa and let my head fall back onto a cushion. Say we *did* go away this weekend . . . we're in the middle of a heatwave and the beach would be the perfect place to be. We could go swimming, get ice cream, sit on the pier. Maybe, after that, we'd reconnect.

The thought of the distraction swims tantalisingly around my head. I'll just check the weather, make sure that the heat isn't due to break. Then I can have a look at some hotels . . .

My phone is in the kitchen, so I absentmindedly pick Katie's up from the table, keying in her PIN to unlock it: 240318 — the day we got together. The phone judders and I sigh, entering it again, assuming I've made a mistake. It vibrates again, clearing the numbers I entered and telling me I have five more attempts. Has she changed the code? I type it slowly this time, saying each number out loud.

Incorrect.

My heart picks up pace, thudding quickly. Why would she have changed the code? She's had the same PIN since a few months after we met. I ignore the alarm bells as another thought occurs to me — she logged my fingerprint alongside her own when she got this phone. It's something we've done since fingerprint recognition became a thing, not due to a lack of trust, but for ease — when she needs me to reply to a text, or I need her to check the map on my phone, it's easier if we can quickly unlock.

I place my thumb over the sensor and it judders again. I try the other thumb — nothing. I adjust my angle, being careful, but the phone stays locked, again and again, until it tells me that fingerprint access is disabled and I'll have to enter the PIN.

I'm on my feet before I can think, running up the stairs with the phone in my hand. I open the bathroom door and Katie gasps, sitting up in the bubbles.

'Adam! I'm in the bath!' Her hair is damp and wisps of it are clinging to her forehead.

'Have you changed your phone code?'

'What?' She wraps her arms around herself.

'And have you disabled my thumbprint?'

'Have you been *snooping*?'

I breathe deeply, feeling the tears building behind my nose. 'Are you cheating on me?'

She stares at me, her mouth open. The bathroom smells of lavender and vanilla, and on the mirror is a heart I drew for her weeks ago, brought to life again by the steam.

'Katie!' I shout, my voice cracking. 'Answer me!'

She stays silent.

I feel something inside me crumble. 'I found all the stuff in your drawers.'

'What stuff?' Her ears are pink.

'You know what stuff!'

'I don't know what you're talking about—'

'You moved it all, after I said I was going to look for my passport. The underwear, the cards, the con—'

'Stop it!' she shrieks, standing up and spraying water across the floor. She snatches her towel from the rail and steps onto the bathmat. 'Just stop talking, Adam.'

'Why? Because otherwise you'll have to admit what you've done?'

She stares at me, her eyes round and her face flushed. She looks so beautiful, I can't stand it.

'What the fuck, Katie,' I whisper.

She pulls her towel tight around herself and pushes her hair from her face. 'I was going to stop.'

Her words don't reach me immediately, it takes a few seconds to process their meaning. And then it comes like a punch, right in my chest. 'It's still . . . you're still . . .'

Her mouth drops open again as she realises what she's said.

How could I be so stupid? I was going to let this slide, book us a hotel, try to see the positives.

'Who is he?' I step further into the bathroom and sink down onto the toilet seat. I put my head in my hands and stare at her toes on the bathmat in front of me; did she put that red nail polish on for him? I remember the night of the awards, her red lipstick and black dress. Her absence. Who was she dressing up for?

When she finally speaks, it's so quiet I can barely hear. 'A guy from work.'

I don't want to know any more. I don't want a name, or an age, or a 'how many times' or 'do you love him'. I know that she doesn't love *me*, and that's enough.

'Adam.' She bends down and rests her head on top of mine, and the damp warmth of her tears me in two. I'll never hold her again.

'I'll sleep in the spare room,' I say, standing up and pushing past her.

'You don't have to do that,' she calls after me. 'I'll go and stay somewhere else.'

No more nights together. I stride into the bedroom, closing the door behind me as my heart cracks and breaks over and over again.

CHAPTER 13

Eve

Subject: Instagram Campaign Update
From: Kirsty.mcclure@florina.co.uk
To: Dev.kalhora@florina.co.uk
13:12:38 — 8 May 2022

Hi Dev,

Just a quick update about the hyacinth Instagram campaign — find attached the numbers, which are up 18% on the last promotion we did back in February. I'd like to extend this by a week, before moving the 10% introductory deal to cyclamens, which we're trying to give a summer revamp. Would love to know your thoughts?

On another note, I'd like to put myself forward for your paternity leave cover. I know it's slightly unconventional, and that the post isn't currently advertised, but I feel that I am more than capable and could bring some brilliant ideas to the role.

Please find attached my updated CV and a PDF of my recent successful campaigns and their figures.

*I have spoken to my manager, Eve Slater, about this,
and she is in support of my application.*
Best wishes,
Kirsty

* * *

Subject: RE: Instagram Campaign Update
From: Dev.kalhora@florina.co.uk
To: Kirsty.McClure@florina.co.uk
15:57:29 — 14 May 2022

Hi Kirsty,
Thanks — will check through this and get back to you.
*With regards to my pat cover: you are right, this isn't
an advertised vacancy and would normally be considered a
'promotion', meaning upper management would decide who
was best to undertake the added responsibility and receive any
corresponding change in pay.*
*That being said, I admire your confidence and know
from Eve that your work is always exemplary. As you have
received her permission, I will keep your name in mind for
the role and will let you know as soon as a decision is made.*
Best,
Dev

* * *

'Six weeks ago!' I click furiously through the desktop calendar, flicking back to the middle of May. 'No, over six weeks! Nearly seven weeks since she emailed to put her application in.'

I push my chair back from behind me furiously, sending it skidding across the room.

'Calm down.' Graham glances through the window to the office. 'People are looking.'

'I won't get you in trouble, Graham, don't worry.' I lean forward, clutching the edge of the desk, my knuckles white. 'I can't *believe* it.'

He shrugs. 'Maybe she felt like she couldn't tell you.'

'Oh!' I pull myself upright and spin around to face him. '*Poor her.* But she could lie about getting my permission, could she? And could cope with me finding out from *Dev*? She was fine with me being humiliated, and with congratulating me at the paternity leave party, and with being a lying, backstabbing little—'

Graham's hand is on my shoulder, and I realise I'm waving my arms in the air aggressively. Somehow, I've made it to the other side of my office.

'I need to log you out now.' He frowns. 'This was a bad idea.'

'No! Wait, give me two more minutes.' I push past him and pull my chair back up to my desk. I click through a few more emails.

'Seriously, Eve, this isn't good.'

'Wait!' I hiss. He sighs and pulls out his phone. I keep clicking, looking through the emails she's saved under the name 'Application Support' — all the praise from upper management, every good piece of feedback I've ever sent her. All tucked into a neat little folder for her to use against me.

'Come on.' Graham pockets his phone and comes over, and I close the screen.

'Fine.'

He checks I'm logged off, and then gives me a look. 'What are you going to do?'

'I haven't figured it out yet.'

'You could just tell Dev she didn't ask for your permission,' he suggests.

'I can't!' I seethe. 'I pretended I knew that she'd applied.'

'Hm.' He frowns. 'Well, maybe just work hard and let the best woman win? You know you'll cinch it.'

'I know I will.' I sigh, running my fingers through my fringe to flatten it. I check my watch and turn to Graham again. 'Thanks, anyway. I'll buy you a drink later. Shall we say seven?'

'Ah.' He looks away. 'I'm busy tonight.'

'Big night in with your mum, is it?' I tease.

'Not quite.' He catches my eye.

'*Oh*.' I raise my eyebrows. 'The girl from Dev's party?'

'Who? Oh, no, haven't spoken to her.' He looks sheepish. 'Hannah, from accounts.'

'Very nice. You move quickly,' I say, rage plucking at my throat again. I sit down and fix my eyes on my computer screen. 'Anyway, I've got to get back to work, so I'll see you later.'

He chews his lip, staring at me for a second, and then moves towards the door. Before he leaves, he turns around. 'Don't be a dick about it, eh, Eve?'

* * *

'I mean, it's just basic etiquette, isn't it? Like, not even on a managerial level, but just as a *friend*. Is she a psychopath? Well? I'm serious, is she?'

We're sitting outside Katsouris Deli on Deansgate, the buses trundling past noisily. Jess is slowly lowering a bottle of organic champagne back into her tote bag.

'I can't believe it, Eve,' she says, pushing the bag out of sight under the table. 'It's mad, isn't it, Will?'

Will nods, holding a bottle of iced tea against his neck. 'It's certainly a betrayal of trust.'

'It's a betrayal of *everything*.' I shake my head. 'How could she do this?'

'Have you spoken to her?' Jess rests her hand on her chin. 'Maybe she can explain.'

'No, I haven't, and no, she can't.' I take a sip of my frappe. 'She's conveniently been out of the office since the news broke.'

'Give her a call?' Will suggests. 'Maybe there's something going on.'

'You're right.' I nod. 'Maybe she's been possessed.'

'You know what I mean.' He rolls his eyes, and I notice that he looks tired.

'How's Benny?' Jess turns her attention to Will.

'He's fine,' he smiles. 'Not sleeping super well, but that's to be expected.'

I tune out as they discuss Will's parenting difficulties. I care, of course I do, but I can't concentrate. I need a brainstorming session, I need tactics, I need everyone focused on how we're going to resolve this.

'I'm calling her,' I say, interrupting their conversation. They turn to me and watch as I put my phone to my ear.

'What are you going to *say*?' Jess whispers.

I hold up my hand as Kirsty's voicemail message chirps in my ear.

'Oh, hey, Kirsty. Just thought I'd check in. I haven't seen you in a while. I had my meeting with Dev on Monday, if you remember? He told me you'd put yourself forward for his paternity cover! That's exciting. Anyway, give me a call when you get this and we can figure out what the fuck is going on. Bye!'

I hang up.

'That went well,' Will says drily.

I take a deep breath. 'I'll be more professional when she calls back.'

My phone starts ringing.

'Is it her?' Jess gasps, peering at my screen.

I nod. Right, this is it. I need to get my head on straight. I'm a professional woman, and I will be getting this job. There's no point giving Kirsty a chance to report me for poor conduct in the interim.

'Hello?'

'Eve.' She sounds down, sombre. 'Eve, I'm so sorry. I should have told you.'

'No problem,' I breeze. 'You're perfectly entitled to apply for any positions that come up within the company.'

But you're not entitled to lie about getting my permission, I think, but bite my tongue. If she finds out I've seen her emails, it's game over.

'I swear I would have come to you, but it was all so quick. Dev spoke to me just before he came to you, it was such a shock.'

A cold fury wraps itself around my neck. *Liar.*

'Of course, it must have been really tricky for you,' I say calmly. 'Especially when you were so supportive of me getting the job.'

'Exactly!' she breathes, and I can hear the relief in her voice. 'I've just felt awful, I haven't been able to get out of bed.'

'Gosh, well if it's making you feel that terrible perhaps you should just drop out of the running?' I say, unable to help myself.

'Well . . . yeah, maybe I should,' she says, but there's defiance in her voice now. 'But I'm sure you'll get it anyway. There wouldn't be much point.'

'No, you're probably right,' I reply, my hand tight around the phone. 'Anyway, Kirsty, I've got to run. I'll see you when you're back in the office?'

'Of course, I'll—'

I hang up.

'Well?' Jess leans forward. 'Is she dropping out?'

'Of course she isn't.' I drain the rest of my drink in one long slurp, and then crumple the plastic in my fist. 'But she's deluded if she thinks she's in with a chance.'

CHAPTER 14

Eve

'Manifestation, Eve.' Jess is sprawled across my living room floor, a pile of books scattered around her. 'It's been scientifically proven to work.'

I pull two yogurts from the fridge and toss one to her, peeling the lid off my own and eating it while leaning against the arm of the sofa. 'So you're telling me that science says you can just wish for something and it'll happen?'

'Not *wish*, Eve. Wishing is for children and Christmas. *Manifest*.' She tips her yogurt up and drinks it instead of asking for a spoon. 'You will the universe to give you what you want and it listens.'

'. . . a wish, then.'

Jess sighs. 'No. Come here and sit down and I'll show you.'

'I need to do my meal prepping for the week.'

'Eve!' Jess gives me her sternest look. 'Sit down. Now.'

'Can I at least make a coffee first?'

She rolls her eyes. 'Fine.'

I take my time, prolonging the inevitable, and then dump myself on a cushion in front of her, popping our mugs on coasters on the floor.

'Right, take this piece of paper,' she rips a sheet from her notepad and thrusts it into my hand, 'and write down everything you want.'

Jess flicks through books while I write, occasionally scribbling something in one of the margins. After ten minutes have passed, she slams her copy of *Chakras for the Soul* closed and turns to me. 'OK, read them out to me.'

'Isn't it supposed to be private?'

'I'm a spiritual teacher, you're allowed to tell me,' she says seriously.

'OK. Number one, get the job.'

'Good.' She nods. 'Keep going.'

'That's it.'

'What do you mean *that's it*?' She snatches the paper from my hand. 'Eve! There must be other things you want.'

I think for a second, and then shake my head. 'Don't think so.'

'What about a man? Kids?'

I roll my eyes. 'Can I manifest for stuff *not* to happen?'

She screws the paper into a ball. 'I thought your Tryst date on Thursday went well?'

'It did!' I say, brightening a little. 'He was completely emotionally unavailable.'

'Oh my god.' She groans and looks at the ceiling. 'Fine, just the job. Have you figured things out with Kirsty?'

'We're being professional, but she's staying out of my way.'

'So you're just going to keep going as normal and hope for the best?'

I consider my answer. There's been a ball of rage in my stomach since my meeting with Dev last Wednesday, and try as I might, I can't seem to put it to bed. But Kirsty is one of my best friends. We should talk about this. But how can we, when she's betrayed me like this? 'Maybe.'

'Oh, Eve, don't. I liked Kirsty.'

'Yeah, so did I.'

Jess lies back on a cushion and I get to my feet, stepping over a book about botanicals and walking back over to the kitchen area of the open-plan living space. I pull some salmon out of the fridge and begin chopping vegetables, loading them into a tray and turning on the oven.

'Since when do you do weekly meal prepping?' Jess calls over.

'Since it became better for the environment,' I lie. Really, it's because I can't sit still, and because there's a small part of me that worries this promotion and the increased income might be snatched away from me. Living on Deliveroo and meal deals isn't financially sensible.

'Oh!' Jess props herself up onto her elbows. 'Guess who I ran into the other day.'

'Go on?'

'Jamie Fishwick.' She snorts.

'The guy from that druggie weekend you went on?' I carve into a red pepper and chop it into chunks.

'It wasn't a *druggie* weekend, Eve! It was ayahuasca.'

'The drug?'

She flips her dreadlocks over her shoulder. 'Well, *yes*, technically, but . . . anyway, never mind.'

'Didn't you fall in love with Jamie Fishwick within three hours and then ditch him after you went through his phone?' I ask.

'It was love at first sight.' She nods. 'We had one beautiful night together before I found out he was a journalist.'

'Oh yeah. He was doing an article and trying to use photos of you when you were off your tits, wasn't he?'

'He was using me as a *case study*,' she corrects me. 'Lying bastard.'

Something nudges at the back of my mind. An idea.

'Didn't you edit his article?' I ask casually.

'Yeah!' She laughs. 'I changed the story a bit, and put the word 'cock' somewhere in the middle where he wouldn't notice.'

I start laughing too. 'God, yeah, I remember.'

The idea is taking shape now, and Jess's voice fades into the background. I cut a butternut squash into pieces, toss it in the tray and drizzle over some olive oil. I add salt, pepper and thyme, like the recipe says, and then put the tray in the oven. My heart starts beating quickly, adrenaline pumping in my throat. Could I? I couldn't. No. But maybe . . .

'Eve? Are you listening to me?'

'Yes, of course.' I drop three salmon fillets into my biggest frying pan. 'Did he ever find out what you'd done?'

Jess looks at me like I've lost the plot. 'I just *told* you, his editor spotted the additions just before it went live. He couldn't prove it was me — I did it from his phone.'

'Attagirl.' I squeeze some lemon over the fish and put it in the oven with the vegetables, before moving into the living room and perching on the windowsill. 'You never saw him again, then?'

'Nope.' She giggles. 'Will you sit down? You're like a bloody budgie.'

'Shut up.'

She rolls over onto her side, repositioning the cushions underneath her. 'God, it's so hot. Do you think Will was alright the other day?'

The sudden change in topic makes me pay attention. 'What do you mean?'

'I dunno.' She stands up and goes to the back door, pulling it open even wider. 'He seemed really tired.'

'He's living with a baby.' I shrug. 'It comes with the territory.'

'Hm.' She flops back down onto the floor and spreads her arms and legs like a starfish. 'Eve, I'm dying.'

'I've got a couple of those cucumber face masks upstairs?'

'Oh my god, yes, please.'

I go up the stairs, noticing a little bit of dust here, a slight mark on the carpet there. I make a mental note to rent a rug doctor while the weather's good.

As I rifle through the bathroom cupboards, my idea comes back to me. It's dangerous, of course, but tempting. Is it too far? I remember Kirsty's emails, the way she used my support as a weapon against me. I *deserve* that job. I've worked harder and put in longer hours than her. I'm a year or two younger than her, sure, but I have more experience, I'm more senior than she is. It's a no-brainer, surely?

Florina's target market might be women, but upper management is an old boys' club. Everyone knows you've got to be ruthless to make it in, to prove that you're willing to go above and beyond and put emotions to the side. But she's my *friend*. How could she do this to me?

'Eve!' Jess calls from downstairs, her voice panicked. 'Eve, there's a cat in your living room!'

I take the stairs two at a time, clutching the face masks in my fists. 'What?' I pant as I skid into the living room. 'Where?'

'It's just run out!' She points to the back door. 'A dead scrawny one.'

I peer through the back door, but there's nothing but the sun-baked patio. 'I can't see anything.'

'I swear!' She puts her hand to her chest. 'It just ran in and jumped on the sofa. There.'

She points to a patch on the cushion, where a few wispy hairs have settled on the fabric.

'It'll be that one from next door again.' I sigh. 'It was in the garden a week or so ago.'

'Aw, cute.' She pouts. 'Do you think it's lost?'

'Who knows.' I shrug. 'Anyway, shall we do these face masks?'

'Sure.'

We paste the cool mixture onto our hot skin and then lie, sighing, on the kitchen tiles.

'What are you thinking, Eve?' Jess turns her head towards me.

'What do you mean?'

'You're plotting something. You're always quiet when you're scheming.'

'I'm not!' I slap her arm.

'Don't touch me, I'm burning to death.'

I laugh. 'Pour a bucket of water over me.'

'And ruin your floors? You'd never forgive me.'

I sigh. 'You're right.'

She looks at me again, but I stay quiet.

'Honestly, Eve.' She taps her foot against mine. 'Don't do anything stupid.'

'I won't.'

She sniffs loudly. 'I think your fish is burning, mate.'

CHAPTER 15

Adam

Just as there are times in life when you are drunker than you believe, there are also times when you are very, very aware of how plastered you are.

Right now is one of those times.

I am sitting in Sinclair's Oyster Bar, on my eighth £2.50 pint of Taddy, and Bil has just had a bright idea to pull me out of my slump.

'Give me your phone!' he roars, his volume-control switch officially broken.

'Why? No!' I clutch my phone like it's my firstborn child. 'You're not deleting her number.'

'Nah mate, it's too soon for that, she still needs to get all her stuff.' He beckons with his hand again. 'Come on, hand it over.'

Through my drunken fog, I vaguely register that I've memorised Katie's number, so all being well I can remember it tomorrow anyway. 'Fine.' I unlock the phone and pass it over.

'Right, where's the App Store on this thing?' He squints at the screen with one eye closed, swiping with his index finger. 'There.'

'Ooh, I know where this is going,' Piotr cackles.

'RIP, Adam.' Ferg pats me on the arm.

'What? What's he doing?' I take another sip of my pint and instantly regret it.

'*Et voila.* You are officially the owner of one Tryst app.' Bil grins. 'Right, let's set up your profile.'

I groan. Online dating is *not* for me. Katie and I met at work, when I was a secondary school maths teacher and she was the school nurse. It was organic and perfect, and made a brilliant story. Secretly, I've always felt a bit sorry for people who meet online. But then again, look where the alternative got me.

'Curly-haired Adonis seeks someone to listen to his boring coffee stories.' Bil giggles as he types.

'No, no, try this: Are you the x to my y? Come and solve this maths tutor's special equation.' Piotr snorts.

They collapse into giggles and I let my head hit the table.

'Forget Pythagoras, let me be the father of *your* triangle.' Ferg quips, and they all explode with laughter.

'What does that even *mean*?' I cry, laughing despite myself.

'Right, come on, enough of that.' Piotr wipes the corners of his eyes. 'Let's get swiping.'

'Alright.' Bil taps a few times. 'Wait, wait, we need a picture.'

'Use the one from my—'

'If you say LinkedIn, I swear I'll kill you,' Bil warns.

I *was* going to say LinkedIn.

'When was that picture even taken?' Somehow, he's pulled it up on my phone and they're all staring at it. '2006?'

'No!' I say. 'Like, five years ago.'

'Bollocks.' Piotr takes the phone from Bil and trains it on me. 'Time for a new one, smile.'

I grin drunkenly, and make a mental note to delete the entire profile tomorrow.

'Right, now let's get down to business.' Bil settles back in his seat and the other two crowd round. 'Ooh, she looks nice. Oh, shit, it's right for yes, isn't it?'

'Pass it here.' Ferg takes the phone. 'Yes, yes, yes, yes, hmmm . . . yes, yes—'

'Ferg, you can't say yes to *everybody*!' Piotr protests.

'They all look nice!' Ferg retorts. 'Look, this one's a doctor.'

'No more medical people.' I shake my head. 'If I smell hand sanitiser on another woman I'll have a breakdown.'

'Quick, Bil, update his profile: allergic to individuals in the care sector.'

I laugh. 'Piss off.'

'Jenny, yes, Roberta, yep, Bella . . . hmm, no, she's got a French bulldog, it's unethical, Grace, yes, Eve, yes, Eleanor, oh god, definitely not, she's a Trump supporter. I didn't even think they existed over here?'

'You know I'm not going to touch this app again once we're done here?' I try.

'You might!' Piotr sits down next to me, leaving the other two to carry on swiping. 'Never say never.'

'Hmm.'

'I am sorry, mate.' He squeezes my arm and I feel the tears rush back to the surface. 'You didn't deserve it.'

'Thanks.' I wipe the end of my nose and he hands me a tissue.

'We thought . . .' He gestures vaguely to the air around him and then shrugs. 'Well. It doesn't matter what we thought.'

'It does, of course it does.' I'm slurring slightly, and I put my drink down. 'You thought we'd have broken up sooner.'

It's only now that it's happened, now that she's gone, that I can even bear to say it. The way the guys reacted to Katie's betrayal, the way they've been this evening with their ploys to help me move on, suggests they had less faith in our relationship than I thought.

Piotr sighs and runs his finger around the rim of his glass. 'You're not alone, Ad. You know that, right?'

'I know. I'll be alright. I just need time.'

'Take as much as you need.' Bil leans across the table, lowering the phone for a moment. 'If you're still feeling crappy by the time we go to Dublin, I've got some tricks up my sleeve.'

'Well that's motivation to get over it if ever there was any.' I laugh snottily. 'I dread to think.'

'You don't need another woman,' Ferg scrapes his chair up to the table noisily. 'I haven't had sex for five years and I'm alright.'

Piotr raises his eyebrows. 'I think the jury's still out on that one, mate.'

We collapse into laughter again, and I wonder, just for a second, if maybe I will be alright after all.

* * *

The hangover is already kicking in by the time I stumble through my front door. It's dark and empty without Katie here, but I bat away the urge to mope. She often worked nights, so this isn't new.

It's gone midnight, but the heat is still heavy and I can feel a headache coming on. I make myself a cup of tea and go to the back door, sitting on the step and sipping slowly. Every so often I lose my balance and almost fall backwards into the kitchen. I am so drunk.

Tomorrow is going to be hell. I have no lessons, so all I'll be able to do is wallow in my hungover shame. I don't know where Katie's gone. I assume she's at his house, but I don't want to think about it. If I let my imagination run, it'll never stop.

Another wave of drunkenness washes over me and this time I don't try to fight it. I let my body fall back until I hit the kitchen tiles with a soft thud. My legs hanging out of the back door, I stare at the ceiling and sigh.

'I loved her,' I say out loud, my voice cracking. 'I love her.'

The kitchen stays silent, the hum of the fridge the only sound above the distant roar of the motorway a few miles away.

My mind drifts lazily back six years, to stolen glances in primary school corridors and unnecessary trips to the nurse's office to request a plaster that wasn't really needed. The staff Christmas night out when, emboldened by eye-wateringly strong tiki cocktails, I admitted to her that the cold compress I'd asked for the week before had sat in the drawer of my desk the entire day, completely unneeded, until it had soaked all of the practice SATs papers for my lesson the next morning. The resulting reprinting had caused the launch of an internal investigation into 'abuse of stationery privileges'.

She had pretended to be horrified, telling me that she was going to report me to Mr Beasley, the school's biggest jobsworth busybody, for abuse of medical supplies, too. Then she'd leaned in and whispered, 'You're a terrible liar, you know.'

And she was right. My disguised attempts to see her were completely transparent. It was her that was the actress all along.

A tear leaks out of the corner of my eye and trickles down onto the cool floor beneath me. My phone vibrates against my leg, and I pull it out and hold it above my face.

Chloe: *Adam, please just answer the phone.*

'AGH!' I roar into the silence.

Something soft brushes against my ankle and I jump, sitting upright, my phone skidding across the floor.

I blink. There's a cat — a scraggly tortoiseshell — sitting on the patio by my feet and swishing its tail.

'Hi?' I croak.

It stands up, arches its back and then trots through the back door and into the kitchen.

'Erm, excuse me . . .' I scrabble to my feet, holding onto the door frame for balance. 'This isn't your house, can you—'

The cat turns and stares at me with huge amber eyes.

I stare back. 'Look, mate, I appreciate the ballsy approach, but now really isn't the time.' I take a few steps forward, crouching down unsteadily and reaching out my hand.

He stands stock-still as I run my fingers through his patchy fur. It's soft, but comes out in thick clumps as I root around, looking for a collar. There isn't one.

'Whose are you?' I ask.

He stares at me, as though trying to convey the message that he answers to nobody. I shake my head. I'm too drunk for this.

'Well, I'm going to bed, so . . .'

He blinks.

'. . . off you pop.' I sweep my hands gently, trying to usher him out of the door. He sits down and sweeps at the tiles with his tail.

I sigh, and then move towards the fridge. 'Fine. I'm going to get a glass of water and a snack.'

I run the tap and unsheathe a Peperami before taking a bite. The cat stares at me some more, and then meows.

'Oh, you want some?' I break a piece off the top as an idea hits me. 'Go on, then!' I throw the chunk out of the back door.

He pads slowly over, tentatively sniffing the air, and then steps gingerly outside.

I shut the door quickly behind him.

'Sorry!' I shout. 'It's just late, and I really need to go to bed . . .' I trail off, realising how ridiculous I must sound. The cat has probably gone; run away to beg for food at some other person's house. I flick off the kitchen lights and take a swig of my water, before leaning over to close the blinds.

The cat is still there, sitting under the floodlight, licking his lips and staring unblinkingly back at me.

CHAPTER 16

Eve

'It's Canada Goose, actually,' my Tryst date for the evening, Jay, says proudly, a bead of sweat glimmering on his forehead.

'It's also thirty degrees,' I remind him.

'Two birds, one stone.' He leans back in his chair, and the resulting pungent waft from inside his coat suggests he hasn't removed it all day. 'Get myself nice and dehydrated before my session tomorrow and the definition will be *mwah*.' He kisses the tips of his fingers. 'Plus, what's the point in spending a grand on a coat if you're never going to wear it?'

I want to remind Jay that spending a fortune on a car wouldn't mean he had to sit in it for the rest of his life, but I bite my tongue.

'How old did you say you were again?' he asks, slurping his cucumber water thirstily.

'Thirty-three,' I say. 'It's on my profile.'

'You know how it is.' He lets out a small belch. 'You swipe past so many, you lose track.'

I nod. I can't exactly disagree. 'And you?'

'Twenty-six.' He catches sight of my face and laughs. 'Don't worry, I like an older woman. And hey,' he leans forward, bringing his stench across the table with him, 'it's on my profile.' He winks.

Jesus Christ. This might be a step too far, even for me. I check the time: 8.48 p.m. Jess will call in twelve minutes, and I'm definitely going to go for the dead dog. The self-obsession I can cope with — I seek it out, actually — but the smell, and the Canada Goose, and the cucumber burps . . . no. There's such a thing as self-respect, and I need to get some.

'Just going for a slash.' Jay scrapes his chair back noisily and rustles his way across Deansgate's latest 'wellness bar' to the bathroom, his coat brushing everyone he passes. People stare at me sadly.

A waitress appears and offers me a shot of turmeric juice, which I politely decline. I pull out my phone and go back onto Tryst. If I line another one up, I won't be tempted to go home with Jay. I swipe quickly, only stopping on a few profiles to gather more information before making a decision.

Chris. 29. Mountain Rescue Volunteer; four miles away. Nice face, but kind eyes and too selfless. Left swipe.

Jonathan. 35. Sales Executive; six miles away. His bio says he's looking for a 'wifey for lifey'. Left swipe.

Adam. 34. Maths tutor; less than one mile away. Gibberish in his bio; something about a triangle and an axis. He looks cute in his photo: messy, curly hair, nice teeth, a huge smile that makes his eyes shine—

'Back.' Jay throws himself into his seat, making the reclaimed bamboo table shudder. I jump, and my fingers skitter across the phone as I scrabble to lock it. 'Texting anuvva luvva?' he drawls in a faux-Cockney accent.

My phone trills in my hand, and I answer it quickly, not even bothering to excuse myself.

Two minutes later, I'm pretend-crying over Boingy, the dead dog I've never owned, as Jay escorts me out of the door.

* * *

'You know it's nine thirty? On a Friday?' Graham huffs as he swipes us into the building and strides over to the lifts. 'We'll probably be sacked.'

'We won't.' I wave him away and stab the button for our floor. 'I work 'til midnight sometimes.'

We ride up in silence, and I wonder when he's going to ask.

'I really don't see why I couldn't update the system on Monday for you. Is it that urgent?' He leans against the doors and regards me steadily.

I mentally organise everything I learned from Google just ten minutes ago: the features I'd only have access to with the new Windows update.

'I need to add new animations to my PowerPoint for the expo.' I step out into the corridor as soon as the lift doors open. 'Only available with the latest software, apparently.'

He grumbles behind me as we make our way across the room and into my office. I weave around my desk and stand by the window, positioning myself carefully. Graham lowers himself into my seat.

'Do you need me to log on?' I ask, crossing my fingers behind my back.

'No.' He taps his fingers on the desk as the machine boots itself up. 'I need to log in as admin to make changes to the software.'

My stomach jumps with excitement.

I toyed with telling Graham my plans — he helped me get into Kirsty's emails the other day, after all — but it would have been too risky. Even Graham has a moral compass, particularly when it comes to keeping his job.

'Where have you been, anyway?' he asks, turning around and looking me up and down.

'On a date with a guy who wouldn't take his coat off,' I sigh, pulling out my phone nonchalantly.

'In this heat?'

'Yeah, I know.' I glance at the screen, but the computer is still turning itself on. 'How was last night? Heather, was it?'

'Hannah,' he says, with an arched eyebrow that tells me he knows I knew. 'It was good. We spent the day together today.'

'Nice. Did I interrupt?'

'Of course.' The computer makes a noise, and he glances over his shoulder before turning back to me. 'Your timing is always inconvenient.'

I pretend to bow. 'Got a second date lined up, then?'

He smiles but doesn't answer, holding my gaze for a second too long. Just as I'm about to look away, he swivels back round to face the screen. I shake myself, remembering why I'm here, and position myself behind his chair quickly, pretending to be interested in what he's doing. The smell of him makes me dizzy.

'OK . . .' He types in the username and password with lightning speed. My desktop appears. I pocket my phone as he clicks around, going into settings and opening and closing the internet browser.

'Right, that'll take an hour or two, so probably best if you come back tomorrow.' He leans back in the chair and raises his hands over his head, stretching.

'Oh, it's OK. I'll wait. I've got my laptop so I can be doing some other stuff.' I dig around in my bag.

He looks at me again, a slight crease between his eyebrows. In the dim security lighting, his blonde hair looks darker, and his eyes shine. For a second, I think he's going to see through me, but then he sighs and stands up.

'I don't feel like going home yet.' He slings his jacket over his arm. 'Fancy a drink while you work? I can go and grab some beers from Londis.'

'Sounds perfect.' I feel the relief course through my body. Just ten minutes alone, it's all I need.

'Alright, back in a sec.' He brushes past me, his thumb grazing against my arm, and walks out of the door. I watch as he goes into the lift and turns around, fixing me with that look again as the doors slide closed.

It takes me a second to ground myself, but once I do I'm quick, running out of my office and over to Kirsty's desk. I pull out my phone and find the video I've just taken, the one of Graham entering the admin login details. I slow it down, pulling my finger across the play bar and following each stroke carefully. It takes me longer than I thought it would, but after six attempts, I'm in.

In the back of my mind, I know I could get Graham in a lot of trouble for this. If they investigated, they'd see that his details had logged onto Kirsty's computer. But what choice do I have? If ruthless is the name of Kirsty's game, I have to match her. Dev wouldn't worry about things like this. Michael wouldn't play fair.

I click through her folders, looking for the most boringly named ones to see what I can find. I keep searching, occasionally opening random folders and finding nothing but PowerPoints and Excel Spreadsheets. Then, just as I'm growing conscious of Graham coming back, I find a folder called 'Tax Returns'.

My heart leaps. Unless Kirsty has a secret card-making business I'm not aware of, she doesn't file her own taxes. I click into it.

There's a single document inside, titled 'F Ups'.

Frowning, I open it.

For a second, I'm not sure what I'm reading. It's out of context, just paragraphs of text.

And then I notice my name.

Again and again.

It's emails. Emails I've sent to Kirsty, dating back over the last two years.

> *. . . just realised I spelled 'chrysanthemum' wrong on the new Facebook click-through campaign . . .*

> *. . . accidentally got accounts to set up the wrong supplier, and now they've paid almost 12k to a random woman in Bournemouth — managed to cover it so Dev shouldn't find out . . .*

... spent three hours this morning trying to get B&Q to come back round after I forwarded them that email by mistake — you know the one where we called their buyer a Z-List Hugh Grant ...

For a second, I think I'm going to be sick. My body is covered in goosebumps and my hands are shaking.

Kirsty has saved all of our correspondence; every time I've fucked up, she's copied and pasted it into a word document. For *two years.*

She's creating a case against me.

I am suddenly blinded by white hot rage. I bring the cursor to the end of the twelve-page document and hit back-space, deleting everything, before saving and then putting the whole folder in the trash. I go back to her C: drive and open up her expo folder. She's presenting, and there are three PowerPoints and four Word documents. I pull my keys out of my pocket and jam my USB stick into the side of the computer.

The lift whirrs behind me; Graham is coming back.

My heart beats in my throat; I've got to be quick. I drag the folders onto my flash drive and glance over my shoulder as the green bar creeps across the screen, loading everything onto the USB.

Come on, come on, come on.

The computer pings: complete.

I eject the drive quickly and stab the computer's off button as the lift doors slide open. I throw myself onto the floor.

'Eve?' Graham walks over, four bottles of Corona dangling from his hand. 'What are you doing?'

'Huh?' I look up from under the desk, pushing my hair from my face. 'Oh, I dropped my favourite pen here the other day, I was seeing if it had rolled between the desks.'

He glances over to my office, where my laptop is still in my bag. 'How long have you been looking?'

I stand up and brush myself off. 'Ugh, dusty. Erm, I was on the phone until a second ago.'

'Right.' His eyes flick across my face, searching.

'Thanks for these.' I take the beers from his hand. 'Shall we go and see how far off this update is?'

I stride towards my office, but he doesn't follow.

He's staring at Kirsty's desk, the blinking light of her computer as it shuts down suddenly bright in the dark room.

CHAPTER 17

Adam

Okie flies through the two-hour A Level maths exam in just over 45 minutes. I check it over and make small corrections in the margins before writing '96%' on the front in red biro.

I grin. 'This is really good, Okie.'

Okie smiles back.

I shuffle through the other papers he's completed since our last session, one of which had only one error. I straighten the booklets into a pile and take a sip of my water, figuring out my wording in my head before speaking.

'You sat your GCSEs a month or two ago, didn't you?' I say, as casually as I can.

Okie nods. 'Six weeks and two days.'

'That's brilliant. How did you find it?'

'I had my own room.'

'OK.' I haven't been able to find any evidence of these kinds of provisions for A Levels, particularly not when they're taken privately. It's what I've been worried about.

'How do you think you'd have felt doing the exams with other people?'

Okie shakes his head but doesn't say anything.

'What about it would be difficult for you?'

'The noise,' he says.

'Exams are really quiet,' I respond. 'In fact, you have to be completely silent during an exam, so you wouldn't hear anyone speaking unless they needed to ask the teacher something.'

Okie looks at the table.

'Also, because you'll be taking them at a different time to everyone else, it'll be even quieter,' I push. 'There won't be as many people there as there are at school.'

Okie taps his fingers on the table. 'I want to go to university.'

'Absolutely.' I nod, and then take a second to weigh up my next move. 'The next set of exams is in November. Do you think we could work towards that?'

He thinks for a second. 'OK.'

'Great!' I have to stop myself from cheering. 'That's great. If I get the dates of them all, we can work from there. How does that sound?'

Okie nods and begins packing up his things. I sit back in my chair for a second. Private fees run at around £75 per exam. That's a huge amount of money, considering Okie will have to take at least two papers for each of his subjects. At the moment, I'm paid £35 an hour, twice a week to tutor him. It's still five months until the exams take place . . .

'How did it go?'

I hadn't noticed Mr Adayemi enter the room. He sits down at the table and places a coffee in front of me.

'Good. He seems happy with November.'

'I'm glad.' Then he frowns, and I see how tired he is.

'I've been thinking about how much the exams cost,' I blurt. 'They're not cheap.'

'No.' Mr Adayemi smiles. 'Nothing seems to be.'

'I was thinking . . . well, I've got quite a lot of work at the moment. And really, most of my time with Okie is spent watching him zoom through past papers. We could reduce my fee, and—'

'No.' He shakes his head fervently. 'Absolutely not.'

'I'm not saying I'd work for free.' I pull out a piece of paper and a pen. 'Look, I've worked it out. If you paid me 50% less, you'd save £35 a week. It's about ten weeks until the payment deadline — that's £350. It might not cover all of it, but it'd help, wouldn't it?'

Mr Adayemi looks angry for a second. 'We aren't a charity.'

'God, no.' I hold my hands up, mortified. 'I'm so sorry, I didn't mean to offend you. I just want to make things easier. It's such a busy time of year for me, I wouldn't usually have this many students, and—'

'You're a kind man, Adam,' he interrupts, tracing a finger down the side of his coffee cup. 'But this is too much.'

He reaches into his pocket and pulls out an envelope, identical to the one he hands me twice a week. Inside is £35 in cash. He stands up and places it in my hand, signalling that our conversation is over. 'We'll be fine. Thank you.'

* * *

As I cycle between places, I always think of Katie. Even when we were together, I'd use the quiet time to wonder about our future, or reminisce about our past. I'd think of what to cook her for dinner when she got in from a long shift, or imagine our next holiday and where we'd be spending Christmas.

This time, as I weave my way towards Hugh's, I think about all the people attached to her who are now also lost to me. Her parents, her brother, her friends . . . My life is so tightly interwoven with hers that her leaving has stripped me of part of my identity.

With yesterday's hangover not quite a distant memory, my mood is lower than I can cope with alone, and a visit to Hugh is exactly what I need. I pull up outside his home and chain my bike to the railings before taking a dollop of hand sanitiser on my way inside. The smell makes my throat feel thick.

Hugh is watching *Moana* again — it's as if no time has passed. I pull up a chair and sit next to him, gently squeezing his arm to let him know I've arrived.

He squeals and waves Hei Hei in my direction. The stuffed rooster looks to have been in the wars since my last visit.

'Me and Katie broke up, Hugh,' I murmur, my eyes fixed unseeingly on the screen. 'She's moved out.'

Hugh claps.

'I should have seen it coming. I mean, I guess I *did* see it coming. I told you, didn't I, that something felt off?' I sigh and put my feet up against the railings on the side of the bed. 'She's coming to get her stuff soon. Hopefully I'll be at work, but there's a weird part of me that kind of wants to be there? I sort of want to know if she's sad about it, or if she regrets what she's done. Is that sick? I mean, what if she doesn't? What if she bounces in all happy and breezy? Then what? I'm just torturing myself.'

Hugh sighs loudly. I don't know whether he hears the sadness in my voice, or whether it's because Moana's grandma has just popped her clogs, but it makes me feel better.

My phone buzzes in my pocket, so I pull it out and see another Tryst match notification on my screen. The little flame icon has been a permanent fixture in my notifications bar since the boys swiped right for every female in Greater Manchester at the pub the other night. I haven't opened the app, and I go to clear the latest notification when I pause.

I could just check, couldn't I? What's the harm in it? It might make me feel better, seeing that there are other women out there.

No. I can't. What would be the point? I'd match someone, go on a date, and then — what? I don't want anybody else.

My finger hovers over the notification. Suddenly, I think of Chloe.

You're so bloody careful, *Adam. You know the sensible choice isn't always the right choice, don't you?*

I click on the icon and my screen lights up with a giant 'H'. It disappears, and a picture of a woman appears. The message box in the corner shows that I have thirty-two unopened notifications.

I tap through, and see an inbox full of names, each of them next to a message: *New Match! Say Hello!*

Sarah, Anna, Freya, Jessie, Eve, Olivia, Beth . . . I scroll down the list, my head spinning. This is *weird*. 'They don't know anything about me!' I say out loud.

I go to my profile, and my own drunken face greets me, filling the screen. Underneath is written: *AreyOu the x axis to my Y? I can be you're triangle dadddy.*

I laugh out loud and take a screenshot, sending it on to the boys before swiping back through to the app.

My own face is making me feel uneasy. I go to the homepage, where there's the same picture of the girl I saw before. Underneath is a love heart and an 'x'. I tap the 'x', intending to close the app, but she disappears off to the left and a new girl takes her place.

Oh, god — have I just rejected her? I press the love heart for the next girl without looking — I don't want to upset her, whoever she is — and another picture slides onto the screen.

I pause, my finger hovering over the heart.

'I know her,' I say, holding the phone towards Hugh. 'Where do I know her from?'

Hugh pushes the phone away — it's blocking his view of the TV — as the door behind us opens and the woman on my phone screen walks into the room.

'Afternoon, Hugh! Oh, hi, Adam.' It's Becky, the nurse I met last time. My face flames, even though I locked my phone before she could have seen. 'It's good to see you again.'

'You too.' I smile, trying to calm myself. Have I just willed her here? Did she get some kind of notification when I saw her profile?

She chats about the weather as she tidies the room, and I try to look at her through single eyes. Objectively, I can see that she's pretty, with blonde hair piled messily on top of her head and alarmingly blue eyes. She's telling a funny story, and her laugh is contagious.

'. . . and I said, "it's not like it can be hot *forever*, Mum!"' She giggles, and I haven't been listening, but I join in anyway.

I smile. 'She sounds great.'

'She is.' Becky blushes, and drops her gaze. 'Sorry, look at me going on. I'll leave you two to it, and I'll be back in a bit to do your meds, Hugh.' She catches my eye again as she backs out of the door, and then she's gone.

I wait a few moments, and then go back to my phone. I tap through to Becky's profile. In the first picture, she stares up at the camera, her lips slightly parted, blonde hair cascading over her shoulders. In my mind I see Katie, Chloe.

You're so bloody careful.

Before I can think twice, I swipe right.

CHAPTER 18

Adam

When we bought this house, it was the middle of a freezing cold winter. The estate agent that showed us round laughed at our reaction to the master bedroom: the owners had had industrial-strength insulation put in to keep the upstairs toasty all year round, and it was like paradise.

Now, in the middle of this never-ending heatwave, the first floor is like hell's furnace: the air is thick and heavy and still, making sleeping impossible, even with the windows open.

It's because of this, and because I am now single with nobody to make sure that I'm maintaining normal standards of living, that I have taken to sleeping downstairs on the sofa — with a fan trained directly on my face and the kitchen window swung wide, I can usually get an uninterrupted night.

But not tonight.

It's four o'clock in the morning, and I have just woken up to a heavy weight on my chest. For a moment, I think I'm experiencing sleep paralysis — Piotr has told me how it feels, and my eyes strain in the dark to find the figure in the corner of the room.

And then, as my brain engages, I see the mass on top of my chest, rising and falling in time with my panicked breathing.

I flail my arms, wailing, and sit bolt upright. Whatever it is falls into my lap.

I scrabble behind me for the lamp, struggling to find the switch, and eventually turn it on, illuminating the scene in front of me.

It's the cat.

'Jesus Christ!' I shout, my heart hammering in my chest.

He's lying on his back, his paws flopped in the air, staring at me.

'Wh-what . . .' I choke on my words. 'How did you get in here?'

He closes his eyes and starts purring.

My eyes dart around the room until they find the open kitchen window. My heart rate begins to slow. There's an outside window ledge on the patio, perfect jumping distance for a cat to get inside.

I reach out one shaky hand to touch his belly, and the purring gets louder. 'There's something wrong with you, mate,' I say, as I look at his legs, splayed in the air with un-cat-like abandon. 'What is it? Are you hungry?'

I wriggle my body a little, expecting him to move, but he stays put, so I stand up and let him roll onto the sofa, where he opens one eye lazily and then closes it again.

I pad over to the kitchen, keeping my footsteps light out of habit rather than necessity, and pull a Peperami out of the fridge. I chop it into pieces and lay it on a plate, and then fill a dessert bowl with water.

'Here.' I go back into the living room and place my offerings on the floor. 'If I give you this, will you go home?'

His eyes open sleepily, and he assesses the meal he's been presented with. Slowly, he rises to his feet, stretches, and leaps off the sofa, his joints cracking.

He must be old, I think, as I watch him sniff at the plate of salami. His fur is patchy and slightly matted, and one of his ears is scabby. God, I hope he hasn't got fleas.

After several minutes of inspection, he eventually opens his mouth to take a piece of salami. As he chews, I notice he's missing a few teeth.

'Ahh,' I stroke the little patch of fur between his ears, 'you've been through it a bit, haven't you? Old sausage.'

It's only a few days since Katie left, but the company already feels like welcome relief from the emptiness of the house. I rock back on my heels, realising how pathetic that is.

The cat moves on from the Peperami after only two pieces, and licks at his bowl of water. I feel a small pang of guilt — how much salt is in a stick of salami?

'What's your name, then?' I ask, uselessly. He gazes at me over the rim of the bowl, as though this is something I really ought to know.

'Well, for now we'll call you Old Sausage,' I say, feeling ridiculous but also a little bit happy.

Old Sausage finishes with his water and jumps back up onto the sofa, curling up right in the middle of my makeshift bed.

'Great,' I sigh.

I should send him home. I'll give him a couple more minutes, just to let the salami go down, and then I'll put him out through the back door.

He purrs again, and without my full permission, my feet carry me upstairs, into the heat and my empty bed.

* * *

Old Sausage has gone by the time I wake up, and I spend a large portion of the morning hoovering the sofa, cleaning up crusty Peperami and feeling a bit deflated.

It's Saturday, so I sit in the garden all afternoon marking papers, a nervous feeling growing in my stomach.

The sun moves lazily across the sky, peeking out from under my umbrella. I stand up to move my chair and a movement catches my eye: something is running across the garden two doors down.

I squint into the distance — is that Old Sausage? Before I can tell for certain, he disappears in through an open back door.

I sit back down and check the time: 17:48. Only an hour to go. My heart rate accelerates again.

I've got a date with Becky tonight.

I practically ran out of Hugh's residential home after matching with her, jumping on my bike and pedalling out of there before we could bump into each other in the corridor. By the time I'd got home, a message had appeared on my Tryst account.

> Becky: *Heyyy — weird q but is this Hugh's brother Adam?*
>
> Me: *Guilty as charged. Is this weird?*
>
> Becky: *Lol no. It's nice*
>
> Me: *I'm glad! Sorry, I'm a bit new to the online dating thing so I'm not really sure what's deemed normal.*
>
> Becky: *Haha oh right*
>
> Me: *Do you want to meet for a drink tomorrow evening?*
>
> Becky: *Yeh sure :)*

Was I too quick in asking her out? How do people usually do these things? I know that Bil has, in the past, matched with a woman mere minutes before meeting up with her for the first time. But is that me? It's under twenty-four hours since Becky and I agreed to our date; is that too soon?

Is this too quick *full stop?* I wonder now, as I wait for the tram into town. Katie's barely been gone a week — is it normal to be dating this early? Imagine if Becky and I *do* click; would I be ready for another relationship so soon?

No. The answer enters my head immediately, clearly, and I involuntarily turn towards the exit. If I'm certain nothing will come of this, what am I doing?

I think of Bil, of his life's purpose being to take life itself less seriously. I'm relatively young and — the realisation hits me with renewed force — single. Why *not?* Meeting for a drink isn't the same as getting married and having babies. Besides, my previous lifestyle of caution and care has hardly led me to relationship bliss.

Just thinking about Katie makes my heart twist. She can't be gone.

But she is. She's not coming back, and somehow, I have to step onto this tram and muddle my way into an unpredictable future.

I walk into the Peaky Blinders bar on Peter Street two minutes before our arranged meeting time, and Becky doesn't seem to be here yet. The place is packed full of people, so I manage to grab an empty table and send her a quick message telling her where I am.

This is insane. This is absolutely bonkers. Two weeks ago, if you'd have told me I'd be here, waiting to meet Hugh's new nurse for a date as a single man, I'd have called you an ambulance. *Hugh's nurse.* A fresh jolt of panic shoots through me. What am I *doing?* This is completely unethical. It's a conflict of interest—

'Adam?' Becky appears in front of me, wearing a short red dress and purple lipstick. I almost do a double take.

'Hi!' I stand up and knock my knee against the table. 'Oops, sorry. I didn't recognise you for a second! Sit down, shall we get a drink? Isn't it busy? Sorry, should I take your coat?'

I'm babbling, and I force myself to shut up as she hands me her denim jacket. There are no coat pegs, so I hold it for a second before folding it and putting it on my lap like a complete freak.

Becky sits opposite me and stares at her hands.

'Sorry,' I say again. 'I'm a bit nervous. I've just got out of a long-term relationship, and — sorry, you probably don't want to hear about that. You look lovely. Have you been working today?'

'Yeah.' She looks up and smiles. 'Hugh's DVD player broke so we've ordered him a new one.'

'Oh, god.' I laugh. 'I always imagined it'd be the DVD itself that'd give out first.'

She giggles, twisting a loose strand of hair around her finger.

We lapse into silence.

'So . . . have you been here before?' I try.

'A couple of times.'

I nod, smiling encouragingly. She seems even more nervous than I am. 'Shall I go and get us a drink?' I ask, standing up. 'What would you like?'

'Oh, yes please. A vodka soda, thank you.' She smiles and her trademark blush creeps up her cheeks.

By the time we're on our second drink, she seems to have come out of her shell a little. 'Do you like holidays?' she asks.

'Love them. I went to Crete last year — have you been?'

She shakes her head. 'Is it one of the party islands?'

'Not really — it's quite historical.'

She looks disappointed.

'Is that really boring?' I laugh. 'I promise I'm not *super* nerdy. I did sunbathe, too.'

'I love sunbathing.' She brightens. 'Have you ever been to Dubai?'

'No,' I say, not wanting to admit that it's bottom of my list of holiday destinations. 'Is it any good?'

'*So* good. Look, I've got pictures.' She pulls out her phone and flicks through a series of photos of her, posing on high balconies with city lights twinkling in the background, a serious expression on her face. An image of Katie comes into my mind — on a boat, her head thrown back, her hat blowing away in the wind. She hated that picture.

Becky keeps swiping — her in a Lamborghini, her on the beach, her at a party — but I can't concentrate. I look at her hands, her perfect nails and smooth, tanned skin. What am I doing? I try to imagine kissing her, going for dinner, talking into the evening. I can't.

A sudden rush of sadness makes my breath catch in my throat. I've lost her, I've lost my person.

'They pay nurses loads in Dubai,' Becky is saying. 'I'm going to go and work there once I've got enough experience.'

I smile weakly. 'Sounds amazing.'

She offers to get us another drink, and I accept. I watch her standing at the bar, surrounded by people, her blonde hair sending my head spinning. For six years, I have sought Katie's chestnut ponytail in a crowd. How will I ever get used to this?

CHAPTER 19

Eve

I'm half asleep, my mind empty. The bed is soft and familiar, and the smell of Graham's detergent makes me feel as though I'm sinking. He starts drawing gentle lines down my back with his finger, circling the dimples at the base of my spine before trailing back up again, under my shoulder blades, at the base of my neck, along the grooves of bone and across the smattering of teenage acne scars across my shoulders . . .

I roll over and he looks at me sleepily. 'What?'

I frown. 'That's a bit . . . intimate, isn't it?'

He rolls onto his back, tilting his chin and laughing loudly. 'Christ, Eve.'

'What?'

He turns onto his side again, shifting his weight onto his elbow and propping his head up with the palm of his hand. '*Now* you talk about intimacy?'

I let my head sink into the pillow again and eye him. The cast of his hair gel has been broken, and one thick strand flops over his eyebrow. He looks vulnerable. An image of Hannah from accounts arrives in my mind, and I close my eyes. When have I ever cared about that?

He cups the side of my face, stroking my cheek, and I snap my eyes open. He twirls a piece of my hair between his fingers.

'OK, enough.' I push his hand away.

'What?' He stares at me, a deep crease forming in between his eyebrows. 'What's going on with you?'

'It's weird.' I sit up, groping around for my bra and fastening it quickly.

He scoffs. 'Eve, we just — I mean, we do this all the time—'

'No, we don't,' I interrupt. 'We don't do *this*, ever.'

I stand up and pull on the rest of my clothes, trying to ignore him staring.

When he speaks again, his voice is quiet, steady. 'What were you doing on Kirsty's computer, Eve?'

'I wasn't on Kirsty's computer.'

He looks at me, his eyes heavy and dark. 'You're not staying, I take it.' It's a statement, not a question.

'No,' I answer anyway.

He rolls onto his back again and blows a thin stream of air through his teeth. 'Jesus. You're a real head fuck, you know that?'

'Thank you.' I check my hair in the mirror. I can feel something building in my throat, like a scream, but not.

He laughs. 'Go on then. You can go back to pretending I don't exist.' There's a catch in his throat, and he looks at me, suddenly serious. 'Until the next time you click your fingers.'

I try to bite the end of my tongue, hard, but I'm not fast enough. 'I'm sure Hannah will keep you company in the meantime.'

His eyebrows shoot up. '*Oh*. That's it, is it? Of all the things, Eve, I have to say I didn't take you for the jealous type.'

'Because I'm not,' I retort, cringing at the childishness of it. 'I've got work to do.' I pick my bag up from the floor and move towards the door.

'You can't marry your job, you know.' He chuckles softly from the bed. 'And you can't fuck it, either.'

'No.' I pull the door open. 'That's what you're here for.'

***

'Kirsty!' I run towards the lift and put my hand between the doors to stop them closing. 'Glad I caught you.'

Kirsty stands back to let me in. Surprise flits across her face, but she composes herself. 'Hey, how are you?'

'Good!' I dig around in my bag and pull out a piece of paper. 'Just got the new numbers through from the Summer Bundle campaign — I thought you'd like them before the briefing.'

'Oh, thanks.' She scans the document quickly. 'This is great.'

'No problem.'

'Listen, Eve,' she turns to me, sliding the piece of paper into her satchel, 'about the paternity cover thing . . .'

'Oh, god, don't worry about it.' I wave my hand in the air as the lift doors slide open. 'I know it wasn't malicious.'

'Absolutely not.' She follows me out into the office. 'It was such a shock, honestly, I had no idea—'

I spin around to face her. She stops in her tracks and stumbles backwards. 'Don't even think about it. I trust you, Kirst. It's not like you *planned* it, is it?' I laugh.

Something flickers across her face, but she masks it quickly. 'Of course not.'

'Great.' I flash her a smile and turn around, striding over to my office. 'See you in a min!'

I sit at my desk, watching through the glass wall as Kirsty does her rounds with the marketing assistants. After fifteen minutes, she checks her watch and begins making her way towards the meeting room. I scoot out of my chair.

'You don't mind if I join for this one, do you?' I say as I catch up with her.

She startles. 'Oh.' She glances towards the room, where Dev is leaning back in his seat. 'No, of course not.'

'Fab.' I move past her and let myself in, taking the seat nearest to Dev.

'You're not doing the update today are you, Eve?' He clicks at his laptop, checking the agenda.

'No, no.' I reach forward and pour myself some coffee. 'My nine o'clock was cancelled, so I thought I'd come and keep my finger on the pulse.'

Kirsty comes in, followed by a couple of the marketing assistants. She sits down at the end of the table.

'Right, shall we get started?' Dev looks up over his screen.

Half an hour of sales numbers and accounting figures passes, until Kirsty is called to give the marketing update.

'Erm,' she stalls as her eyes flick around her screen, and I wonder what she'd have said if I weren't here. She seems to be reorganising her presentation. She falteringly lists off a few figures, and Dev's mouth flattens into a thin line.

'Do you have a more concise overview for us, Kirsty?' he asks.

'Yes, of course, sorry.' I haven't seen her this flustered in a long time. I experience a sudden flash of guilt: my god, she's my *best friend*. What the hell am I doing? She reaches into her satchel and pulls out a piece of paper. I remind myself of *F Ups*, and my pulse quickens. No going back now. 'I have the final figures for the Summer Bundle campaign here.'

Dev sits up in his seat and beams. 'Great, let's hear them.'

'The mixed rose basket on a blue background had a twenty-three percent click-through rate,' she says, more confident now. 'And engagement on the red azaleas in the pink pot was twelve percent higher than the green. With the corresponding sales—'

'Um,' Jenny, one of the more confident marketing assistants, shifts in her seat. 'The rose basket actually had a nineteen percent click-through rate. And the green azalea pot got twenty-six percent more engagement than the pink.' She frowns, her cheeks reddening. 'Sorry, I — I've got the figures here.'

The room hums a little as people shift in their seats.

'Eve sent the final figures over this morning, so I can look now,' Dev sighs and taps at his laptop tersely, clearly signalling that this kind of fact-checking is below him. 'You're right, Jenny — those are the numbers I have, too. Kirsty, are you sure you're up to date?'

'Yes, I—'

I feel mildly sick.

'What do you have for engagement on the succulent set with the rose gold background?' Dev fixes his gaze on Kirsty, who runs her eyes frantically over her paper.

'Thirty-six percent, which we were really happy with—'

'I have twenty-two percent here.' Dev raises his eyebrows. 'Where have you had these figures from?'

'Eve gave them to me this morning,' she says, her voice shrill. She looks at me, panicked.

For a moment, I'm tempted to confess. The way she's looking at me, the confusion on her face — how can I be doing this to her?

She is in support of my application.

I take a breath. 'I emailed the figures round.' I frown, pretending to be confused. 'Dev, can I just have a look . . .' I lean over and check Dev's screen. 'Yes, that's the document I sent. I'm not sure what—'

'You gave them to me!' Kirsty yelps, and the room falls silent. 'You gave me this piece of paper in the lift!'

Awkwardness ripples around the room. Someone clears their throat. Kirsty's face has changed now: her eyes have hardened — she knows what I've done. It's do or die. I look around incredulously. 'Kirsty, I really don't know what you're talking about.'

'Right.' A deep crease has formed above Dev's eyebrows. He taps the desk impatiently. 'Eve, do you want to take over?'

Kirsty stands, frozen.

I sigh and purse my lips, returning her gaze.

'Of course.' I take Dev's laptop as he passes it to me, and then smile across the room. 'It's a good job I turned up, isn't it?'

CHAPTER 20

Adam

The heat wakes me and I lie for a moment, feeling the dampness of my sweat on the duvet. Katie's arm is draped across my chest, her skin clammy against mine.

I close my eyes again and roll over. The draft from the movement cools my skin and I shiver. Katie shifts and I curl my arm around her, my hand flat against her collarbone. Her hair tickles my face and I move my head, wrinkling my nose. She's using a new shampoo — it was always strawberries, but now it's . . . peach? Apricot?

Images of fruits pass across my mind as I drift between waking and dreaming. Is it pear? Apple?

My eyes flicker open as I think, and an unfamiliar brightness hits me, waking me up.

Blonde hair. Not brown. Not Katie.

Becky.

I startle, pulling my arm from around her and shuffling backwards across the bed. It all comes back: another pint for me, another vodka soda for her. Searching in her eyes for Katie, or for something new. Convincing myself, as the night wore on and empty glasses piled higher, that there was something there. Her laugh: contagious. Our differences: surmountable. Linking her arm as we stepped out onto the street, feeling the strangeness of the height difference, her mannerisms.

Asking her to come back to mine.

Sleeping with her in our bed.

I roll onto my back and stare at the ceiling. Katie isn't the last person I've slept with anymore. She isn't the last anything; Becky has taken her place.

'Morning.' Becky stirs and turns to face me, her eyes sleepy.

'Good morning.' I smile, and swing my legs out of bed before anything happens. 'Do you want a coffee?'

Her eyes widen as she tucks the duvet around herself. 'Sure. I'll come down in a second.'

I go to the kitchen and flick the kettle on, thinking. I hear Becky's feet creak across the floorboards upstairs, and it's impossible to imagine it's anyone but Katie. The boiler kicks in as the shower starts running, and I pull out my phone.

There's another text from Chloe. It came in last night at midnight.

You can't ignore me forever, Adam.

I swipe off it quickly and tap through the call screen.

'Hey, Ad,' Piotr answers the phone on the second ring.

'I've fucked up,' I say, running one hand down my face. 'I slept with someone.'

Piotr cheers. 'That's not a fuck up, mate! That's great!'

'No, no, it isn't.' I pace into the living room and back again, keeping one ear trained on the boiler. 'I don't like her.'

'So? You don't always have to be in love with the people you sleep with.'

'I don't mean I should *love* her, I mean . . . she likes me, I think, and now I've led her on—'

'Ad, calm down. It's fine. These things happen. Just be upfront with her,' Piotr soothes.

114

'She's a nurse at Hugh's care home,' I hiss.

'Oh, shit, the new one? Rebecca, is it?'

'Becky, yeah,' I say quietly, and then pause as I stand at the bottom of the stairs, listening.

'Well, mate, she seems like a really nice girl. I'm sure she'll understand.'

I press my head against the cool wood of the banister. 'OK. OK, yeah, I'm sure you're right. I'll speak to her.' The boiler clicks off, and I hear the shower door opening. 'I've got to go, I'll speak to you later.'

I end the call and go back to the kitchen, pouring the coffees and setting them on the table. I'm putting bread in the toaster when Becky comes in, freshly showered and fully dressed.

She smiles and stares at her feet. 'Hey.'

'Morning again.' I gesture towards the kitchen table and she sits down. 'I made you coffee, do you want sugar?'

'No, thanks.' She takes a sip.

'Toast?'

'I'm OK.'

We fall into silence until the toaster pings. I carry the plate over to the table.

'I had a really nice time last night,' I say as I sit down. I haven't done this in so long — years — I'm not sure where to start.

'Me too.'

'I've . . . well, I just got out of a long-term relationship, as you know,' I start. 'And I'm not sure . . . well, I don't think I can do this again for a while.'

Becky smiles sadly. 'Wow, straight into it.'

'I know, I'm sorry, I just . . .'

'It's OK. Maybe we can try again when you're in the right headspace,' she suggests.

'Maybe,' I begin, but I shake myself. I need to be honest. 'I think — I mean, we're quite different people, aren't we? I'm not sure this would work at all.'

Her face hardens. 'So what is it, you've just got out of a relationship, or you don't like me?'

'It's not that I don't like you!' I say, floundering. 'We're just . . . we're not compatible, I don't think. It's not your fault — you're brilliant — sometimes it just doesn't . . . *click*.'

She nods. 'So it's both. You're unavailable and I'm unattractive.'

'No!' I say, panicked now. 'You're beautiful! When I saw you last night, I mean, wow, you were—'

'So it's my personality?' she challenges.

She's sort of right on this one, but I don't want to hurt her feelings. 'Definitely not! You're great. I just think our personalities *together*—'

'Don't worry about it.' She stands up and pulls her bag up onto her shoulder. 'I should be going anyway.'

'Oh, you don't have to leave . . .' I follow her out into the hallway. 'Don't you want to finish your coffee?'

She swings the front door open and turns to face me, flicking her hair across her shoulder. 'Goodbye, Adam.'

The door slams behind her, and she's gone.

* * *

'Well, that's two women who've left my house hating me in as many weeks,' I say, my legs sticking out of the back door.

Old Sausage looks up from licking his paws and regards me steadily.

'I know, I know.' I sigh. 'I'm cursed. And now I'm dreading going to visit Hugh in case she's there. How ridiculous is that?'

I pluck another treat from the bag I've bought from the corner shop and toss it in his direction. 'I've got this really horrible feeling, you know. Like history's going to repeat itself. What if her hating me affects Hugh's care? What if I've fucked things up for him?'

Old Sausage nibbles on his treat and ignores me.

'You're right, I'm overthinking it. I always overthink things.' I pull my phone out of my pocket. 'I need to distract myself.'

I pull up the AQA examinations page and look up the November exam times. There's a college near Okie's house that hosts the maths and physics papers twice a year, so I take a screenshot to show him.

'I'm brewing up, you want one?' I ask Old Sausage. He blinks.

I get a dish of water and make another coffee for myself, keeping my eyes trained on my phone as the kettle boils. No texts from Becky, but that's to be expected. Still nothing from Katie, either — she said she'd come and get her stuff and let me know about the mortgage, but so far, nothing.

I fire off a text to her, asking when she's planning on coming over, and then take my drink back outside.

Old Sausage isn't where I left him, and the garden is empty. I peer over the fences, to where I saw him the other day, and sure enough, he's sitting at the back door of the same house two doors down. That must be his owner.

I make a mental note to go and knock on later in the week, in case they've been missing him, and then sit back down on the back step, willing the hint of a breeze to come my way.

My phone vibrates in my pocket: a text from Katie. My heart leaps.

I'll be over tomorrow at 6 to get my stuff. RE: the house, I'd like to sell it, if you're happy with that.

My stomach drops. She's not going to change her mind. She's not coming back.

I stand up, unsteady on my feet. Something new and unfamiliar burns in my belly.

She can take my trust, my life, everything we had.

But she isn't taking my home.

CHAPTER 21

Eve

> Me: *Eve 1–0 Kirsty*

Jess: *Do I want to know what you've done?*

> Me: *Nothing as bad as what *she* was planning on doing*

Will: *You know you're just feeding your emotional addiction, Eve*

> Me: *I don't have an emotional addiction — I'm a very logical person, you say so yourself*

Jess: *Don't you ever feel like just crying about things instead of burning the building down??*

> Me: *You know I haven't cried since I was 17*

Will: *I would never tell a client there was something wrong with them*

Will: *But Eve*

Will: *There is something wrong with you*

Me: *Is that a formal diagnosis*

Will: *I wouldn't even know where to start*

Jess: *I think meditation would be good, Eve. Try sitting and really tasting your food*

Me: *OK great speak later*

I tap out of WhatsApp and into the notes folder on my phone, half a takeaway burrito wedged in my mouth. As I pace around the room, I read through the key points of Kirsty's expo presentation. There's a familiar fire burning in the back of my throat — a mix of anger, determination and satisfaction — and I draw energy from it.

I'm working from home today, a luxury I allow myself once every couple of weeks, so that I can make progress away from prying eyes. Every so often, a tiny part of me wonders whether I'm taking things too far, but then I remember *F Ups* again, and I push forward.

My laptop pings with a new email, so I walk over to the kitchen to check.

From: Dev.kalhora@florina.co.uk
To: Eve.slater@florina.co.uk
Subject: Summer Bundle mix up and expo prep
13:47 — 29 June 2022

Hi Eve,

I've received a formal complaint regarding the incorrect Summer Bundle figures in yesterday's update meeting. For obvious reasons, I can't tell you who the complainant is, but as a result, we're trying to get to the bottom of where the falsified numbers came from.

Unfortunately, this complaint has been lodged directly against you, and while I'm sure there was no foul play on your part, it is company policy to investigate any allegations of misconduct. I am confident this will amount to nothing, not least because the document containing the numbers can't be found on the internal printing log, but you have a right to be aware of any complaints filed against you.

A quick additional heads-up: your slot for the expo has been bumped up — I still hope to be there, but am unwilling to commit 100% to travelling/speaking when it's so close to Eleanor's due date, so you will now be presenting in my place, and Kirsty in yours, etc. Big ask, I know, but I have every faith you'll pull it off.

Any qs just pop in when you're next in the office.
Best,
Dev

I throw my head back and laugh.

A complaint. *A complaint!* Is she crazy? Did she think I wouldn't find out?

A memory swims into my mind: Kirsty and I, stealing two bottles of champagne from the office Christmas party and escaping up the emergency exit staircase onto the roof of our building.

She was panicking, worried we'd get caught.

'I'm shit at being sneaky,' she'd hiccupped, sitting down on a vent and staring across the city.

'I'm really good at it.' I'd leaned my head on her shoulder. 'We make the perfect pair.'

And then later, when Dev was recruiting the new Head of Finance, and the competition for the role became our own personal reality TV show: Paula, a meek but experienced accountant, was pitted against two men ten years younger than her.

'What's the point in her even going forward for it?' I'd asked one day as we sat in my office, watching Paula fawning over Dev. 'You can't just . . . be yourself. You've got to play the game.'

'Maybe she wants to change the system,' Kirsty had suggested. 'Prove that you get to the top through merit and hard work, not peacocking and bullshit.'

I'd shaken my head and laughed. 'That's cute.'

120

Paula didn't get the job.

I slap my laptop lid shut. Yes, the complaint was a rookie move, but her little evidence stash suggests she isn't as naive as she pretends to be. Was this her plan all along? Lure me in and then stomp on my head as she climbed her way past me?

What is this turning into? What is it turning *us* into? There's no going back from this now. We'll never slip easily back into what we had before. I've boarded the train, I might as well see it to its final destination.

My burrito is cold, so I throw it in the bin and then ease my laptop open again, paying attention to the final paragraph now.

I'll be presenting Dev's slot at the expo.

I drum my fingers on the table. This makes things trickier — the expo presentation I'm currently editing on Kirsty's behalf is the one she was *originally* going to present; now she's doing my topic instead, I'll have to start from scratch.

Standing up, I begin pacing again. Perhaps I was too quick in showing my hand; I can't go to Kirsty and offer to give her a falsified version of my work now, not after I gave her those Summer Bundle numbers.

I'll have to hack into her desktop again and see what she's doing — try to fiddle with things that way. Unless . . .

Unless I just stopped all of this. Played fair. But the complaint — she's not going to play fair, is she? And there's another potential idea . . .

I am pacing so quickly now, so lost in my thoughts, that when I trip over something I don't have time to catch myself. A yowl pierces through the room as I fly forward, grabbing onto the fridge door and smacking my back against the countertops as the momentum swings me round.

'Agh,' I wince, blinking and reaching round to rub my shoulders. 'What—'

I spot the cat under the kitchen table, cowering.

'You!' I shout, hoisting myself up onto my knees. 'You nearly killed me!'

The cat blinks back at me, her eyes sticky.

'Shoo!' I climb to my feet, glad to feel that there doesn't seem to be any permanent damage, and pull one of the dining chairs out from under the table. The cat streaks past me, darting into the living room and leaping up onto the sofa.

'No!' I yelp, hobbling after her. 'You don't live here! That's not your bed!'

The cat yawns, and then begins kneading the sofa, her claws clicking as she plucks strands of fabric out of the cushions.

'Oh my god.' I reach forwards and hold her gingerly around the waist. 'Off!'

I pull her upwards, but her claws are embedded in the sofa, and she mews shrilly.

'Shit, sorry.' I drop her again. 'No, stop it! Stop ruining my sofa, you vandal!'

She turns her head to look at me. As though she realises she's gone too far, she tugs her paws away from the fabric and sits down.

'Thank you.' I slump to the floor, sitting cross-legged and assessing the damage. 'You've fucked up my sofa.'

She regards me steadily.

'Whose are you?' I ask, reaching forward to touch her neck. She lets me. 'No collar, hm? Little nomad.'

She meows, and I look at her properly. Her ears are scabby and dry, her fur patchy and matted in places. I feel a small pang of pity — does nobody own her?

I shake myself and stand up. 'I'm too busy for this,' I tell her, and pick her up, carrying her over to the back door. 'Go on, go home.'

I drop her and she lands lightly on the patio. She stares at me accusatorially.

'God, *fine*.' I take my half-eaten burrito from the top of the bin and plonk it on a plate, placing it outside the door. 'Bon appetit.'

I swing the door shut again and the house immediately feels cloyingly hot. I'll give the cat a couple of minutes to take herself off, and then crack the window.

I open the fridge, intending to bin the Tupperware boxes of vegetables and salmon. The mixture is charred and dry and, by now, probably outside the range of safe human consumption. But I glance out of the window, and see the cat, skinny and sad-looking, still outside, staring forlornly at the burrito. I take the salmon from the box and pile it on a chopping board, remove the salty exterior and flake most of the remainder with a fork into a new tub. The last bit I scoop onto a plate and take outside to replace the burrito. The cat still doesn't move, but she licks her lips.

Back inside, my little idea nudges at my mind again as I'm scraping at a rogue piece of butternut squash with a fork. I won't need Graham for this one, which is useful as he hasn't spoken to me since I left his house the other night. I should apologise — even I can admit that what I said was out of order — but we haven't crossed paths at work. Sometimes, it feels like a sudden emotion overwhelms my common sense, and I'm unable to control my mouth. I feel a stab of guilt and push it down.

When I'm not with Graham, he doesn't enter my mind. *You can go back to pretending I don't exist.* He's right; at work, we don't fraternise, but I always assumed that was a mutual decision. In any case, what we have is casual, and we don't owe each other anything.

My phone beeps with a message and I dump the empty Tupperware in the sink.

Will: *Is anyone up for a drink at some point? It'd be nice to catch up properly*

Jess: *I'd love to — just name a date. Is everything OK?*

Will: *I'm fine. Do you want to come to ours? Nina could do with some fresh faces*

Me: *Sounds good — do you want to do a poll?*

Jess: *Can't we just say Thursday?*

Will: *Works for me. 7pm?*

Me: *Maybe — send me a calendar invite*

Will: *No*

I put my phone back down and go upstairs to change into my running gear. As I come back down, my phone beeps again.

Kirsty: *Have you heard about the expo changes?*
Can we meet to discuss?

I put my AirPods in and leave through the front door. Closing Kirsty's message, I open the Independent Women playlist on Spotify, setting off quickly and pounding the streets, until that questioning little voice trying to hold me to account in the back of my mind stops bothering me.

CHAPTER 22

Eve

I sit behind my desk, my eyes trained beyond my computer screen and through the glass wall. Kirsty is leaning back on her chair, gesturing to Dev, who is manspreading on the edge of the desk, his head thrown back in laughter.

I twirl a pen around in my fingers, counting to three, over and over. It's nearly 7 o'clock in the evening, and I'm due at Will's house. I refuse to leave first, though — what kind of message would that send?

Suddenly, Kirsty turns her head and looks directly at me. I hold her gaze, and she turns back to Dev, her eyes not leaving mine, and says something. His head swivels my way, and he says something back and then puts his hand on her shoulder briefly. Kirsty smiles, her eyes still locked on mine.

I click angrily at my original expo presentation, typing the words 'Kirsty McClure, Deputy Head of Digital Marketing and Chief Backstabber' under the title page before deleting it and mentally slapping myself for being so childish.

I watch as Dev strides purposefully towards the lift, giving Kirsty a quick wave over his shoulder. I wait five minutes, until I'm sure he's gone, and then log off and gather my things.

I smile, as I walk past Kirsty's desk. 'See you tomorrow.'

She glances up. 'See you.'

I press the lift button and wait.

'Oh, Eve.' I hear her swivel on her chair, and when I turn around she's facing me.

'What's up?'

'Did you get my text? Can we meet? To discuss the expo presentation?' Is that hope in her eyes? I falter. Or is it scheming, calculating hardness?

I take a breath as the lift pings open. 'Of course. Tomorrow morning? Shall we get a coffee before work?'

'Sure.' She nods. 'Thanks.'

I step into the lift as she turns away, back to her computer.

* * *

It's quarter to eight by the time I knock on Will's door, and the moment I see his face, I know he isn't happy about it.

'I'm sorry.' I hurry after him up the corridor and into the kitchen, where Jess and Nina are sitting around the island. 'Something came up — have I kept you from eating?'

'Don't worry about it.' He turns and gives me a tight smile. 'Wine?'

'Yes, white, please.' I briefly hug Jess and then turn my attention to Nina. She looks thinner than the last time I saw her, although it can't have been more than a couple of weeks, and her eyes look dark with exhaustion. 'Hi, Nina, I'm so sorry.' I reach down and peck her on each cheek. 'You look great, how is everything? Where's Benny?'

I scoot backwards and settle myself onto a bar stool as Nina rakes her hand through her hair. 'Don't apologise, you're a busy woman. He's asleep.'

'Brilliant!' I accept the wine that Will offers me, my voice overenthusiastic in an attempt to soften the awkwardness of my late arrival. 'Is he settling, then? Getting into his . . . routine?'

'No, not really.' Nina takes a gulp of her wine and I notice that the stilted atmosphere seems to be out of proportion with my crime. Jess is staring at her hands and Will is moving pans off the draining board a little too loudly. 'Shush, Will! You'll wake him up,' Nina snaps.

Will shuts a cupboard door with exaggerated softness.

'How's Johnny?' I ask Jess.

'It's her night tonight, so . . .' She shrugs. 'I'll find out tomorrow, I suppose.'

'Are you finding it any easier?' Will asks, drying his hands on a tea towel.

Jess sighs. 'I don't know. Not really.'

'Well, you know what I think,' I say, clinking my glass down on the island countertop. 'I don't think it's good for you.'

'But I *love* . . .' she starts, but her heart isn't in it. 'Whatever. I don't want to talk about it.'

I glance around the room. This is dire. What's wrong with everybody?

'Pizza or Chinese?' Will pulls a stack of menus from down the side of the microwave. 'Sorry, things got on top of us a bit today.'

'God, don't apologise.' Jess shakes her dreadlocks. 'I'm good with pizza. What about you, Nina?'

Nina is staring out of the window, but at the sound of her own name she turns and looks at us all, as if she's forgotten we're here. 'I think your relationship sounds brilliant, Jess,' she says, her voice a little too loud. 'Lucky you, sending him packing for half the week.'

There's an excruciating silence. Jess turns to face me, her eyes wide, subtle as ever.

'Right, let's go with pizza then.' Will slaps the menus down onto the counter and picks up his phone. 'Two larges and a garlic bread?'

We nod, and a smattering of chat takes place regarding toppings. By the time the order's in, the wine glasses need topping up, and the mood has lifted slightly.

'How are your mum and dad, Eve?' Nina asks, peering into the baby monitor. 'Will, do you think he's breathing?'

Will closes his eyes briefly and lets a thin stream of air out of his nose. 'Of course he is.'

'I need to go and see.' Nina stands up quickly and places her glass on the side.

'Is he not breathing?' Jess asks, panic in her voice.

'He's definitely breathing.' Will sighs heavily, passing the monitor over to us. 'She does this about twelve times a night.'

I stare at the grainy image of Benny on the screen, his chest visibly rising and falling. Nina enters the shot and cranes into the cot, her head to one side, listening.

'God.' I pass the monitor back. 'Who'd have kids, eh?'

Jess nudges me. 'Not helpful.'

'What?'

Nina reappears, tucking her hair behind her ears. 'He's fine. Sorry about that.'

Jess and I mumble half-coherent platitudes, and she settles back in her seat. 'Sorry, Eve, I was asking about your parents. How are they?'

'Fine, yeah.' I shrug. 'Still living the life of Riley in Spain.'

'Bring on 2040.' Will laughs, and I join in.

'What? Why 2040?' Jess asks.

'Benny turns 18,' Nina says, her eyebrows raised. 'Can't wait to get rid of him, can you, Will?'

'Oh, come on, Nee. I'm only kidding.' Will wraps his arm around her shoulder, but she doesn't yield and turns her face away from him.

Silence descends again, and Will holds his arm stiffly around Nina's back. Jess goes back to staring at her hands.

'So, um, when's this pizza arriving, then?' I ask, my tolerance for the awkwardness reaching its limit.

Will moves away from Nina and checks his phone. 'Forty minutes.'

Forty minutes of this? 'Could I top myself up?' I ask, rising to my feet and moving towards the fridge.

'I'll do it, don't worry.' Will pulls the bottle out and refills my glass. As he goes to put it back, Nina makes a point of leaning around him and taking it from his hand, filling her own glass almost to the brim.

I sit back down, and my chair scrapes loudly into the silence.

The fridge door thumps softly closed as Nina takes a gulp.

This is unbearable.

'I found something on Kirsty's computer,' I announce.

Jess gasps. 'How?'

'Doesn't matter.' I wave her question away. 'It turns out she's been keeping track of every mistake I've ever made. All our chatty email back and forth, she's been copying and pasting my fuck-ups into a Word document for over two years.'

'What?' Will frowns. 'That's really messed up.'

'Christ.' Nina looks animated. 'Have you asked her about it?'

'No, because she doesn't know I've seen it.' I take another sip of my wine.

'How *did* you see it?' Will asks.

'I just told you, it doesn't matter,' I stress. 'But it's fine, I've got a plan.'

'Oh, Eve.' Jess cradles her head in her hands. 'Don't.'

'What?'

'I think you'd be better actually sitting and processing this before you do anything at all,' Will declares, his therapist eyebrow-crease emerging. 'And then you should speak directly to Kirsty.'

The baby monitor chirps, and Nina grabs it.

'And let her get one step ahead of me?' I ask. 'No thanks.'

Neither Will nor Jess say anything. I look between them both. Why aren't they with me on this? I feel that sense of nagging doubt again: what am I doing? I've never been one to care too much about what other people think of me, but Will and Jess are being openly unsupportive. Does that mean I'm wrong, or do they just not understand how awful Kirsty's being? How much of a betrayal all of this is?

'God,' Nina puts the monitor back on the counter, laughing bitterly. 'Who'd be a career woman, eh?'

CHAPTER 23

Adam

I'm in the foyer of Hugh's home, waiting for the receptionist to answer my question. She's searching on her database, tapping slowly, and I crane my neck to the left, glancing up the corridor.

'Sorry, are you in a rush?' She frowns sympathetically at me. 'Monday morning, the system's slow.'

'No!' I shake my head emphatically. 'Not at all. I was just . . . have you changed the wallpaper?'

She looks behind her, as if she might not have noticed. 'I don't think so . . .'

I look up the corridor again. A nurse with black hair, a plump, older lady, a man with blue epaulettes. No sign of her.

'Right, do you have a pen and paper?' The receptionist finishes tapping and looks at me.

'Erm.' For a second, I forget what I asked her. 'I'll just jot it down on my phone.'

She reads out Hugh's NHS number to me — I already have it written down on a million doctor's letters at home — and I thank her.

'Is he with anyone at the moment? I don't want to interrupt,' I ask.

She frowns at her watch. 'I shouldn't think so . . . he had his wash an hour or so ago, and his meds are done. No other visitors on the log.'

'Great, thank you.' I flash her a smile and dart up the corridor, rushing into Hugh's room and slamming the door behind me.

Just Hugh. Thank god.

I am being completely pathetic. I take note of this fact as I ruffle Hugh's hair and sink into the chair next to his. What am I doing, surveilling my own brother's care home in the hopes of avoiding a woman I slept with?

'I'm such a coward,' I sigh. Hugh gurgles delightedly.

I have been known, in the past, to be a bit of a doormat. When I went freelance and started tutoring, I thought I'd really taken the reins. I was in charge of my own destiny, I'd escaped the misery of my old job and created a fulfilling — if less well-paid — life for myself, and I really believed I'd proved that you didn't have to be a dick to get what you wanted. You could be kind, and nice, and still have it all and be happy.

But what Katie did, and my reaction to it, is making me question myself. Several times my instinct was to sweep it under the rug and pretend it wasn't happening; other times I wanted to confront her and forgive her. That's chief doormat behaviour, isn't it? If I had asked her to stay, would she have?

Chloe's texts swim into my mind again. Her face, the things she said. *You're so bloody* careful, *Adam.*

I shake the memory away.

'And now, all of this with Becky,' I continue out loud. 'I'm being doormat-y again, aren't I? I'm not facing things head on.'

Hugh throws Hei Hei at my head.

'Thanks, mate.' I laugh. 'I needed that.'

I half watch *Moana* for half an hour, idly swiping through A Level resources and university admissions rules, before standing up to leave. If I see Becky, I decide, I'll say hello. She's looking after my brother — I want us to be civil.

I reach down to give Hugh a hug, but as I pull away, I notice a faint, round bruise on his forearm.

'What's this?' I ask, holding his wrist. It's the size of a finger-print, faded and grey. Hugh shakes his arms, shrieking happily.

Something icy cold pools in my stomach. I weigh up my options. If anything is happening, I need to know so that I can move him immediately. But if it's nothing, if it's an accident, an accusation like that could upset all the people who work so hard to look after him.

I make up my mind and drop a kiss on Hugh's head before walking out into the corridor. The woman at reception looks surprised to see me again.

'Hi, sorry. I just wanted to flag something really quickly — my brother seems to have a bruise on his left forearm. It's small, but I'm just a bit worried about it. Would someone be able to have a look?'

She raises her eyebrows, looking concerned. 'Oh, good-ness. Of course. Let me see when the doctor's due in . . .' She taps at her computer. 'He'll be here at three. I'll ask him to have a look first thing.'

'Great, thank you. He's very energetic, so I'm sure it's self-inflicted, but . . .' I hesitate, and then decide to push. 'If you could just make a record of it?'

'Absolutely.' She nods. 'It's protocol to log anything like this. I'll put it in the system now.'

'Thank you.'

* * *

In a bid for distraction, I pack for Dublin early. I don't want to think about potentials with Hugh, or about Becky, or about the fact that Katie will be here in less than ten minutes . . .

I pull the suitcases down from the top of the wardrobe; they're zipped inside one another like Russian dolls. I unzip Katie's hard-shell silver case to reveal my lightweight, practical bag with wheels and backpack straps. I stare at the two cases lined up next to each other on the bed. The contrast is unnerving. Am I boring? Is this what made her leave, this sad metaphor for my dullness?

I shake my head and pull Katie's case to the floor, leaving it open for her to fill with her things when she arrives. My stomach somersaults. Would I take her back, if she returned with her tail between her legs? I hate myself for not having a definitive answer to that question.

I unzip my own bag, splaying it open on the bed. Inside is the tube of sun cream I've been looking for all summer, and the phone charger I assumed I'd left at the hotel. Is *this* why she left? My scatter-brained incompetency?

I pull open the wardrobe, sliding shirts off their hangers at random and rolling them into tubes. Two nights, three shirts — one for contingency purposes. I open the drawers and grab a handful of boxers, stuffing them at the bottom of the bag before nestling the shirts on top. What else? Trousers. Shorts? Will it still be hot in Dublin? I go to check my weather app, but there's a knock at the door.

I take the stairs two at a time, nerves and giddiness rolling around in my stomach. She's here. For the last time?

As I reach the bottom of the stairs, I stop. I need to compose myself. Adrenaline is pumping around my veins. I feel lightheaded, I'm not thinking straight. I take a deep breath, before remembering that the glass partition in the door allows anyone outside a blurry view of the hallway. She can probably see me, standing here. I can see her, her outline is as familiar as my own in the mirror.

I slide the chain back and twist the key, pulling the handle down.

And there she is.

'Adam.' She smiles, her face bright. Her hair is lighter, curled, and as she moves to pull it away from her forehead, I notice her nails are buffed and shiny. 'Can I come in?'

CHAPTER 24

Eve

I can feel the weight of concealer dragging my eye bags further into my cheeks. I'm five minutes away, on foot, striding across St. Peter's Square with my phone pressed against my ear.

'Lots of little Spanish children, aren't there, Mike?' my mum is saying, and I hear my dad's muffled agreement in the background. 'Not much fun for the British kids. A lot of them come on holiday to make friends, you know? And how can they do that when they don't speak the language?'

I am too tired for this. I pulled an all-nighter working on Kirsty's expo presentation, and when I finally took myself to bed at 3 a.m., I was awoken half an hour later by the cat curling up beside me. I'd left the downstairs window open a crack to let the air circulate, and the bloody thing had jumped in to come and find me.

'Oh, and you should see the size of the prawns, Evie. It's not natural, it really isn't,' my mum is murmuring down the phone, as if the King of Spain might hear her and have her arrested for hate speech.

'Genetic modification!' my dad shouts from somewhere else in the room. 'Tell her, Carrie, Joe from the diner's sure of it.'

'Oh!' I swear as someone's bag smacks me across the arm as they run for the tram. 'Sorry, Mum, I'm meeting Kirsty for coffee — can I call you later in the week?'

I stop a few steps away from Starbucks, leaning against the arches of Manchester Central Library and rubbing my forearm. Lack of sleep has made me irritable and weary, and I need a moment to compose myself.

'Oh, is that your friend from work?' Mum chirps, and I come to, surprised that she remembers. 'The one we saw on FaceTime a few months back? Be sure to say hello from us!'

I assure them that I will and end the call quickly, conflict nudging at my resolve. A memory surfaces: Kirsty and I having lunch in my office, my phone ringing, her insisting she stayed to virtually meet my parents. We were friends, and not only in the forced-colleague-closeness sense. We were *friends*.

I take a step forward, and then push myself on with renewed force. I'm tired and it's making me emotional. I repeat my mantra to myself: *F Ups*, false permission, complaints, betrayal. She'd do this to me tenfold — she *is* doing this to me tenfold. She's slagging me off to Dev, playing just as dirty as I am. There's no space in this plan for nostalgia and sentimentality. If I don't fight my own corner, who will?

Kirsty is waiting for me at a little round table in the corner, two steaming coffees placed in front of her. I note this and almost stop — she's bought me coffee, undoubtedly my usual order. Is she trying to make amends? A momentary flash of how things could be if we stopped this now, apologised and made up, crosses my mind. It's tantalising.

'Hi.' I sink into the seat opposite her and she sits up.

'Hey, how are you? I got you an Americano, triple shot.'

'Perfect, I need it.'

As I take a sip I can feel her watching me, no doubt taking in my over-concealed under-eyes. Is she feeling as bad as I am? Is she regretting what she's done?

'So,' I say, putting my cup down. 'What did you want to talk about, specifically?'

She grimaces. 'I know it's awkward, after the confusion with the job vacancy.' *Not a vacancy*, I think. 'But we still need to do the best we can at the expo, don't we? For the company's sake. So I hope we can help each other.'

'Oh.' I raise my eyebrows, the coffee suddenly feeling cheap. She thinks I'm stupid enough to trade my dream job for a £3.45 Americano. I feel idiotic for thinking she might want to move on from this. This is why I never let my guard down. 'Do you have something for me?' I ask, managing to keep my voice neutral.

She reddens. Of course she doesn't. 'Well, no . . . I mean, I thought maybe you could give me a hand with my stuff, seeing as you were presenting it originally. I could try and help out with yours, but I'm not sure what use I'd be . . .'

In another life, I'd tell Kirsty that putting herself down is a shit way of getting what she wants, and that she should value her contributions and own the knowledge she's worked so hard to accumulate. But this isn't another life, and what she thinks of herself is rapidly becoming something I am not able or willing to assist with.

'Of course.' I sit up straight, switching to manager mode. 'Have you got a notebook? Or your laptop?' I pull my computer out. 'I can tell you what I've got.'

'Yes, brilliant, that'd be great.' She scrambles for her laptop and I watch her carefully. After the Summer Bundle drama, there's no way she's drinking this in like she appears to be.

I give her accurate information, going through the presentation I prepared weeks ago and reeling off data protection laws and future security development plans.

'That's a really good idea,' she muses. 'Making a campaign entirely *about* how we protect our customers' data.'

I nod. It *is* a good idea. It's the kind of idea that makes a great Head of Marketing. I'd have given it to her with no strings, if she'd asked a few weeks ago.

She scribbles a few notes down and taps at her laptop, and I drain my drink. 'Just nipping to the toilet,' I say, scraping my chair back.

I close the single-stall bathroom door behind me and lean against the sink. Kirsty's positioned herself so that she's facing the door, so there's no way I can look to see what she's doing, but I've left my cursor directly over the word 'encryption' on my PowerPoint presentation, and I have a tissue folded in the top of my bag, right below the zip. I'll know if she's been digging.

I look in the mirror and tap under my eyes, smoothing out the makeup that has found its way into the creases. I wash my hands slowly, rubbing the soap under my nails, and then dry them, watching as the paper towel drops softly into the bin. When a good amount of time has passed, I swing the door open and stride back across the café. Kirsty is bent over her laptop, typing. As I sit down, she closes it.

'This has been great, thank you,' she says, and for a second, her eyes make it seem like she means it. If only.

'No problem. Just give me a shout if you need a hand with anything else.' I smile. 'I'm going to grab another coffee and fire off a few emails, so I'll see you in the office?'

'Sure.' She packs her bag and then hesitates, her eyes flicking towards me. I think she's going to say something, but then she swings her bag onto her shoulder and walks out of the door.

I watch her through the window, her steps confident and her head high. When she disappears round the corner, I finally look at my computer screen.

The arrow of the cursor is still hovering over the word 'encryption'. I pull open my handbag, and the tissue snags against the zip. Something in me sags with relief. I gave her good information; it was her loss if she decided to double-check it. Now neither of us have done anything wrong. I go to close the lid of my laptop, half smiling, but as I do, I notice that two new words have been added randomly

138

into the middle of the paragraph, making the sentence nonsensical.

Good luck.

* * *

I am so angry as I reach my front door that I almost walk straight into Will.

'Shit!' I stumble backwards, grabbing the fence post for balance.

'Sorry.' He holds up his hands and rises from where he's been sitting on the doorstep. 'I wanted to catch you.'

I hold my hand to my chest, my pulse slowing. 'Couldn't you have called?' Will looks hurt, and I mentally slap myself. *What kind of thing was that to say?* I'm all over the place — it's beginning to scare me. 'I mean, I'm sorry, no, it's OK. What's up?'

'I just needed a break. Jess is in a session, so I thought I'd come over and see if you were working from home.'

'Right, of course. Are you alright? Do you want to—'

I stop as a movement down the street catches my eye. It's the cat. She pads softly up the path of the house two doors down and slinks through their open front door.

'Oh, hang on.' I hold my hand up to Will as I walk backwards towards the street. 'Can you give me five minutes? Literally, five minutes? I just need to speak to those people about that bloody cat.'

Will opens his mouth to respond but I'm already moving, rushing quickly up the road. 'Go and sit in the garden!' I call over my shoulder, realising belatedly that I should have given him my keys. 'Five minutes, I promise!'

I stride up the garden path of the house the cat went into and knock loudly on their open front door. I can see directly down the hallway, and raised voices are filtering down the stairs.

'Hello?' I call. The voices stop. I look back down the street to my house. Will has gone, he'll be in the garden.

Footsteps sound on the stairs, and I turn my head back around. Piece by piece, a man appears: dark, curly hair, sharp blue eyes, a short, untidy beard.

He stops when he sees me, and we stare at each other. There's something familiar about him.

I shake my head, suddenly forgetting what I'm doing. I pull myself up. 'I need to talk to you about your cat.'

CHAPTER 25

Adam

'God, Adam, it's a bit depressing in here.' Katie stands in the middle of the hallway, the front door wide open behind her. A tickle of a breeze filters through and the bottom of her dress ripples in response.

I take her in. Her eyes are bright and alert, her legs smooth and tanned. On one wrist she wears a bracelet I haven't seen before, and the thin straps of her dress trail down to meet at the base of her back, exposing a new tattoo.

'What's that?' I ask dumbly, pointing.

'Oh.' She laughs, and it's strange: light and girlish. 'I thought it was about time I bit the bullet. Embraced the change, you know?'

No, I don't know. Who is this woman?

'Shall I go and get packing, then?' She asks, turning around to face me. Her perfume — new, unfamiliar — tickles my nose.

'If you like.'

She wanders the rooms downstairs like a beautiful ghost, collecting bits and trinkets I barely pay attention to, and I stay rooted to the spot. It's only when she starts climbing the stairs that I snap out of my trance and follow her.

'Oh, thanks for getting my case down.' She heaves it up onto the bed next to mine and partially fills it with an ornamental elephant, a flower-themed coffee table book and a favourite coaster of hers that she found downstairs. 'Are you going somewhere?'

'Dublin. We booked it a while back.'

'Ah, yeah.' She nods, and I notice that she averts her gaze, looking bashful for the first time since she arrived. The passport. The memory washes over me again, and I breathe deeply.

'Shall I leave you to it?' I ask. Being in the same room with her when she's like this, when I don't recognise her, is making me nauseous.

'No, stay.' She starts bundling clothes from the wardrobe into her case. 'I won't be able to take everything today. I'll come back at some point, when you're at work.' She tests the lid of her case, and when it closes easily, adds another few items. Before I've had a chance to reply, she's speaking again. 'We need to talk about the house.'

'I'd like to keep the house,' I say quickly.

She turns to me. 'And how are you going to afford that?'

I shrug. I can't come up with a plan, not now, not when she's just confirmed that she's gone for good.

'Right.' She turns back to her clothes. 'Well, if you're serious, I can buy you out. You could get somewhere smaller, an apartment, maybe? Somewhere less expensive.' She moves to the chest of drawers now, pulling out t-shirts and under-wear. I look away. 'There are some nice ones down by the high street — you'd have more than enough for a 10% deposit . . .'

I watch her talking, stunned. How can she be so flippant? Every word she says is like a thump in the chest. Has she been thinking about this for a while?

'What about the beach?' I whisper, unaware I've said it out loud until she turns to look at me again.

'The beach?' She frowns. 'You'd have a bit of a commute on your hands, wouldn't you? I suppose you could—'

'No, you asked me to come to the beach with you. Before . . . before we broke up.'

She raises her eyebrows. 'Oh. Yeah. I think that was . . . it was an attempt. To sort this. Or come clean, or something.'

It was a breakup trip, then. I feel my heart fold in on itself. 'You said you missed me.'

'Christ, Adam!' She spins around from where she's gone back to packing. 'I slept with someone else! I cheated on you!'

I step back. 'I know.'

She rolls her eyes. 'Have some fucking self-respect.'

All the breath leaves my body. She moves around the bed to her bedside table and crouches down to open the drawer. Something simmers inside me, bubbling up in my stomach, slowly, and then uncontrollably.

'I'm sorry,' she says, not looking at me. 'That was harsh, I—'

'Need something from in there, do you?' I ask, my voice shaking. 'I thought you'd already taken all the important things.'

'Oh, grow up,' she snaps. 'This is hard for me, too.'

'Yeah, I bet it's *really* hard,' I growl, my voice loud now. 'How's this for self-respect? Give me your keys and fuck off.'

There's a small pause as she turns around, slowly, to look at me. 'Adam—'

'You'll get your half of the house. Just don't ever come near me again.' My hands are clenched so hard, I can feel my nails puncturing my palms.

She stands up. 'What's up with you?'

'*Me?*' I yell, despite myself. 'What's up with *me?*'

'Yes!' she shouts. 'You just swore at me!'

I hold my hands up in the air. 'Oh, I'm sorry. I'm so sorry. How dare I? Can you forgive me? Because I sure as hell can't forgive you.'

Katie opens her mouth to respond, but a noise downstairs makes her pause. There's a knock, and someone calls something downstairs.

'Keep packing,' I snap, turning on my heel and jogging down the stairs.

The front door is wide open. A woman stands there, framed by the sunlight: wavy, chin-length black hair and green eyes.

She stares at me for a second, as though she's lost her train of thought, and her mouth hangs open, a confused frown between her eyebrows. I go to speak, but she straightens her shoulders and her face smooths.

'I need to talk to you about your cat,' she says.

I shake my head, my argument with Katie clouding my thinking. 'My cat?'

'Yes, the scabby one? It keeps coming in through my window.' She raises an eyebrow at me, and I take in her tailored blouse and folded arms. Something tells me she isn't to be messed with.

'Old Sausage?' I say, stupidly. My head feels like mashed potato.

'What?'

'Sorry.' I shake my head. 'I'm in the middle of something. I'm . . . do you mean the tortoiseshell one?'

'Why, how many have you got?' she asks.

'None,' I say. 'I don't have a cat.'

'What about that one, right there?' She points beyond me, and I turn around. Old Sausage is sitting at the bottom of the stairs, swishing his tail.

'Oh, Jesus. No, he isn't mine. He just lets himself in. He belongs to someone down the street, I think.' I step around her and poke my head out of the door, my arm brushing hers as I point. 'That house, two doors down. I always see him going through the patio doors.'

'That's *my* house,' she says incredulously.

I step back, conscious of how close we are. 'Oh.'

Footsteps thunder down the stairs and Katie appears, dragging her suitcase behind her. 'Hello.' She stands beside me, studying the woman in the doorway. 'Who's this then?'

'Eve,' the woman says, holding out her hand, and something niggles in my mind.

'I see. Well, don't let me keep you.' Katie smiles at me. 'I'll come by for the rest in the week. Keep the furniture. We've—' She catches herself, assumedly before she starts talking about quite how little she needs our chipped IKEA offerings in her new life. 'Well. Doesn't matter. I'll make sure you're out, so I'm not . . . interrupting.' She casts a quick side-glance at Eve.

I open my mouth to correct her, whatever her assumptions are, but she's halfway down the path, moving towards a waiting Uber.

As she reaches the gate, she stops, hesitating for a moment before turning back around. 'Chloe called, by the way,' she says, an unreadable expression on her face. 'You might want to get in touch.'

She turns on her heel, swings open the gate and drops her case into the open boot of the car. Two seconds later, she slams the door behind her and the car drives away.

I stare after her, my brain struggling to process the enormity of what's happening. I don't realise I'm still staring until Eve clears her throat.

'This feels uncomfortable,' she says, and I come to, dragging my eyes away from the road.

'Feels worse than uncomfortable to me.' I shake my head. 'Sorry, not a great time.'

'No worries,' she says, peering shamelessly down the corridor. 'If it's not your cat, it's not your cat.'

'It's not my cat,' I confirm, looking behind me, but Old Sausage has gone. 'I'm actually starting to wonder whether it's anyone's cat at all.'

'Yeah.' She looks thoughtful. 'I feel a bit bad for her, but she is sort of ruining my life.'

'Her?' I smile. 'You reckon it's a girl?'

She looks down, her severe expression melting into something that looks a little like embarrassment. Dark eyelashes flash against her cheeks for a second before she looks back up. 'I just assumed.'

'I thought he was a boy.' I scratch my beard. Something about this woman is putting me on edge.

'Right, here's what we'll do.' She straightens her back again, her eyes focused, and the transformation is mesmerising. 'We'll take her to the vets, and if she isn't chipped, list her on some missing animal sites, then update each other if her owner is found. OK?'

It feels like I don't really have a choice. 'Yeah, OK.'

'Here's my number.' She holds her hand out and I look at it dumbly, expecting to see something written there, before realising she wants my phone. I unlock it and open the 'new contact' screen before passing it over.

'Great.' She taps her number in quickly and hands it back. 'One-bell me. Get in touch if you hear anything.'

She turns and walks determinedly back down the path, and I watch her leave, feeling like something has just happened, but not precisely knowing what.

CHAPTER 26

Adam

It feels a little bit like I'm a snow globe, sitting on a shelf with all the other snow globes, and a child has just come along and shaken me.

Hugh is distressed; his arms flailing and mouth wide. I give him Hei Hei, once, twice, three times, but he lasts five seconds before he's flung across the room. My head is full of thoughts: Katie, Becky, Chloe, Old Sausage, Eve, Okie, Hugh, the house, Dublin . . . three weeks ago, my life was still, and now there are things falling everywhere, and I can't decide which parts are beautiful and which are a mess.

I try to soothe Hugh, fast-forwarding *Moana* to his favourite part, but he is appeased for only a minute before he begins shrieking again. While he's quiet, I quickly roll up his sleeves. No bruises, nothing. So why is he behaving like this?

I shovel all of my other thoughts into a box in my head, focusing only on this. Is something happening? Is he OK? If only he could tell me — if only I could *see* . . .

My experience with Hugh's last home is making me paranoid; understaffing and lack of training meant that I pulled him out of there underweight and clinically unhappy, but since being here he's been better than I've ever seen him. The doctor came to see me as soon as I arrived this morning, telling me that Hugh's bruise was likely the result of him catching his arm as he moved it, and nothing more sinister. But if something were to happen again . . . I stop my imagination in its tracks. It won't. But I need to be prepared.

I cycle from Hugh's to my first student's house — a struggling and highly-pressured girl whose parents want her to be a doctor — and then on to three more before I reach Okie's as my last call of the day. I use most of our session to show Okie the exam times I've found; we write them in his planner and make a flow chart of actions before they occur. As we wrap up, Mr Adayemi hands me my envelope and wishes me a good afternoon.

My sessions finished for the day, I cycle in the opposite direction of home. I stop in a shop and find what I need, before continuing on, back to Hugh's.

He's no better when I return, sullen and downcast, which to me is worse than the screeching. At least when he's loud he's fighting, trying to tell me something.

'Right, we're going to get to the bottom of this,' I tell him. 'Let's see what's going on.'

I sit on the bed and unwrap the box I bought at the shop, quickly scanning the instruction manual and connecting the device to my phone. Then I stand on my tiptoes and place the tiny camera on top of the wardrobe, feeling a thin layer of dust that tells me it's unlikely to be disturbed for a while.

I check my phone and make some adjustments, until I can see Hugh's chair and the bed clearly. The battery icon in the corner of my screen tells me the camera is on 100%, but I'll bring spare batteries with me next time just in case.

'Hi.' A voice from the doorway startles me, and I lock my phone quickly, spinning around. It's Becky.

'Oh, hi!' I say, unnecessarily enthusiastically.

'How are we?' she asks, avoiding my gaze and focusing on Hugh.

'Not good, actually,' I reply, my words tripping over each other, caught between the awkwardness and the need to protect my brother. 'He's not been great today, which is really unusual for him.'

Becky crouches down next to Hugh. 'Hugh?' She touches his arm lightly. She studies his face for a second, and then stands back up. 'He's not himself, is he?' she says, a crease forming between her eyebrows.

'No. Can we — I don't know, I'm not accusing anyone of anything, but he isn't usually like this, and I found a bruise on his arm the other day, and—'

If looks could kill, Becky would be murdering me again and again. 'We all love Hugh. There's no way anything like that's going on.' She glares at me a second longer, and then turns away.

'Of course, no, but you understand that I have to be vigilant. I'm the only person he has—'

'What about your parents?' she says, almost accusatorially. 'Where are they?'

I falter. 'Becky, I'm sorry. If you're still angry with me . . .'

'No, I'm sorry.' Her face goes red and she runs a hand through her fringe. 'That was too far. It's none of my business.'

'No,' I agree. 'But our parents aren't around, so it really is just us. Us and the guys, when they pop in.'

She nods. 'I'll see if I can get therapy to come to him first thing in the morning.'

She leaves, closing the door behind her, but I stay where I am, staring at the space where she stood. I feel deeply unsettled; something is nudging against the edge of my mind — the way she snapped at me, the look she gave me. The tiny tattoo on her wrist. Was it Becky I didn't like . . . or was it who she reminded me of?

I sink onto Hugh's bed, resting the back of my head against the windowsill. Holidays: Katie's sunbathing, the beginning of our end. Becky's sunbathing, a sign of irreparable differences. Does Becky just remind me of the person Katie has turned into?

My thoughts are interrupted by the beeping of my phone. A stream of new WhatsApp messages, from 'Eve Cat Neighbour'.

Eve: *Hi, it's Eve, from down the road*

Eve: *I don't think I got your name*

Eve: *I've put Old Sausage on Animal Search UK*

Eve: *Can you do Facebook — not really my remit*

Eve: *Thanks*

> Me: *Hi Eve, I'm Adam. Should I trust you or are you going to get me kicked out of the garden?*

I delete it all and start again.

> Me: *Hi Eve, I'm Adam. Trying to think of a joke about our names that doesn't sound weird and I'm failing. Yeah, I'll put it on Facebook — didn't realise there was a remit for these kinds of things if you were under 50, but what do I know?*

I check on Hugh, handing him Hei Hei again, before another message comes through.

Eve: *Ha. Careful, I might get you kicked out of the garden.*

I mentally slap myself for not getting the joke in there first.

Eve: *Great, let me know if you hear anything*

Eve: *Have you seen her recently?*

> Me: *Not since he appeared in my hallway while you were there. Have you?*

150

Eve: *Nope*

Eve: *Hope she's gone home*

Eve: *It's a girl BTW*

> Me: *I sort of hope HE sticks around — I like it when he comes and disrupts my day*

Eve: *Keep *HER* then!*

Eve: *Let me know when you've put the ad up*

> Me: *Will do — speak soon*

My phone stays silent, and I turn it over in my hands. I take one last look at the camera, plant a kiss on Hugh's head, and then leave, to go home to my empty house.

CHAPTER 27

Eve

The plane to Dublin is packed full of expo attendees and lads making the most of the £15.99 Ryanair summer deals. I've walked the 83 miles through Manchester Airport's terminal buildings to find that I've been allocated a seat on the front row, right next to the emergency exit door.

I quickly message Will again. When I got back from Adam's the other day, he'd gone, and he hasn't answered any of my texts since.

The safety procedure demonstration ends, and a flight attendant clips herself into the seat opposite me. I glance around me quickly; there are two flights to Dublin today, and I'm almost certain Kirsty had booked onto this one. But I arrived late, running up to the gate as the stragglers were boarding, and I haven't seen her.

As soon as we're in the air, I pull out my laptop and load up my presentation again. It's the one I left open for Kirsty the other day: my original PowerPoint, before Dev changed the schedule.

My plan was simple — it was a basic double bluff. I changed everything on the presentation, falsifying figures and writing out bogus campaign ideas that would never come to fruition. Then I added notes to each piece of information, things like 'Make Kirsty believe this is actually achievable' and 'Tell Kirsty this is actually 83%'. Before I went to the toilet, and before she started snooping, everything I told her was accurate. I gave her all the correct information. She was only in danger if she decided not to trust me.

Adrenaline pulses in my throat. What I've done is fine. I was honest, genuine, as long as she was, too. I gave Kirsty a choice: take the correct information I told her at face value, or dig around and uncover imaginary lies that would ruin her presentation. She made her decision, and, whatever it was, now she'll have to live with it.

Just fifteen minutes into the flight, we begin our descent. I close my laptop and pull out my phone, desperate to make plans for the evening. As soon as the wheels hit the tarmac, I tap out of airplane mode and fire off a message to Graham.

> Me: *You arriving this evening? Fancy a drink?*

My phone beeps a response almost instantly, but it isn't him.

> *New alert from Animal Search UK*
> *Hi I think this is my cat does it have a collar like*
> *this please let me know thanks*

There's a picture attached, and I open it. In front of a Christmas tree sits a large, black cat in a pink jumper and a sparkly silver collar. Its eyes are amber, but the similarities end there. I type back:

> *Hi, I'm sorry, the cat we've found is a tortoiseshell.*
> *I hope you find yours.*

I screenshot the interaction and the photo, and send them on to Adam. A phone beeps loudly from the back of the plane, and the noise triggers people to rustle in their bags for their own.

I'm first off the plane, and I stride quickly into the terminal building, hoping to avoid Kirsty and anyone else from work who might be onboard. Passport control is empty, so I sail through and straight into an awaiting taxi.

I have twenty-five minutes of peace before we pull up outside the Cosgrove hotel, a standard-issue, three-star establishment that Florina decided was cheap enough to be coverable by expenses. I walk quickly inside and over to the reception desk, where I give my name and wait for my keys.

I check my phone again. Twelve emails, but no response from Graham. I load up Tryst; fresh faces, Irish accents . . . that would be one way to spend an evening. I swipe through, trying not to think about how Kirsty and I spent the evening before last year's expo: drunk on a boat up the Liffey.

Once I've matched a few, I look through my inbox. The names continue endlessly — *New Match! Say Hello!* — hundreds of unopened connections from back home trailing behind a few new potentials from Dublin: Ross, Cian, James, Donal, Freddie, Ben, Adam—

'Hiya.'

I glance over my shoulder, certain whoever it is isn't talking to me.

It's Kirsty.

'Oh, hi.' I lock my phone quickly, but she's seen.

'Fishing for local talent?' She leans against reception and drums her fingers against the desk.

'Just seeing what's out there.' I smile tightly. 'How are you feeling about tomorrow?'

'Fine, yeah. All of your stuff was really helpful.' She smiles at me sweetly. 'Thanks.'

'You're more than welcome.' I turn back to reception. 'I'm sure you'll blow them all away.'

'Here we are, madam.' The receptionist hands me a key, the number 304 in faded lettering on the side.

'Thanks.' I take it and turn back to Kirsty. 'See you tomorrow.'

She nods, and I move towards the lift. I step inside.

The doors begin sliding closed behind me, and I turn back to face reception. Kirsty looks at me. When only a slither of light remains, and the doors are almost shut, she grins.

'Good luck!' she calls.

* * *

I pace my room, beating a path into the carpet from the bed to the desk to the bedside table. I start running a bath, and then stop. I do some squats, some sit-ups, and have a shower. I check my phone, and resist the urge to message Graham again.

Tryst notifications light up my screen sporadically, but I ignore them all. If Kirsty sees me out with a random man . . . I couldn't give her the satisfaction. Why is she *doing* this?

Eventually, I order a pizza to my room and open my laptop, plunging myself into my real presentation for tomorrow. My anger at Kirsty is at eruption point. I want to find out her room number, go over there and smash her door down. I want to ask her why she's stabbing me in the back over and over, blatantly now, and what I've done to deserve this. I want to know why our friendship meant so little to her.

There are boys in the room next to mine; they keep shouting and playing music. Occasionally I catch snatches of words, they have Manchester accents, and I assume they're racking up their holiday bill on the mini-bar.

My pizza arrives, and as I open the door, I see a man stood in the doorway of the room next door. He leans inside, shouting, 'Come on, Piotr, for Christ's sake! The taxi's here!'

A voice calls back, 'Ferg's chundered all over the bathroom!'

I pay the delivery guy, and the man in the doorway turns to face me. 'Evening.' He smiles.

I nod, and retreat into my room.

I sit back at my computer and funnel pizza into my mouth, clicking through emails and fantasising about tomorrow. I haven't thought much about my own presentation, but I am constantly picturing Kirsty's. I imagine it like the Summer Bundle meeting, but on a colossal scale: fudged numbers, bumbling mistakes, ripples around the audience and Michael Peters pursing his lips, texting Dev to say that Kirsty has to go.

My phone vibrates and I snatch it up from the desk, my eyes seeking Graham's name, a room number for me to go to. It's Adam, and I suddenly loathe myself for being so needy.

> Adam: *If that's Old Sausage, he probably ran away to avoid wearing that jumper. Thanks for the update — sorry for the late response, away from home at the moment. Saw OS this morning and gave him a tin of something stinky.*

I consider not replying — there's nothing to say — but something makes me engage.

> Me: *Seconded, but that is 100% not OS*

> Me: *I give her criminally overcooked salmon so you win*

> Me: *Hope you're away somewhere nice*

My phone stays silent, and I pick at a pizza crust as I hear the boys next door finally emerge from their room and thunder loudly down the corridor. When they're gone, it's silent, and I stand up again, pacing, waiting for tomorrow.

CHAPTER 28

Adam

'WHEYYY!' Bil roars, pumping his fist in the air.

'Oh Christ,' I bury my head in my hands.

'Shut up, Bil.' Piotr thumps him on the arm. 'Don't make us those people.'

'What people?' Bil looks around the plane incredulously. 'The *fun* people?'

'The dickheads screaming at the back of the plane,' I correct him. 'We'll get chucked off.'

Ferg swivels around in his seat and raises a smug eyebrow. 'Thanks for sorting the seating plan, Piotr. I'm really comfortable.'

I am less than comfortable, wedged in on the back row between Bil, who is intent on making us all look as laddish as possible, and Piotr, who keeps sticking his legs out into the aisle and accidentally tripping up the air stewards. Ferg, as the only member of the group who was principally against pre-booked seats, seems to have come off the best. He's a row in front and on the other side of the aisle, so he can quite easily pretend he doesn't know us.

Bil is pacified as the drinks trolley comes around, mercifully reaching us first. The plane is full of people on their way to some flower event; it's all anyone's talking about.

'. . . looking forward to seeing the Florina talks,' someone in the row in front is saying.

'Might be nice to see some of the smaller brands, too. They always seem to dominate the whole event . . .' their friend replies.

'Adam?' Piotr is nudging me. 'What do you think about Chicken Cottage for tea?'

'Are you serious?'

A small argument erupts over the merits and downfalls of Chicken Cottage as a holiday tea option, and by the time we've decided on Nando's (which nobody wanted, but which was chosen because chicken had, by this point, become the focal point) we're touching down in Dublin.

I rush to turn my phone on, wishing I'd put it on airplane mode rather than switch it off completely, desperate to check that there's no news about Hugh.

'Ad, everything's going to be OK,' Piotr murmurs to me. 'Keep it on extra loud, and we'll stay where there's signal, but try not to obsess.'

'I know,' I say, grappling for another excuse. 'I've got my students as well, though.'

'On the weekend?' Piotr looks at me kindly as the intercom reminds us all to stay in our seats.

'Yeah. Okie — the one who's hoping to go to uni — he might need me for something.'

My phone starts up and beeps loudly with a new message. People turn around to stare.

'Anything?' Bil asks.

'No,' I say, smiling at the picture of the cat Eve has just sent me. I start to reply, but remember my promise not to stay glued to my phone, and pocket it.

* * *

'Goodbye to Katie!' Bil raises a can and droplets of beer splash across my duvet.

'Goodbye to Katie!' the others cheer. I join in.

We've just got back from Nando's, and the drinks are flowing. Tonight, it has been decided, is my first foray into a Katie-less world. We're in my room at the Cosgrove hotel, drinking cans of BrewDog and researching the best pubs on Temple Bar.

'Ooh, a *concept* bar.' Bil shows his phone to Ferg, who grimaces and snatches it off him.

'Traditional, please,' he says, swaying on his feet. 'Let's try and be a little bit cultural.'

They begin to bicker, and Piotr sits next to me on the bed. 'Bil's ordered the Uber, so drink up,' he says. 'How are you feeling?'

'I'm good.' I nod, smiling. 'Yeah, I think I'm OK.'

He nudges me. 'Knew you would be.'

'Yeah. Thanks for this.'

'Any time.'

There's a pause as Piotr looks at me, a strange expression on his face. His mouth opens slightly, and then he sighs. 'You know Chloe's been in touch.'

I meet his gaze. 'I don't want to speak to her right now.'

'Alright.' He nods. 'OK. But do you think—'

'Not now.'

Bil thuds into the chair opposite us and takes a swig of his drink as Ferg goes into the bathroom. 'What are you two doing next Friday?'

'I've got a session with Okie, but think I'm free in the evening.'

Piotr and Bil share a glance.

'What?'

Piotr opens his mouth to speak, but Bil jumps in.

'Do you think you're getting a bit too . . . involved? With Okie?'

I sit back. 'What?' I say again.

'Not in a bad way.' Bil leans forward. 'I mean . . . offering to work for free, organising his exams . . . it's more than going above and beyond, isn't it?'

A rare feeling of defensiveness rises up inside me. 'And the alternative would be?' I challenge. 'Let him fall behind because he can't afford it? Withdraw help when I'm perfectly able to provide it?'

Piotr holds his hands up. 'Ad, that's not what we're saying. We're just worried, that's all. You give such a lot of yourself to people.'

I run my hand through my beard, all my energy leaving me. 'If someone had offered to do this for Hugh, before . . . it's important to me that he doesn't miss that opportunity.'

When we were young, we had no money. Hugh lived at home with me, Mum and Dad, and there wasn't even wriggle room for specialist provisions. Hugh didn't even have a proper bed — just a wide sofa a family friend donated — and Mum was his sole carer. With only Dad working, money was tight, and Hugh missed out on a million opportunities simply because we couldn't afford them. It's only now, with the insurance money, that he can have the life he always deserved.

Bil places a hand on my shoulder. 'I get it. I get it. We're just looking out for you.'

I nod. 'I know.' I slide my phone out of my pocket, ready for the conversation to be over. 'I'll just check the cameras, and then let's go.'

'Alright.' They stand up.

Bil walks over to the bathroom and raps hard on the door, his phone held in front of his face. 'Uber's here, Ferg! Come on!'

He opens the door to my room and stands in the corridor, gesturing to us all to hurry up. Piotr drains his can.

I quickly open my phone while we wait for Ferg, clicking onto the camera app. Hugh's room is dark, and I can see the shape of him in his bed, curled up, asleep. I cycle back quickly — the camera records twenty-four hours of footage before overwriting it — and manage to catch the moment before the lights are switched off. Becky stands in the doorway, saying something; Hugh is lying sleepily in his bed. She pulls the door to, flicking off the light, before closing it.

I close the app and quickly tap out a response to Eve, smiling as I look at the photo of the cat in the jumper again.

'Guys!' Bil roars.

'Ugh,' comes a moan from the bathroom.

Piotr rattles the bathroom door handle until Ferg lets him in.

Bil checks his phone again, standing at the door. 'Come on, Piotr, for Christ's sake! The taxi's here!' he calls.

'Ferg's chundered all over the bathroom!' Piotr shouts back.

A muddled twenty minutes pass as Ferg is thrown into the shower and force-fed a pint of water. Another taxi is ordered, three more cans of BrewDog are opened, and then we're on our way.

* * *

'The free stuff's this way.' Bil pounds the stairs ahead of us, yanking Ferg by the sleeve.

'No! No, Bil, we haven't even seen the hop room!' Ferg protests shrilly, his face the colour of a custard tart.

'The beer isn't free if you've paid €15 entry just to get to it,' I add, dragging myself up the stairs, my head pounding.

The Guiness Storehouse is heaving with families and couples taking selfies, and this, paired with a rapidly growing hangover from last night, renders me unable to fight.

'The problem with you, Bil,' Piotr says as we reach the top and join the back of the snaking queue for the bar, 'is that you're the bad influence *and* the only one who doesn't get hangovers.'

Bil cranes over the crowds of people to see how far off we are. Ferg starts arguing that we should go and see the exhibition about the history of Guinness while the queue quietens, but he's quickly shot down.

We make it to the front, and after a few gut-wrenching sips, the beer slips down nicely and my headache starts to ease.

'Hair of the dog sorted.' Bil grins, and starts his descent towards the exit.

'You're joking?' Ferg scrambles after him. 'We're actually not going to see anything?'

Piotr joins in the debate, flitting from one side to the other: 'We've paid to get in, we should at least get out money's worth', 'but then again, it's full of tourists and it stinks a bit'.

My phone beeps loudly in my pocket, and I pull it out. It's a comment on my Facebook post about Old Sausage.

Glenda McDonald: *Shared in Devon. Hope he turns up.*

I snort, and screenshot the response. I send it on to Eve, with the message:

Thanks, Glenda. Note: 'he'.

She doesn't reply immediately, so I pocket my phone. While I've been typing, the boys have moved towards the exit. I catch them up and we emerge outside, the bickering continuing.

'What's the *point*?' Ferg is wailing. 'Fifteen euros for a pint of Guinness!'

'We paid seven last night on Temple Bar!' Bil retorts. 'It's an *experience*, Ferg.'

We meander through the small side streets until we come out onto the main road. People bustle past in every direction, shouting down phones and jostling each other. Women on stilts dressed as giant flowers saunter down the pavement, and outside a bar is a huddle of people wearing lanyards, the words 'UK and Ireland Floristry Expo 2022' printed on the front.

'Reckon we should crash the conference?' Bil grins mischievously.

'No!' Ferg cries.

We keep moving, wandering aimlessly, back-and-forthing about where to go next, and I think about how much I needed this; how just 24 hours of distance has given me a good shift in perspective.

Katie has gone, and it's time to start afresh.

'. . . quite embarrassing, really.' I catch snippets of conversation as people pass. 'They're the biggest retailer in the country, it was a complete shambles . . .'

'. . . and you'd have thought they'd be better prepared. That girl really showed herself up. Thank god the other one was more professional about things . . .'

I spot a bar across the street, the words 'FREE POOL TABLE' emblazoned on the front. 'Guys,' I nudge Ferg, 'Fancy a game?'

Ferg begins to respond, saying something about the Little Museum, but he's drowned out by the loud ringing of my phone.

I dig into my pocket and pull it out.

'Hello?'

'Hi, Adam Parks?'

'Speaking.'

'This is Janet calling, from Rosegreen Residential Care. I'm afraid Hugh has been taken into hospital. You might want to come down.'

CHAPTER 29

Eve

Graham sits opposite me in the hotel breakfast room, his hair tousled, a small smile playing at his lips.

'Good night?' I ask, flattening my fringe with one hand.

'*Very* good.' He spears a piece of sausage with a fork and pops it in his mouth.

I stare at my fruit bowl, willing myself to hold my tongue and keep my face impassive. 'I'm glad.'

'So why did you want to meet?' Graham asks, looking up at me through narrowed eyes. 'Oh. Is it about me not texting back last night?'

'No,' I scoff. 'I messaged a few people.'

'Who did you end up going out with?' He regards me steadily.

'No one, I had to make some big changes to my presentation so I cancelled.'

'Cancelled who?'

I take a deep breath. I won't let him bait me.

'Are you doing the lighting for our talks this morning?' I ask, checking my watch. Two hours to go.

'Yeah. Why?' He spreads jam on his toast.

'I wondered . . .' I bite my lip. It's risky. 'I thought you might be able to make some changes. To the second presentation.'

Graham stops spreading and looks at me. 'Kirsty's presentation.'

'Yes.'

He laughs, shaking his head. 'You're not serious.'

'Do I look like I'm joking?'

He stops smiling and drops his knife onto the tablecloth, a smear of red swiping across the linen. 'Eve.' His voice is low, warning. 'What the fuck are you doing?'

I wiggle my tongue around my teeth, trying to dislodge a string of pineapple. 'Forget about it.'

He sits back in his chair. 'You know, I'm really glad I didn't text back.'

'What?'

'Well, this was it, wasn't it? Use me to get your way. Ask me to risk my job for you.'

'No.'

'Yes.' He shakes his head. 'That's cold, Eve, even for you.'

'And I suppose you spent all night pining over me, did you? Watching the porn channel and ordering room service?'

'That's not the point.'

'It is, Graham, and you know it.' *Is it?* I push my bowl away from me, my defences rising tall. The words whip out of me before I can stop them. 'You can't fuck whoever you want and expect me not to play the same game.'

'Oh, because that's what's happening here.' He glares at me, and I scrape my chair back, standing up.

'I'll see you at the expo,' I say, and I walk away.

* * *

An hour until Kirsty's talk, and half an hour until mine. I sit in the corner of the main hall, checking through the bogus presentation she found on my computer and trying to predict which parts she might include. With Graham out of the picture, I can't have a look at what she's done, or add anything of my own to ensure she bombs it. I'm just going to have to pray.

The Convention Centre is packed already; smart professionals and small-business florists mill around, looking at the stands and checking their programmes. I tap my foot, impatient, and gaze around the space.

To the left is the largest lecture hall, where we'll be speaking. I don't know my presentation well, but it's fine, I can wing it. I'm not usually so unprepared, have never spent less time on a presentation, particularly not one this important. I put more work into last month's team briefing, but I have had to prioritise. Once Kirsty speaks, any fumbles I make will be forgotten.

I'm packing my bag when I notice a familiar shape looming towards me.

'Eve.' I spot Dev's perfect teeth first; the artificial light of the lobby makes them shine.

I stand up. 'Dev,' I beam, 'so glad you could come.'

'I got the early flight. The doctor says Eleanor should be good for another few days.' He checks his phone. 'Happy to be here, but also praying I don't miss my first child's birth for the sake of appearances.'

'You still want me to present, though?' I ask, as something cold swoops in my stomach. If he bumps us back down, Kirsty won't present what she's supposed to.

'Hm? Oh, yes, yes, no changes.' He waves his hand, his eyes still glued to his phone.

'Great,' I say, relief coursing through me. 'Shall we go through?'

We make our way over to the theatre, where people are taking their seats.

'I'm really looking forward to seeing what you've come up with,' Dev says as we near the front. 'There's a lot riding on this, as you well know.' He winks.

'Mmm.' I look around me; Kirsty is nowhere to be seen. 'I'll catch up with you afterwards?'

He nods. 'Of course.'

I put my bag by the speakers' seats at the front and ascend the stage, checking the laptop and inserting my USB as the hall fills, the seats almost full.

'All ready?' Kirsty has joined me on stage, and is brandishing her pen drive. 'Mind if I pop mine on there as well?'

'Be my guest.' I step away and watch as she drags her presentation onto the desktop.

'Ladies.' I turn my back to Kirsty as Graham climbs the steps towards us, his eyes trained on me. 'Is there any specific lighting you're after? Just spotlights all the way through?'

'A following spotlight,' I say, glaring at him. 'Please.'

'That would be great, thanks, Graham,' Kirsty says from behind me. I turn back around. She's bent over the computer.

'Hi, everyone.' Michael Peters has now appeared. A headache begins in my left temple. 'I'll be doing the introductions in a minute, so if you could all skedaddle. You've got your presentations lined up?'

'On the desktop,' I say.

Kirsty finally moves away from the computer and Michael ushers us off the stage. 'Good luck, ladies.'

Kirsty and I sit next to each other. The hum and chatter of the hall sends adrenaline shooting through my body; thirty-three minutes until she goes on.

Michael taps the microphone, and a hush descends over the room.

'Hello, everybody. For those of you who don't know me, my name is Michael Peters . . .'

The introductions are long and drawn out: what a year we've had, Dev's contributions, our domination of the market. My heart pounds. To be a part of this — to be in Dev's seat . . .

'. . . our in-house Head of Digital Marketing, Eve Slater.'

Applause rains around the room. Kirsty shifts beside me as I get to my feet and climb onto the stage.

'Good morning.' I begin my presentation, trying not to get thrown off by Kirsty, who is staring intently at the slides on the screen behind me. An uncomfortable feeling runs through me, but I shrug it off.

I glance at the laptop for the first few slides, checking that what I'm saying is in sync with my clicks. I falter a few times — tripping over my words and turning back, re-explaining context that I forgot to give properly the first time round — but eventually, I find my rhythm, and move into the middle of the stage, the clicker in my hand.

'As you can see, Florina's share of the market totals almost 46% at last check. We've been the biggest floristry retailer in the country for six years, but never as big as we are now. Our growth is reflected in our customer satisfaction, which we collect by . . .'

I click, describing our feedback attainment methods, but people begin shifting in their seats. Am I boring them? I attempt to speed up, surveying the audience, injecting more energy into my voice.

The shuffling intensifies, and a hum reverberates around the room. I talk louder, my eyes darting from person to person as they murmur in each other's ears and crane their necks forward.

I look to Dev; his face is like thunder.

'Overwhelmingly, the majority of our respondents . . .' I turn to look behind me.

My voice dies in my throat. My stomach drops.

On the screen is a template presentation slide, the title box empty, and underneath, a list of bullet points.

[Insert Title Here]
-Something here about how we're improving our metrics
-Don't mention complaints related to poisonous foxglove recall
-Something about how fucking brilliant Dev is blah blah
-Also don't mention how sturdy the office desks are for shagging IT managers

'I'm so sorry.' I rush towards the computer, my feet skidding across the stage. I stab the escape button, again and again, closing the presentation, catching a glimpse of the side bar where, three slides ago, my presentation merged into this tampered version. Nausea swells inside me.

I return to the desktop. 'I do apologise; if I could just find the correct presentation . . .' I roam the cursor around, going to open my PowerPoint again, to see if something has changed, but a hand lands on my shoulder.

'Technical difficulties happen to the best of us!' Michael booms into the microphone. He guides me, firmly, towards the stairs. 'It's probably best if we have a small break before we move on to the next talk.'

He looks out to Kirsty, who is standing up, a slow smile creeping across her face. I hold the banister tightly, my legs threatening to give way, and walk past, feeling every eye in the room boring into me.

CHAPTER 30

Eve

'How could you?' I push my way through the door of the tech room, where Graham is sitting fiddling with the controls.

He spins around and holds up his hands. 'Eve, I swear to god, I didn't do anything.'

'You did! Of course you did! You've teamed up with her to ruin my career!' I hiss.

Graham stands up and grabs me by the shoulders. 'I didn't touch that computer! You saw!'

'I know you can access them remotely,' I push his hands away. 'Don't lie to me.'

'I can't! Not that laptop, not from here.' He shakes his head. 'Someone went into your presentation after you put it on there. They deleted half your slides and replaced them with new ones.'

I stand in the middle of the room, breathing heavily. Kirsty. She must have done it when I left her alone with the laptop. While I was talking to Graham and Michael. Rage pulses in my throat.

'You can't think I'd do that?' he says, his voice heavy. 'Eve, it's got my fucking job title on it.'

I turn to face him, and his eyes are round and serious.

'It's fine,' I shake my head, moving away. 'Fine. She's going up in a minute. It'll be a car crash.'

'Christ,' Graham sits back down, running his hand through his hair. 'You're both insane.'

'She started this,' I retort, leaning against the control deck and peering down at the stage. What she's done — humiliating me personally in front of the whole floristry community — is unthinkably malicious. I grip the edge of the control deck. 'She deserves everything she gets.'

Graham turns to me, his face unreadable. 'Eve.'

'What?'

'I think you should go and explain. Don't let this fester.'

'I'm not going down there until she's done.' I walk around the small room, from one wall to another, my teeth clenched. 'Once she's hammered the nail in her own coffin, I can say she panicked and sabotaged me. I'll say she was out of her depth, that she didn't know what she was talking about, so she had to draw the attention away from herself.'

'Do you realise how mental you sound?' Graham is staring at me, his mouth open. 'What have you *done*?'

'I haven't done anything.' I lean towards the window again and watch as Dev, Kirsty and Michael stand in a huddle, their eyes searching for me.

'Go and explain, Eve. If you haven't done anything, you can sort this.'

I watch as Kirsty speaks to Dev and gestures towards the stage. She's writing her own narrative, solidifying my culpability. Graham's right: I have to go down there.

I move towards the door, but Graham stops me, grabbing my arm and dragging me back as he turns down the lights. Michael is on the stage again.

'Again, everybody, we apologise for the earlier mishap. We'll move quickly on now to Kirsty McClure, our Deputy Head of Digital Marketing, who is going to tell us about Florina's plans for successful marketing in a data-conscious digital world. Kirsty, over to you.'

Kirsty mounts the stage, a vision of confidence. She introduces herself, and then seamlessly segues into her presentation.

As I watch her talk, a coldness creeps from the base of my spine to the top of my head. She's regurgitating my ideas — my good ideas, the ones I gave her — but with added flair. She's taken what I did and improved upon it, making it more doable, more accessible. The nonsense figures and questionable plans I tried to feed her aren't there, there's nothing but innovation and cool, clear self-belief.

'No,' I whisper. 'No, this isn't happening.'

'What?' Graham keeps his eyes trained on the stage, moving the spotlight to follow Kirsty as she moves backwards and forwards, the image of a seasoned presenter.

'She's smashing it. She's taken my ideas and she's doing it better than I did.'

Graham sighs. 'I'm sorry, Eve.'

'Thank you all so much for your time and attention today.' Kirsty begins to wrap up. My heart sinks. 'But before I go, I'd like to share with you some exciting new products that might be making their way into your stores, both physical and virtual, very soon.'

She clicks onto the next slide, and I frown.

It's plant pots. Pretty plant pots housing cacti and succulents; sandy beiges and terracotta. Mismatched edges and wonky shapes.

My pulse quickens.

'I've been working closely with our design team to create our new and exciting student-centred plant range. The colour scheme and low-maintenance plant types will appeal to Gen Zs as they head off to university. We're so proud of this new direction, and think it will contribute towards the fresh, organic brand image that Florina is so well known for. Thank you.'

She dismounts the stage.

'That's mine,' I say, my voice shaking. 'Those are my designs.'

'How did she get them?' Graham asks, flicking off the lights and swivelling towards me.

'I gave them to her.' I sink into an empty seat and bury my head in my hands. 'I literally handed them to her.'

'Oh Eve.' Graham looks at me, and the pity in his eyes makes me want to scream.

I stand up and open the door to the tech room, moving down the stairs on autopilot, not stopping, not thinking, until I'm out of the building and onto the street, swallowed up by the crowds.

* * *

The bar is busy, but not with people from the expo. I've purposefully picked somewhere off the beaten track, where nobody will see me.

I'm three gin and tonics down, and I'm in full scheming mode. How can I pull back from this? I can collect the evidence; not all of it, but some, and present it to Dev. Surely, if I'm upfront about the part I played, it will count in my favour.

I mix the ice cubes at the bottom of my glass with a paper straw. Admitting to anything would see me out of the running for the promotion, but so would letting things stand. Unless I pin everything on Kirsty, which would seem petty and unbelievable, it's all over.

I feel the unfamiliar pressure of tears collecting behind my eyes, and swallow them down. It's sixteen years since I last cried; I won't be starting now.

My phone buzzes across the table, and Dev's name appears on my screen.

'Hi, Dev.' I answer because I am tipsy. I don't have a plan.

'Eve,' he sighs.

'How are you?'

He laughs softly. 'How are *you*?'

'Fine, thanks.'

There's a pause. 'What happened, Eve?'

I don't speak for a minute. 'I know what happened, but it wasn't me.' I sound like a child who's been caught stealing sweeties.

'Right.' I can hear the noise of the conference in the background, the excited babble and shouting. 'I think you know what this means, don't you?'

I close my eyes.

'We're going to have to do a proper investigation,' he continues, 'but for now . . . the cards are stacked against you, Eve. I go off in less than a week. We need someone—'

'I know,' I whisper.

'I'm sorry.'

'Me too.'

I hang up, and signal to a passing waiter to bring me another drink.

My phone buzzes with a message from Adam: a screenshot of a response to his Facebook post. I put it face down on the table.

'Drinking alone?' I look up — a man is looming over me. He's attractive, slightly drunk, a little older than me.

I carve a deep scratch into the surface of the table with my fingernail. 'Take a seat.'

CHAPTER 31

Adam

The fluorescent lights of the corridor flash — blink, blink, blink — as I run, the maze of Manchester Royal Infirmary disorienting me. I flick my eyes towards the signs above the doorways as I pass, seeking Ward AM1, looking for directions.

I skid to a stop in front of a nurse, who is pinning something on a noticeboard.

'Excuse me,' I say, breathlessly, 'where's AM1?'

'Up there, first left,' she replies, pointing in the direction I've just come from.

I take off again, my heart hammering in my chest. It's two in the morning. After I got the phone call, the boys dragged me into a café and fed me water and strong coffee until I was coherent enough to book the last seat on the late flight back to Manchester. The waiting, and the flying, and the pure, piercing terror have sent my mind into overdrive.

I find the ward and push the buzzer at the door.

'Hello?' A voice comes through the intercom.

'I'm here to see my brother,' I pant, 'Adam Parks, I mean, it's Hugh Parks, I'm here to see him.'

'Visiting hours start at 8 a.m.,' she chirps back.

'No, please, he's just been brought in. I need to see him.'

There's a pause, and I think I might scream, and then the door buzzes open.

'Hugh,' I call, running down the ward, my head turning this way and that, checking the bays for a familiar face. A nurse stands up behind reception and shushes me.

'This is a hospital, and it's the middle of the night,' she scolds.

'I'm sorry,' I say, tears building in my eyes. 'Please, tell me where he is.'

She slides behind the desk and beckons me to follow her.

What have they done to him? I can feel my pulse in my throat. Where is he? How has this happened?

The nurse leads me into a side room, and suddenly, there he is.

He's lying on the bed, tubes and wires snaking up and down his arms and across his body. His face is pale, his breathing shallow.

'Oh my god.' I dive forward, clutching the edge of the bed, taking Hugh's hand in mine. 'Hugh? Hugh, it's OK. I'm here.'

The door clicks behind me as the nurse leaves me to it.

'He's better than he was.' A voice comes from the darkness, and I whip my head around.

'Becky?' She's sitting in the corner, her face drawn.

'Sorry.' She shakes her head. 'It didn't feel right to leave him on his own.'

I look between her and Hugh, my head spinning. 'What's wrong with him?'

'Chest infection. Pneumonia,' she says. 'It came on so suddenly.'

I sink down onto a plastic visitors' seat.

'I'm going to go.' Becky stands up.

I can't think of anything to say, so I just sit, my eyes trained on Hugh, as she closes the door softly behind her.

The room is dark and silent, save for the beeping and dripping of the machines. Hugh looks at me through half-closed eyes.

'Get some rest, buddy,' I say, pulling his blanket up under his chin. Next to his arm is his Hei Hei toy, and I clutch it, suddenly, to my chest. A tear leaks out of my eye I sit back down, wiping my face, and pull out my phone. I quickly message the group chat to update them. They reply immediately:

Bil: *We'll come straight from the airport*

Ferg: *How is he doing? Have the doctors said anything?*

Piotr: *Give him a gentle squeeze from us*

I swipe off the chat, not wanting to respond until I have more information.

On impulse, I tap into the camera app. Hugh's room sits empty and dark, and I swallow. I pull the footage back, further and further, until something moves. It's the paramedics, carrying Hugh out of his room on a stretcher. I squeeze my eyes shut, and swipe my finger back further. When I open them, the late-morning light is streaming through Hugh's curtains.

He's coughing; I can see that. He's not in his chair, but his bed, and his face is red with the effort of it all, spittle collecting on his chin. My heart twists.

On the screen, the door opens, and Becky comes in, her face creased. She sits next to Hugh, taking his blood pressure, his temperature, shining a torch into his eyes. She leaves again, and then returns with a cool flannel, and mops his forehead gently. She holds his hand, and I see her mouth moving, and then she's still and she just sits.

I fast-forward; she sits, and sits, and sits. Sometimes she leaves, and brings something back, some medication or another cold compress, but then she sits again. Hugh's coughing gets worse, and I can see him struggling to breathe. I see her notice too, and she leaps to her feet, running out of the room. When she returns, she strokes Hugh's forehead, murmuring something, and stays, soothing, until the paramedics come.

I lock my phone, tears streaming down my face. I should have been there; that should have been me. But I wasn't, and she was. She stayed with him, and cared for him, and loved him.

The door clicks open again behind me, and I turn around. It's the nurse from the front desk.

'Hello again,' she says, her voice soft in the dark. 'How are we in here?'

'What's going to happen to him?' I'm on my feet, my voice panicked. 'Is he going to be OK?'

She takes Hugh's chart from the end of his bed and flicks through it, her eyes darting to and from the machines, and then slides it back into its holder and turns to me.

'He's responding well to the antibiotics at the moment, but pneumonia can be complicated.' She frowns. 'He wasn't in a great state when he got here.'

'Oh, god.' I rub my hand through my beard, my heart hammering.

'Your brother has cerebral palsy,' she states. 'These infections . . . he's much more susceptible. His muscles aren't as strong as yours or mine; his breathing is shallower, he can't cough up as effectively.' She pauses, and looks at me. 'If he continues to respond the way he is doing, everything will be OK. I understand he's had chest infections in the past?'

I nod. 'When he was younger. Only once recently, but we caught it in time.' Hugh got a pretty nasty chest infection at his old home; it was the calling card for me to pull him out of there after too many red flags went unheeded.

'That's testament to the care he's getting.' She deftly folds a second blanket and places it gently across Hugh's legs. 'A good diet is really important. And physio, proper holistic therapy.'

'He gets all of those things.'

'Oxygen therapy could help, too.'

I nod, only half participating in the conversation. *Everything will be OK . . . he's much more susceptible.* What is she trying to tell me?

'So he's going to be OK?'

'We'll know more over the next twenty-four hours.' She looks at me kindly. 'The best thing you can do is look after yourself. It's unlikely anything will change over the next few hours. Why don't you go home and get some rest, and come back in the morning, when the doctor's here?'

I nod, and then shake my head, torn. My mind is all over the place; I can't think straight, and I can't take in what she's saying to me. I don't want to leave but if I don't sleep, or shower, or give myself a second to process, what use will I be when the doctor comes?

'OK,' I say. 'I'll be back as soon as possible.'

CHAPTER 32

Eve

'Will!' I hammer again on the door, craning my neck to peer through the slither of unfrosted glass that allows a glimpse of the hallway. It's empty.

I knock again, loudly, and squat down, lifting the flap of the letterbox. 'Will, open the door!'

I prise the bristles surrounding the letterbox apart with my fingers, and watch as the hallway remains still. I bang once more, and then see Will's socked feet begin padding slowly down the stairs.

He opens the door and I scramble up quickly.

'Why weren't you answering?' I run my fingers through my fringe.

'I was asleep.' He's angry, his face twisted.

'Shit, sorry. Can I come in? Where are Nina and Benny?'

Will looks at me for a second, and then steps aside to let me pass. I lead the way into the kitchen and flop myself onto a bar stool.

'Well, I've officially fucked it all up,' I say, my fingers tapping against the granite of the island. 'But before you say "I told you so", she was worse than me. *Way* worse. Like, Will,

180

you would not believe the things she has done. But it's fine; I've slept on it. I typed up an action plan on the plane home, and I know how we're going to fix this.' I reach down and pull my laptop from my bag and open it up. 'OK, so, her original email about the "promotion" was on the 8th of May, right? But I'm not supposed to know about that—'

'Eve,' Will interrupts me, and I look up.

'What?'

'I don't want you to take this the wrong way.' He runs a hand through his hair. 'But I really don't want you to be here right now.'

I stare at him. 'What do you mean?'

'I don't have the space for you,' he taps his head, 'here. I don't have space for all the scheming and self-centredness and emotionless drive . . . I just . . . I need a friend, and you're not being one.'

I can't speak for a second; this feels like it's coming from nowhere. I slowly lower the lid of my laptop. 'What . . . I don't know what I've done?'

Will shakes his head. 'That's the problem, isn't it? You don't know what you've done, or how you make people feel, or whether anyone else around you might be going through something—' He cuts off suddenly, his voice cracking.

I frown at him. 'But if there was something going on, why didn't you just say?'

He barks out a laugh. 'I did say! I said it a hundred times. I turned up on your doorstep, do you remember? But you were so wrapped up in what you were doing, so focused on your little missions . . .'

'That's not fair,' I say, but something inside me is telling me it might be.

Will holds his hands out, palms up, his face sad. 'You still haven't even asked.'

Something cold and hard drops into my stomach. 'I'm sorry.' I stand up and walk over to him. 'I'm sorry, you're right.' I put my hand to my chest. 'Please, tell me what's happening.'

Will shakes his head again. 'You need to stop, Eve. This isn't another one of your tick-box problems to solve.'

I throw my hands up. 'So you want me to understand you, to be there, but you won't tell me what's wrong?'

'I don't want you to do anything until you've figured out how to just . . . be. How to listen.'

'Don't throw pop psychology at me, Will, it's patronising.'

He laughs bitterly. 'Go home, Eve.'

I stand in front of him, my mind turning. 'Just tell me what's wrong.'

'You don't want to go home, do you?' There's a hint of sympathy in his voice now. 'You can't bear to sit with your thoughts.'

I shake my head. 'That's not true. I'm always at home.'

Will nods. 'OK.'

Frustration bubbles up inside me, tightening my jaw. I can't leave; I don't want to leave. I don't want Will to cast me aside.

'I'm going back to bed.' He turns around and walks out of the kitchen. I scamper after him.

'Please, can't we talk about it?' My heart is racing, my head spinning.

'Not now.'

He climbs the stairs, leaving me in the hallway to show myself out.

* * *

'What's going on with him?' I gabble down the phone, my feet heavy on the pavement. 'Is he OK? He wouldn't tell me . . . he said I was being selfish, or that I didn't listen, or something.'

Jess is quiet at the end of the line.

'Jess?'

She takes a deep breath. 'I understand where he's coming from, Eve.'

'What?' I stop in the street, a few paces away from my front door.

'I love you, you know I do. But you can be a bit . . . self-involved. You're like a dog with a bone sometimes.'

I clench the phone in my hand. Everything feels like it's tilted; like the ground is moving slowly under my feet.

'I get you, Eve.' Jess is still talking. 'We both understand where this comes from, the abandonment issues and unwillingness to get attached to anything, to invest in something that might walk away. But we're your friends; you can't keep friends if you don't invest in them.'

'*Abandonment* issues?' I scoff. 'Have you been on the ayahuasca again?'

'And now you're being defensive,' Jess sighs. 'You don't have to be on guard for every possible threat. I'm saying this from a place of love.'

'Of course you are.'

Jess is silent, and I start walking again, mindlessly fishing in my bag for my keys. A few doors up, a taxi pulls in, and I watch as Adam gets out. I don't have the time — the headspace — for interaction, so I move quickly up the path and unlock the front door.

'Have you ever thought that not crying for sixteen years might not be healthy?' Jess asks tentatively.

'You're on a roll here, aren't you? Is this years of thoughts about me pouring out, or just a few months?'

I hear her sigh again. 'I'm going to go. I love you. But Eve, not everybody's going to leave you. Not unless you push them to.'

She clicks off.

I stand in the hallway, listening to the ticking of the clock above the mirror. The heat is cloying and my heart pounds, my head heavy.

I drop my bag to the floor and walk through to the kitchen. I swing open the back door and sit on the step, staring out into the soulless emptiness of the garden.

CHAPTER 33

Texts

Eve: *Sorry I didn't reply — got caught up in something*

Eve: *Have you seen OS recently?*

> Adam: *I haven't been home much, and no sightings when I have. Hope everything's OK.*

Eve: *No problem*

Eve: *All fine, let me know if you have any more messages*

> Adam: *Will do.*

* * *

> Adam: *Just got this sent through from Facebook — could be him?*

Eve: *No, ours has a yellow bit next to the scab on her ear*

184

Adam: *OK, I'll let them know.*

* * *

Adam: *OS at mine now. Seems skinnier — have you been feeding him?*

Eve: *Tin of tuna yesterday*

Eve: *I was away all weekend*

Eve: *Maybe a sign that she really is homeless?*

Adam: *Can we decide on a definitive gender for this cat please, it's confusing me.*

Eve: *Don't put her in a box like that*

Eve: *She can be whatever she likes*

Adam: *I'm not sure she engages in this kind of complex thinking*

Eve: *You just called her 'she' :)*

Adam: *Shit.*

* * *

Eve: *Sorry to message so late*

Eve: *I'm worried about OS*

Eve: *I haven't seen her in a few days*

Adam: *Morning. I don't mind the late messages, but one sentence being broken up into three separate chunks is a *little* annoying at 3 a.m.*

Eve: *Sorry*

Eve: *But fine now, right?*

Eve: *Seeing as it's 9 o'clock*

Eve: *And you're obviously up*

                                       Adam: *Do I have a choice?*

Eve: *Not really, no*

       Adam: *I suspected as much. Do you want to come over for a cup of tea? We might want to think about next steps, seeing as no one's claiming her.*

Eve: *You said 'her' again*

Eve: *Be over in ten minutes?*

CHAPTER 34

Adam

Despite everything, all the other shit going on, I feel a prickle of anxiety at the prospect of this woman, Eve, turning up on my doorstep at such short notice.

I got back from the hospital twenty minutes ago, and this afternoon I have an appointment with a mortgage advisor before my next session with Okie. When I suggested a cup of tea, I thought she'd name a day, or say that she'd let me know when she was free . . . but I should have known. The way she was when she stood in my hallway a couple of weeks ago made it clear what kind of person she was when it came to getting things done.

There's a rap on the front door, and I check my phone. She's two minutes early, which I also should have expected.

'Hi.' I swing the door open and she stands there, her formal attire replaced with a simple mid-length dress and Converse. Her short hair is tied back in a stubby ponytail, that unruly fringe framing her face. Her green eyes seem duller, somehow, than when we first met. 'Come in.'

I stand back to let her pass, and she walks straight past me through to the kitchen before spinning around.

'Sorry!' She claps a hand to her mouth. 'The layouts of our houses are exactly the same, so I sort of knew where to go.'

I laugh. 'Don't worry. Make yourself at home.'

She pulls a chair out from under the kitchen table and sits down. I marvel at her boldness — I'm a hoverer, I won't take a seat until I'm explicitly told to — and flick the kettle on.

'Tea?'

'Hmm . . . coffee?' she asks. 'Extra strong.'

I laugh loudly, despite myself, and she frowns at me. 'Sorry, you're just really . . . direct.'

She shakes her head, running her fingers through her fringe. 'That seems to be the theme of the week.'

'I have always imagined that direct people must get told they're direct quite a lot.' I get out the cafetière and pull the good stuff out of the fridge. The stuff I usually save for Sundays. 'Illy?' I ask.

'What?' She looks up at me suddenly, her eyes crinkled in confusion.

I hold up the jar. 'Illy coffee?'

'Oh my god.' She slaps her leg and laughs, her mouth wide. 'I thought you were saying you loved me in text speak.'

It takes me a second to get it, and when I do, I snort. 'No!' I splutter, laughing, feeling my cheeks heat up.

'Then Illy would be great, thanks.' She smiles, and I quickly turn away.

We discuss a few people on the street as the coffee brews — she knows surprisingly little about any of the neighbours, despite having lived here almost as long as me — and I question her about why I haven't seen her around much.

'I'm usually in work for about twelve hours, and I get taxis on the weekends as a general rule.' She shrugs. 'Does that sound pretentious? I can't always tell.'

'No,' I say, placing our mugs down on the table. 'Why aren't you in work today?'

She stands up and takes the milk from the fridge without asking. 'Long story,' she says, splashing some in her cup and then putting it back.

I nod, deciding not to enquire any further.

'What do you do?' she asks.

'I'm a maths tutor.' I grimace. 'Used to be a teacher, but OFSTED sucked the joy out of it for me.'

'A common story, I hear.'

'Sadly, yes. Loads of parents were asking me about private sessions anyway and I just thought — sod it. Less money, sure, but you know. Life's too short to wake up dreading every day.'

'Yes,' she says, after a moment. 'I imagine it is.'

God, what am I doing going on about my career motivations? I've only had the woman in my house three seconds and I've already managed to bore her.

'Well, cheers,' I tap my cup against hers, and she taps back and then looks down at her fingernails.

'Right.' She slaps her hands on the table suddenly, and I jump. When she looks up, that fierceness is back in her eyes. 'I think Old Sausage needs an appointment with the vet, so we need to catch her. I'm thinking some kind of box with a stick, and a bit of food inside it. You know like on *Looney Tunes*? The box will fall when she nudges it and we'll have her trapped.'

Eve looks very satisfied with her plan, but I decide to cautiously offer my own suggestion. 'What if we just pick her up?'

She stares at me for a second. 'We could do that, I suppose.'

I grin. 'Might be a bit easier.'

She nods, biting her lip as if she's trying to suppress a smile. 'Fine, yes, let's do that. Do you have a car?'

'No.'

'Me neither.' She taps her chin with her finger, her eyes gazing beyond me. 'We'll get a taxi. Whoever catches her, I mean. We can split the fare.'

'Sounds good.'

She takes a sip of her coffee. 'This is really good.'

'Yeah, I love it.'

'Who was that woman who was here the other day?' she asks.

I am thrown by the suddenness of the question. 'Oh. That's my ex.'

Eve grimaces. 'Sorry.'

I wave my hand. 'Don't worry about it.'

Our eyes meet for a moment, and something stirs inside me. Something vaguely familiar, but before I can identify it, she looks away.

She straightens her shoulders — something I've noticed she does when she's about to pull things back to where she wants them to be — and pushes her chair back. 'Right, so—'

'What do you do?' I ask, suddenly, realising she didn't tell me earlier, and feeling like the conversation can't end here, like I need to know more about her.

She stands up anyway, and her face becomes impassive. 'I work in marketing.'

The energy has shifted now. She's closed things down, and the easy back-and-forth we just had seems out of reach.

'Do you enjoy it?' I ask, as one last-ditch attempt, as she pulls her bag onto her shoulder.

Eve stares out of the window, her hand reaching for her fringe again. 'I do, yeah.'

I stand up too, feeling suddenly as though I've said something wrong. 'Well, should we . . .'

'Yes.' She turns to me, nodding. 'Right. We'll keep our eyes peeled for her, and whoever finds her first, take her to the vet. OK?'

'I can hardly expect you to drop work if she comes by in the middle of the day.'

'It doesn't matter,' she replies hastily, and turns towards the door. I follow her through the living room and into the hall where, as though something has just occurred to her, she turns quickly towards me. 'Of course, that wouldn't be fair for you, either. I'm sure you can't just drop whatever you're doing.'

'If I'm here when she comes over, it usually means I haven't got a student. But if I can't for any reason, I'll let you know?' I smile at her. 'I don't think the plan needs to be too rigid. We'll figure it out.'

Her eyes search my face for a second, and then she nods. 'Yes, no, definitely.'

'Great.'

We stand, facing each other. There's something charged in the air around us: awkwardness, but something underneath, too.

Unexpectedly, she holds out her hand. 'It was nice to meet you again.'

I laugh at the formality, and she smiles shyly, shaking her head. I take her hand in mine, only for a millisecond, and register the soft warmth of it. My pulse quickens.

'Bye, then.' She pulls her hand away and opens the front door, giving me one final glance over her shoulder as she leaves.

CHAPTER 35

Eve

I walk away from Adam's house feeling unsettled. My legs feel strange, and my balance is off; as I reach the end of the front path I stumble and grab onto the gatepost to stop myself from falling.

I feel unnervingly self-conscious, like I'm on a catwalk and an audience is reviewing the way I move. My arms swing awkwardly by my sides as I make the short journey down the street. I am hotly aware of the glare of Adam's windows behind me, that he might be watching.

I don't know why I went over. I don't feel right, my head isn't functioning properly after everything that's happened. I messaged Adam as a distraction, and when he suggested going over I jumped at the chance to step outside the house and get my mind on a task — a *mission*, Will would probably call it — and refocus myself.

Thinking of Will brings a fresh wave of discomfort: was he right? How can I claim to be content with alone time if I happily forego it to pursue a hopeless cat-rehoming mission with a neighbour I barely know?

As if she's read my mind from afar, Old Sausage is sitting on my doorstep, and I scoop her up and carry her inside. I briefly wonder whether her owner might be watching — one of the neighbours, maybe — but then I remember that Adam knows everyone around here, and he hadn't seen her around until recently.

'Right, come on then.' I shut the front door behind me and place her on the floor. 'We can be alone together, can't we?'

Something uncomfortable throbs somewhere in the back of my mind. Am I this desperate? Now that I don't have work, the day feels slow and endless, and it seems I've resorted to coaxing stray cats into my house to fill the void.

I think about our plan to take her to the vet, and my mood buoys. That's what I'll do — I'll sit for a minute, maybe two, feel what it is to be quiet or whatever and then call a taxi and go. Old Sausage follows me through to the kitchen, where I spend a long time making a cup of tea and wiping down the sides. When I can put it off no longer, I sit down on one of the dining chairs and stare at the fridge. Within three seconds, my fingers are reaching for my phone, and I catch myself just in time. I can do this. I can sit here in silence.

I tap my foot against the floor. My mind is suddenly a flood of thoughts: Kirsty, work, cleaning, Mum and Dad, Dev, exercise, Graham, the cat, Will, Jess, food deliveries, flowers, marketing, Adam.

Old Sausage sits at my feet and stares at me. I notice a smear on the door of the oven, and the handle of a carrier bag poking out of the cupboard. I push it all away, hard.

Without physical distraction, my mind begins making plans — what I'll do about work, what I'll say to Kirsty next time I see her, what evidence I can gather to fix my predicament. And then, afterwards, problem-solving — when I was in Adam's kitchen earlier, I recognised him from somewhere. It was the same sense of familiarity I felt the first time I went over. I mentally filter through potential connections: friends, colleagues, dates. I can find no link to a maths tutor.

I realise that planning and problem-solving are along the same vein. I'm trying to focus, to find a purpose and something to latch onto. This is what Will says is wrong with me, but when I push this away too, new, unfamiliar thoughts creep in. Hurt, at how Kirsty has treated me. Shame, for how I behaved. Guilt, for how I let Will down. Embarrassment, for the things he and Jess think about me.

My phone vibrates on the table and I snatch it up, my breath catching in my throat. Kirsty's name flashes on the screen. The temptation to answer it is strong. Let me have it out with her, let me have something to work on, some kind of purpose . . .

I let it ring out.

In the silence, the thoughts crowd back in, like tiny needles stabbing at my self-image. The way I behaved at Adam's house, rudely letting him note it might inconvenience me to take Old Sausage to the vet, without giving a second thought to whether it would affect him to do the same. Walking straight into his kitchen, as if I owned the place.

Humiliation washes over me, and the feeling is so unfamiliar, and so consuming, that I'm on my feet before I know it, heading to grab an old cardboard box from the boiler cupboard, scoop Old Sausage up and set off for the vet.

But my sudden movement causes her to leap three feet in the air, and before I can blink she has scarpered, up onto the counter top and then out of the open kitchen window.

Shit.

CHAPTER 36

Eve

I have completely given up trying to be still. My mind is a blur of plotting and scheming. I lie awake at night, turning things over in my mind, my phone on the bedside table. Every so often I roll over, unlock it, and take notes.

When I wake up in the morning, I clean again. I clean things that are already clean, and then I work on the garden. All of the crispy plants are gone, replaced by fresh, green foliage that I water twice a day. I've scrubbed the patio by hand, and repainted the fencing.

While I clean, I turn my options over in my mind. I've taken a two-week holiday from Florina while the investigation is conducted, but have been checking my emails every half an hour, watching and seething as congratulatory messages flood through for Kirsty.

The first Wednesday into my leave, Eleanor has her babies. Two boys, identical. I send Dev a gushing text, which he responds to with what I can tell is a hastily rattled off 'thanks'.

When I'm forced to stop, because I'm in the shower, or trying to sleep, Will and Jess occupy my thoughts. Their comments, about me being unwilling to be alone, now strike an exposed nerve.

I remember Jess's words in particular: *You don't have to on guard for every possible threat.* But the thing is, I do. The evidence is clear: even when I am prepared, there's always something that could knock me sideways out of the blue.

I am thinking about this as I hoover under the stairs. The thoughts give me a strange feeling, like worrying at a loose tooth. It hurts, and it's frustrating.

My phone buzzes in my pocket, muting the sound of the podcast I'm listening to for a couple of seconds. I check it.

Kirsty: *Hey. I really think we should meet. 12 in
St Peter's Sq?*

I stand up and check the time. I turn off the hoover, disconnect my headphones and slide on my shoes, and leave to catch the tram.

* * *

Kirsty is waiting for me under the library arches. Already I can see the change in her. Her hair, which usually falls around her shoulders, is swept low into a slicked clean-girl bun, and she wears a linen blouse and wide-legged tailored trousers that I've never seen before.

As soon as I see her, fury engulfs me. I clench my fists, hard, and then release them, before walking over. I don't say anything, waiting for her to speak first.

She meets my gaze head-on. 'Afternoon. Shall we walk?'

She sets off under the arches and I follow, walking parallel to the tram station and heading towards the war memorial. I watch her as she marches one pace ahead of me, and I am suddenly sucked back in time; back to when I was a fresh graduate in my first big meetings, the men seemingly towering over me, steely and at ease with — or oblivious to — everybody around them.

We reach the memorial and she turns, crossing the square and then looping back. We're like nineteenth-century ladies, taking a turn of the grounds. The air is tight with tension. Neither of us speaks until we're on our second lap.

'You must be angry with me,' she says, staring straight ahead, one hand buried in her trouser pocket.

'Not at all.' I keep my head high. 'You only sabotaged my career — mistakes happen.'

She doesn't respond. We keep walking, around and around. Each lap takes just a few minutes, and I feel my footsteps get faster as the frustration builds inside me.

'Did you ask me here for a reason, or did you just want a walking buddy?' I finally challenge her, when we've passed the statue of Emmeline Pankhurst for the fourth time.

'This needs to stop,' she says.

'Does it? Now that you've got what you want?'

She sighs, and her eyes flick towards me. She keeps walking. 'Yes.'

'I thought we were friends,' I say, and the patheticness of it makes me cringe. 'I don't—'

'And you were the innocent party, were you?' she fires back, her nostrils flaring, her pace quickening. 'You're the victim?'

'Yes!' I stop to turn to her, but she keeps moving, and I hurry to catch up again. 'You started it, Kirsty.'

'How?'

'By applying for the position in the first place! By lying about getting my permission—' I stop myself, realising what I've said.

She stops. 'How do you know that?'

I hesitate. 'Dev told me. When we met in my office.'

She doesn't buy it. She knows I know more; I can tell from the way she looks at me from the corner of her eye, her mouth turned down at the corners. 'This is what I mean, Eve. I learned from the best.'

Suddenly, the pressure of it all builds inside me and I can't keep my mouth shut. 'You kept a fucking *list* — you

197

recorded every time I messed up. Kept it to use it against me.'

She stops in her tracks and a pigeon startles, flapping noisily away. She swings around to face me. 'What?'

'F Ups?' I throw it at her, and I realise I've been dying to confront her about this since I found it. It was only a matter of time. 'Every time I emailed you, telling you about something that had gone wrong, you kept it. For *two years.*'

She stares at me. Swathes of people skirt around us, tutting. 'You hacked into my computer.'

I shrug. 'You hacked my presentation.'

'This is pathetic.' She almost spits the words at me. 'That was an insurance policy, Eve. For the both of us. Did you read it carefully, or did you not have time during your covert mission? I kept a record of *our* mistakes, in case we were ever challenged. It was due diligence. I was the one that called the buyer a Z-list Hugh Grant, wasn't I? And yes, I hacked your presentation!' She throws her arms into the air. 'It's no more than you would have done in my position.'

She lets her arms drop to her sides, her breathing heavy, glaring at me. 'How do you get to the top, Eve?' she continues, her eyes boring into me. An uneasy feeling washes over me.

'I—'

'How do you get to the top? You set a goal, and you go for it. That's what you say, isn't it? You set a goal, and you get there by *whatever means possible*. You don't let anything stand in your way.'

'Kirsty, that doesn't mean you can crush your friends in the process—'

'And you wouldn't have done the same?' she challenges me. 'You haven't literally been *doing* the same, these past few weeks?' People walk and scoot and run past, conversation ebbs and flows around us. Three women drink coffee on a bench a few feet away, their eyes trained on us.

I can't answer. Would I have? If she hadn't started this? If I'd been in her position?

'I applied.' She fills my silence. 'I applied, and that was all. You took it to the next level. Sometimes, you have to fight fire with fire, Eve.' Her eyes finally leave mine, and she stares behind me, toward the Midland Hotel. 'I did feel guilty about it. I still do. But every time I doubted what I was doing, I remembered how Dev got where he is. How *you*'d got where you are.'

I feel like I've been punched in the stomach. I shake my head. 'Nothing I do is as calculating as this.'

She raises her eyebrows. 'Do I need to ask how you got access to my computer?'

I feel sick. 'What about it?'

She laughs. 'Don't tell me you don't use people, Eve. Don't tell me you don't trample all over everybody to get what you want.'

'The thing between Graham and me is mutual,' I say, my voice quiet.

She scoffs. 'When has he ever used you?'

I shake my head, taking a small step back. 'We sleep together — we both get the same—'

'Just stop it, Eve, for fuck's sake.' She sighs wearily. 'I've got to go. Come and see me when you're back in the office.'

She turns and walks away. I stand in the middle of St Peter's Square, the sun beating down on my head, and watch her leave, her head high. My former friend. My manager.

CHAPTER 37

> **Adam:** *Hey, is everything OK? You haven't replied to my last couple of texts. I can take over the OS stuff if it's too much?*

Eve: *Hey*

Eve: *I'm sorry — things have been a bit all over the place*

Eve: *I still want to sort this vet thing*

Eve: *Have you seen her?*

> **Adam:** *Not for a few days now. I hope she's OK. Shout if you spot her?*

Eve: *Of course*

* * *

Eve: *Just seen her on my patio and she ran in your direction*

Eve: *Can you check??*

> **Adam:** *I'm not home, sorry!*

Eve: *Educating the masses?*

Adam: *Ha. I'm actually at the hospital — work would be preferable.*

Eve: *Oh, sorry*

Eve: *Are you OK?*

Eve: *You don't have to give details if it's something embarrassing*

Eve: *Or at all, actually*

Eve: *I've made this weird, haven't I?*

Adam: *Haha, don't worry, I can take it. It's not me, though — I'm still fit for service for the stray cats of Greater Manchester. My brother's in with pneumonia.*

Eve: *I'm really sorry. Do you need anything?*

Adam: *Honestly, I'm fine, but thank you for asking.*

Eve: *Offer stands whenever you need it*

* * *

Adam: *Did you leave a burrito on my doorstep?*

Eve: *Yes*

Eve: *I thought you might need some tea*

Adam: *Thank you. Seriously. It's really good.*

Eve: *No problem*

Eve: *See — I can be neighbourly!*

Adam: *I believe you ;)*

* * *

Eve: *I can hear meowing*

Eve: *Can you?*

Adam: *It's two in the morning . . .*

Eve: *But can you hear it?*

Adam: *Nope. Why are you awake?*

Eve: *I'm not sleeping too well at the moment*

Eve: *You?*

Adam: *My phone vibrated.*

Eve: *Sorry!*

Adam: *Why aren't you sleeping well?*

Eve: *Busy brain*

Eve: *How's your brother?*

Adam: *He's much better — thank you for asking. He's got Cerebral Palsy, so it was a really tough time.*

Eve: *Sounds like it was really scary*

Eve: *I'm glad he's OK*

Adam: *Thanks, me too. I hope you manage to get some sleep!*

Eve: *I will, eventually :)*

CHAPTER 38

Adam

As Hugh's condition improves, I start taking walks around the hospital corridors. I inspect all the vending machines until I find my favourite, and manage to locate the nicest visitor toilet on the other side of the building. When the boys visit, we walk together. Today, Piotr has come.

'It's looking good, Ad.' He bashes his shoulder against mine as we squeak up the corridor.

'I know.' I let out a breath I didn't know I was holding. 'He'll be going back home soon.'

'Pfff.' Piotr puffs his cheeks out and blows a thin stream of air through his teeth. 'He really had me worried for a second.'

'Me too.' I stare at my shoes. 'It's never going to be OK, though, is it?'

We reach the vending machine, but Piotr blocks my view of what's inside, standing directly in front of me. He holds my shoulders. 'Mate, you can't think like that. You just can't.'

'How can I not?' My voice cracks, and I swipe at my eyes. 'He's a ticking time bomb.'

'A ticking time bomb in the gentlest, most knowledgeable hands.' Piotr looks at me intently. 'Ad. I can't tell you it's all going to be OK for ever and ever. But *nobody* is OK for ever and ever. We've got over this hurdle, let's cross the next one when we come to it.'

I nod. 'Yeah. Yeah, you're right.'

We wrestle with the vending machine, Piotr's crisps getting jammed against the glass, and then begin to make our way back to Hugh's ward. We're halfway up the corridor when a familiar face rounds the corner.

'Becky!' I call, waving her over.

'Hey.' She gives me a small smile.

'How are you?' I ask as we begin walking together.

'Good. How's Hugh?'

'He's better every day. Thanks for visiting.'

She nods.

We get into Hugh's room, and he lights up when he sees Becky, his arms flying out, a huge grin plastered across his face.

'Hey!' She laughs and takes his hand. 'Look at you.'

Piotr turns to me. 'I'm going to head off. I'll be back tomorrow if he's still in.'

'Alright. Thanks, mate.' We hug, and he squeezes me hard.

'One thing at a time, right?'

I smile. 'One thing at a time.'

Once Piotr's gone, I pull up a chair on the other side of the bed. Becky turns to me.

'I spoke to the therapists about Hugh's mood,' she says. 'I didn't get a chance to tell you the other day.'

'Oh.' I'd put Hugh's despondency down to a brewing illness. 'What did they say?'

'You won't believe it.' Her mouth twitches. 'It's *Moana*.'

'Eh?' I look at Hugh, who has tossed Hei Hei down the side of the bed, all but forgotten. 'What do you mean, it's *Moana*?'

'He's bored of it. It frustrates him.' She shrugs, smiling. 'He's ready for something new.'

I laugh, surprising myself. It's so simple — so innocuous — that it's funny. A relief. 'How do they know?'

'Apparently it happens a lot. Poor communication skills mean it's not always easy to know what someone with CP wants, even if they're really vocal about being unhappy. He's been trying to tell us that he's sick of that bloody film, but we haven't been listening.' She grins.

I throw my head back, laughing louder than I have done in a long time. Hugh shrieks delightedly. 'Oh my god. *Moana*.'

Becky joins in, her contagious laugh filling the small room. 'They put a different film on and he was a changed man, apparently.'

'Christ.' I wipe tears from my eyes.

Our laughter dies down, and the room goes quiet. Becky studies her fingernails.

'Thank you,' I say, turning to her.

She frowns. 'For what?'

'For looking after him. For caring for him. I'm sorry about the accusations. I . . . Hugh wasn't treated very well at his last place. It's a bit of a sore point.'

She stares at her lap. 'I get that. I'm sorry I was so unprofessional about it.'

'It's alright.' I shrug. 'I guess this isn't a straightforward job, is it? There are feelings involved.'

'Yeah.' Her eyes meet mine, and she looks away.

'And I'm sorry about . . . you know. Us. What happened,' I carry on, feeling like I want everything cleared up and put behind us.

She nods and looks at me sadly. 'Shit happens, doesn't it?'

'I suppose it does.'

* * *

When I get home, Old Sausage is sitting on the patio. I throw my backpack onto the sofa, all thoughts of an afternoon doing Okie's university application forms evaporating, and slowly open the back door.

He pads into the kitchen tentatively, sniffing at the air. 'Hey,' I say.

Old Sausage meows.

I reach into the fridge and grab a piece of steak from a tub of leftover stew. I place it down in front of him and he inspects it, before picking it up and starting to chew.

I pull out my phone.

Me: *Got OS in my kitchen! I'll take him to the vet now.*

I wait a minute or two, but Eve doesn't reply.

I let Old Sausage finish chewing — which takes an unsurprisingly long time, considering his lack of teeth and my unwillingness to fork out on good stewing steak — and then pick him up gingerly.

He allows it, and surveys the room from his elevated position. 'Shall we go and get you checked over?' I ask him.

I step out into the garden, looking across at Eve's house. The back door is open; she must be home. Maybe she'd want to come. I feel my heart rate accelerate a little at the thought. I could go down and ask her, let myself in through the back gate and pop my head in. Would that be weird?

Since she was here, it's felt like something has shifted inside me. I've thought about Katie less and less, and when I do, it's while I'm on the phone to the bank, trying to sort the mortgage. My in-branch meeting the other day went badly; our original mortgage was given to us on the basis of our combined salaries as employees of the local school. Now that it's just me, and I'm self-employed, my options have been reduced.

I pull out my phone. She still hasn't replied.

'Looks like it's just you and me, pal,' I say to Old Sausage, scratching him under his chin.

He gazes at me steadily, and then, like a ninja, he jerks his body around 180° and flips out of my arms, landing on all fours on the patio.

'Hey!' I cry, but he's running, leaping up onto the fence and throwing himself onto next door's lawn. He scales the next fence, and walks along it precariously, until he's next to Eve's garden. He gives me one last look, and then jumps down and slinks through the open back door.

I don't think. I unlock the back gate, and run up the alleyway.

CHAPTER 39

Eve

I can feel it coming, all the way home.

I sit on the tram, feeling the physical space between Kirsty and I growing by the second, but rather than receding as the distance increases, the feeling builds even more.

My house seems so far from the tram stop, I half run to get there. It's an unfamiliar sensation, one I haven't had to deal with for a long time, but I already know I'm going to cave.

I open the front door with shaking fingers and kick off my shoes. I go into the kitchen and swing the back door open, trying to stave it off, but it's impossible. The first tear I've cried in sixteen years rolls down my cheek as I lean over the sink, and as though a seal has been broken, I am suddenly sobbing.

I fold in on myself, slumping onto my barely-used sofa. My body heaves, and I panic — now that I've started, I worry that I won't be able to stop.

I pull one of my decorative blankets up over my knees. My eyes are sore and puffy, but the tears keep coming. *What kind of person am I?* Words rattle around my brain: selfish, calculating, driven, manipulative, *user*.

It's a man's world. The boardrooms, the jokes, the detached indifference to anything not directly connected to profit margins. There's no space for weakness, for emotions, for stopping and considering the full picture. *Just get there.*

But god, this can't be the only way. This *war*. Losing friendships, pitting women against each other. Who pitted us against each other? Nobody: the answer comes to me in a stomach-punching instant. We did this to ourselves.

Memories flit through my mind; Kirsty and I at parties, at my place, at hers. Years of laughter concealing . . . what? A ruthless drive that we'd both convinced ourselves was more important than anything else.

As soon as I think it, my brain bats it away. What's the alternative? Softness? Kindness and consideration? Through my tears, I almost laugh. I try to picture Dev and Michael having an open and honest chat about an upcoming position they're both interested in. The image won't come.

I imagine work with Kirsty as my manager. The humiliation. I can't do it.

I can't do it. I haven't thought this way in so long.

I lie on my back, the tears streaming down the sides of my face, and wonder when I was last still for this amount of time. I wonder if what Will said really was true — do I ever slow down enough to feel anything?

There's a soft meow behind me, and I sit up quickly and turn around, wiping my face. Old Sausage has come through the open back door and is standing on the tiles, staring at me.

'Hi,' I croak.

She pads over, sniffing, her eyes trained directly on mine. She stops when she reaches the edge of the sofa and sits down, her tail swishing.

I sigh and lie back down, tipping my head back and letting it drop softly into the cushion. I think about the plan to take her to the vet, but now really isn't the time.

As I stare up at the ceiling, there's a soft thud next to me on the sofa. I lift my head. Old Sausage has jumped up next to me. She paws along the remaining sliver of cushion, and then curls up next to my shoulder, her head resting against my chest.

Without thinking, I reach up a hand and run my fingers through her fur. She begins purring. I am suddenly paralysed by the stillness of the moment; it feels like I've been running for miles and miles, and have just this second stumbled upon an oasis. Tears leak steadily from the corners of my eyes again.

I've never noticed how comfortable this sofa is. I turn my head and let my cheek rest against the softness of Old Sausage's back. Her fur dampens with my tears, but the warmth of her makes my heart swell. It's so long — so long — since I've felt a closeness like this, unconditional physical contact just for the sake of it.

I'm openly sobbing again now but Old Sausage stays put, the noise of her purring battling against my squalling.

'Eve? Oh.'

I almost think I've imagined it, but there's a shift in the room that tells me I'm no longer the only person in the house.

I sit up quickly, grabbing Old Sausage and clutching her to my chest. Adam is standing in the doorway, his hands hanging by his sides. I can feel the swell of emotion still sitting in my chest, next to the shame and embarrassment of him seeing me like this, and the shock of his arrival. Through swollen eyes I take in his face — it only takes a millisecond — mouth hanging open, a flush up his neck, a tiny line of pity across his forehead.

'Get out.' The words tumble out of my mouth before I have time to think.

'I'm so sorry. I thought—'

'Get out!' I shout now, and Old Sausage mews frantically, wriggling in my arms.

Adam steps backwards, back onto the patio, his hands in the air.

'I'm sorry,' he says again, and then he turns around and leaves.

* * *

I stay on the sofa for almost two whole days. I try to keep Old Sausage with me by closing the door and providing water and tins of tuna, but eventually she leaves through the window. I stare at the TV — properly watching something for the first time in a long time, instead of having it on in the background — and think and think and think.

I sleep a little, and drop in and out of dreams. Sometimes I dream that Adam is here, sometimes I think Old Sausage is lying on my feet. Every time I wake up, I'm alone.

By the end of the second day, dehydrated and starving, I make soup and tea and sit myself on the rug next to the coffee table, my back straight. I call Jess.

'I'm sorry,' I say, simply.

'Are you OK?' She's somewhere busy. I can hear the tram screeching along the tracks in the background.

'Are you?'

I can hear her smiling. 'Baby steps, eh?'

'Please tell me what's wrong with Will. Is it Benny? Is he alright?' I babble, sensing her softening and diving in.

She hesitates. 'It's not my place, Eve.'

'I know.' I want to push for more, want to really dig, but I force myself not to. 'How's Johnny?'

'Ah.' Her tone becomes awkward. 'We broke up a couple of weeks ago.'

'Shit.' I feel wretched.

'Do you feel bad?' she asks. 'I don't want you to, but do you?'

'Yeah, I do.'

'Well.' She laughs softly. 'It's OK. I forgive you. Use it to make changes instead of beating yourself up.'

I nod, even though she can't see me. 'Did you cry?'

'For about a week.'

'I'm sorry, Jess.' I pause, trying to restrain as much of myself as I can, but I fail. 'He really was a twat though.'

She cackles. 'Ah, I do love you.'

There's a small pause. 'I cried,' I say, eventually.

'*Did* you?'

'Yeah. For ages.' I swallow. 'A proper cry, as well. There was snot and everything.'

I can practically feel her beaming down the phone. 'You should have called me! We could have cried together.'

I snort. 'No, thank you.'

'It's healthy!' she tries, and then realises it's fruitless. 'I'm proud of you.'

'Don't be,' I say. 'Not yet.'

My words hang for a moment before she speaks again. 'Speak to Will.'

'I will. I've tried. I'll keep trying.'

'Yeah.'

'Love you, Jess.'

'Love you, too.'

CHAPTER 40

Adam

Okie's focus is razor sharp, but I'm not with it. I'm tired — Hugh moved back into his residential home yesterday evening, and I stayed until the early morning to make sure he settled. Every time my mind veers onto something practical, like A Levels and mortgages, Eve is pushed into my mind — the way she looked, crying on the sofa . . . my stomach twists.

Okie has already packed up his things and is halfway out of the door by the time I remember what I'm doing, and Mr Adayemi is walking through with two cups of coffee.

He sits down opposite me.

'He's done really well again today.' I say, trying to find something new to add. 'But you probably guessed that.'

Mr Adayemi doesn't respond. Instead, he gazes out of the window. 'Perhaps the exams aren't such a good idea.'

It takes me a second to compute what he's said. 'What? But he's doing so well, there's only—'

'They've cut my hours.' It seems difficult for him to say this, as though sharing something so personal is painful. 'It's just not possible.'

I shake my head, dispelling the memory of Bil's suggestion that I'm getting too invested. 'Let me help.'

'No.' He looks at me for the first time, and his eyes are
determined. 'He'll take the exams next year, or in two, with
everybody else.'

Mr Adayemi reaches his hand into his jacket pocket and
pulls out my envelope. 'Thank you again, Adam.'

'Please, this isn't insurmountable, we can—'

'I think it'd be best if you came once a fortnight from
now on. Until the situation improves.'

'If I'm not tutoring Okie for his A Levels, there's nothing
I can do for him,' I say bluntly.

He looks at me, and then nods. 'Then it's settled.'

I grip the back of my chair, helplessness washing over me.
'Please — there's got to be a way.'

'I'm grateful for all of your help.' Mr Adeyemi pushes
his cup to the side and stands up, straightening his jacket.
'Goodbye, Adam.'

* * *

I rattle through my last two students' sessions, but my heart
isn't really in it. I can't process the unfairness of the situation: finances shouldn't stand in the way of education. They
shouldn't stand in the way of a fulfilled life, whatever that
means. I understand that Okie goes to school, that he's generally considered too young to go to university, but it's such a
waste. A waste of a year or two of his life, time that he could
be spending happy. A waste of potential.

I cycle home the long route, passing through the park,
pedalling hard. I'm taken back to the last time I felt this fired
up, when I was riding my bike on the phone to Katie, telling
her that I'd been given the go-ahead to tutor Okie into university. That feels like such a long time ago now.

I briefly wonder what Katie is doing — I haven't heard
from her, but I know it won't be long before she wants an
update on the house — and I push the thoughts from my

mind and bear down on the handlebars. My thighs are burning, and I focus on the pain as I try to think about how I can salvage this.

I need the money that Okie's sessions give me, of course I do, especially now I'm trying to buy half of my own house. But that isn't the point, it's a busy time of year for me, and there are other students on the waiting list. I could add extra sessions to make up for the lost income. What's really eating at me is that we were so *close*. We almost got there, and now we won't.

I eventually arrive home and as I open the door, I immediately notice that something feels different. There's a smell — perfume — and the air is off somehow, like things have been moved. There's an envelope on the side by the front door, with nothing written on the front of it.

I pick it up and step through into the living room as I run my finger under the flap, and my suspicions are confirmed. I might not have noticed, if it weren't for the envelope and the smell of perfume, but things are missing. The pink and green scatter cushion on the sofa; half the contents of the book case; the pointless little wooden bowl filled with pointless little wooden balls that used to sit on the coffee table. All of Katie's stuff. I don't need to go upstairs to know that the wardrobe will be mostly empty now, too.

The edge of the envelope slices into my finger, and I rip it open in frustration. It's as if I've willed this here by thought.

Dear Mr Parks,

I have been instructed by my client, Miss Katherine Dean, to inform you of her intentions to place the below-mentioned property, of which she owns 50% of the equity, on the market . . .

I screw the letter up and throw it onto the now-empty coffee table. I call Katie.

'Hello?' She answers as if she doesn't know who it is. Perhaps she's deleted my number. Get the stuff, drop off the letter, delete the contact. Clean slate.

'Katie, it's Adam.'

'Oh.' There's a pause. 'You got the letter.'

'And you got your stuff, I see.'

I always wondered how ex-partners got into such bitter disputes over possessions — thought I'd be better than that, more rational and benevolent — but right now, I get it.

'I thought it'd be better if I came while you were out—'

'You want to sell the house?' I interrupt. 'I thought I was buying you out?'

She sighs. 'We both know you can't do that.'

'Oh, you know that?'

'Adam . . .'

'Tell your solicitor to back off. This isn't a divorce.' I can't control the anger in my voice. 'You could have called me.'

'I wanted things to stay simple. Amicable.'

'Right, and formal letters are renowned for their friendly approach.' I run my hand through my beard, tugging at the moustache hairs that are creeping over my top lip. 'I'm buying it, Katie. Just give me a few weeks to figure things out.'

I hear her sigh, and it grates on me. That sigh — that irritability at everything I say — how didn't I see it? 'I really could do with things moving along. Rich and I are buying—' She stops herself.

'That sounds sensible,' I chirp, my voice false and bright. 'Buy a new house with the guy you've been dating for two weeks. Rich, is it? Pass him my *very* best wishes.'

'Grow up, Adam. People move on, there's no time—'

I hang up. I'm angry with myself for being childish, for rising to the bait and getting petty. *Rich.* The thought of him doesn't cut as deeply as I thought it would. I'm not trying to picture him. Instead I'm picturing this house, being mine. A more solid foundation for Hugh and me to build our lives upon.

I stalk through to the kitchen and flick the kettle on. The letter caught me at a bad time, after the news about Okie's exams. I'll be better prepared next time I talk to Katie. It's Friday, so I can do my marking at the weekend and spend this evening looking at mortgages, loans, exploring my options.

The kettle rises to a noisy boil, and I don't hear the knocking until I've filled the cafetière. When I register it, I put the kettle down and walk through to the front door.

'Hello.'

It's Eve. She's standing on my doorstep, her face calm, her hair curling up around her jaw. She's wearing jeans and a black t-shirt, and there's a plastic box by her feet.

'Eve, hi.' I take a breath. 'Sorry, I wasn't expecting you, are you OK?'

'I'm fine.' She smiles broadly. 'Old Sausage is from Windermere. Do you fancy a trip?'

I'm trying to process what she's saying, but it sounds like gibberish. 'Windermere? How — what do you mean?'

'I took her to the vets. The chip is registered to . . .' she checks her phone, 'Brierfield Close.'

I look down at the box by her feet. There's a grate on the front, and through it I can see Old Sausage, peering at me. 'In Windermere.' I'm parroting her, trying to process the fact that she's here, that she has information.

'Yes, in Windermere.' She looks impatient now. 'Well?'

'It's almost five o'clock, shouldn't we—'

'Adam.' She meets my gaze and her eyes glint. 'Are you coming or not?'

CHAPTER 41

Eve

'Is she comfortable, do you think?' I crane my neck to look into Old Sausage's crate. I've put her next to me at the four-person table seat we've managed to bag on the train. Adam is sitting opposite me, and our feet keep touching.

He leans forward. I can see a few tiny flecks of grey in the curly hair above his ears. 'She's fast asleep.'

I smile. He said 'she' again, but I don't want to push the point.

I look out of the window. The train from Manchester Piccadilly to Windermere takes two hours, and we're only just pulling out of the station.

'What time's the last train home again?' Adam asks.

'Ten to ten,' I say. 'If we get there for eight thirty, that gives us about an hour to find her house.'

Adam nods.

I still don't know if bringing Adam with me was a good idea. After he found me the other day, I swore I'd never see him again. When Old Sausage came through my back door again, her ribs showing and her eyes crusty, I decided I had to take her to the vet straight away, and when the microchip said she was from Windermere, I planned to go alone. But something pulled me to his house, past the shame and the awkwardness. A sense of loyalty to our shared quest. He hasn't mentioned what he saw.

When he doesn't think I'm looking, he frowns, looking off into the distance. I watch him out of the corner of my eye, taking in his dark eyebrows and strong nose. Every so often the smell of him drifts across the table, and I bite my lip.

Suddenly, he looks at me, catching me staring. I flick my eyes away.

'Are you OK?' he asks.

'I'm fine.' I look anywhere but at him. 'Why?'

'The other day . . .'

My pulse quickens a little. I shouted at him. 'I'm sorry. Can we not talk about it? I shouldn't have shouted, but can we leave it?'

'Sure.' He gazes out of the window. The train rattles along, and at some point we enter a tunnel. I narrow my eyes to see through the reflection of the train lights on the glass, and I catch him looking at me. This time, he's the one who turns away.

'How's your brother?' I break the silence, raising my voice over the noise of the train thundering through the dark.

His face breaks into a grin. 'He's good. Getting there. Thanks for asking.'

'I'm glad.' I smile. 'Sorry, I don't know much about you, really, do I?'

He looks at me steadily. 'I think you know more than I know about you.'

My stomach jumps. 'Probably.'

He leans his elbow on the ledge of the window and props his head up with his hand. His fingers disappear into his hair. 'Go on, tell me something.'

'Like what?'

'Like . . . who you are, where you come from, all that jazz.'

'Well, I'm Eve,' I start, stupidly. 'I'm from Manchester, born and raised. My parents still lived there up until a year or so ago. They emigrated to Spain.'

Something like pain flashes across Adam's eyes, but before I can be sure, it's gone. 'That must be nice for them. Have you visited?'

'No.' I look outside again. We've emerged into the dusk. 'I don't really have the time.'

I can feel him watching me. 'What else? Friends? Hobbies?'

'I have two best friends, really,' I say. *Used to be three, now perhaps just one, if that*, I think. 'Will, he's married with a new-born, and Jess, who's a chaotic spiritual healer and one of the most brilliant people on the planet.'

He smiles.

'What about you?' I ask, as an afterthought. My self-centredness is becoming obvious to me now, and it's embarrassing when I catch myself.

'Tight group of four. We've known each other all our lives.' He looks happy when he talks about his friends, and I listen as he gives me their names and describes what they're like. 'They're really supportive with Hugh, as well. That's my brother.'

I smile. 'That's brilliant.'

'Yeah.' The conversation ends there, and I watch carefully as his face drops again, that frown reappearing.

'Tickets, please.' A conductor looms over us, and we show our phones. He scans them, and then moves on. I drum my fingers on the tabletop.

'Are you alright?' I ask, eventually. 'Sorry, I don't want to pry. You just look a bit . . . worried.'

Adam sighs. 'Sorry. Just before you arrived I got a letter from my ex's solicitor. She wants to put the house on the market.'

'Shit.' *Is he moving?*

'Yeah. And also, the dad of a kid I was tutoring into university has just pulled him out of his exams because they haven't got enough money. So that sucks, too.'

His openness makes me feel suddenly comfortable, at ease. 'I thought A Levels were free?'

'He's only fifteen.' He smiles at the look on my face. 'Gifted.'

'Wow.'

I can feel my brain firing up, and I try to resist it. What was it that Will said to me? *This isn't another one of your tick-box problems to solve.* I can't treat life like a series of obstacles to be overcome. As I'm pondering, my mind is already drafting solutions, actions, plans. I try to bite my tongue, but fail.

'What about a fundraiser?'

'What?' Adam has gone back to looking out of the window. I didn't realise how long I'd let the silence hang.

'A fundraiser. Drum up some money for his exams.'

He frowns. 'I'm not sure his dad would like that.'

'Why not?'

'He's very adamant about not accepting charity. Okie — that's the kid — gets some financial support from the council, but that's about as far as it goes I think.' I must look confused, because he continues. 'He has autism.'

My brain ticks over again. I jiggle my leg. I want to pace, but Old Sausage is blocking my way to the aisle. Something more acceptable, something quiet, with no fanfare . . . 'Charity grants,' I say.

This time, he seemed ready for my input. I could feel him studying me as I thought. 'Charity grants,' he repeats.

'Contact local autism charities. See if there's any finance available for education, or even career development. It wouldn't be charity in the sense of publicly asking for donations — just applying for something that he might already be entitled to.'

Something lights up in his eyes, and something else clicks into my mind. He has the motivation, and I have the solutions. He's got the heart, I've got the brain. I'm not sure how that makes me feel.

'That's not a bad idea.'

I raise an eyebrow at him. 'I know it's not. I don't have bad ideas.' He laughs.

We sit in silence until the train pulls into Windermere station, my mind forming plans as Adam looks out over the landscape, his frown a little smaller. As I think, I absentmindedly take him in — a fine layer of dark hair covers his forearms, and his hands are large and slender, his fingernails short and round. He wears a white t-shirt again, and through it I can faintly see a smattering of chest hair. His arms are toned, but not huge. He's not my type.

We stand up together, and Adam reaches over to take the crate so I can pass. I step forward as he lifts it, and his arm brushes against my ribs. His eyes lock onto mine.

'Let's go,' he says.

CHAPTER 42

Adam

We trudge along the pavement as the sun lowers further in the sky. Eve strides a few paces ahead, her phone held out in front of her, and I walk behind, Old Sausage's crate banging against my shin with every step.

'Left here,' she announces, following the blue line on her screen. 'And then . . . first right, I think.'

'Can you slow down?' I ask, as the crate makes particularly painful impact with my knee.

She apologises, and hangs back a bit until we're walking next to each other. The sudden proximity of her makes my heart jump, and I clutch the crate tightly. Whenever I'm around her, my head feels muddled. There's a reservedness about her that intrigues me, like she's a puzzle that needs untangling, but every time I feel like I'm cracking the surface, that fierceness returns to her eyes and knocks me sideways.

'Can we speed up just a tiny bit?' she asks. 'I'm conscious of the time . . .'

'How far off are we?'

She glances at her phone. 'Thirteen minutes.'

I check my watch. It's now nine o'clock. We've been walking for more than half an hour.

'I'm not flaunting my maths genius here or anything,' I comment, 'but the timings don't really add up, do they?'

She frowns. 'I thought we'd be able to get a taxi . . .'

When we got to the station, there were no black cabs, and the nearest Uber was ten minutes away. I wish we'd waited for it now.

'We can't turn around now,' she says decisively. 'We'll get a taxi back when we're done.'

We keep walking, only stopping once to check on Old Sausage, who had some water and tuna when we got off the train. He sleeps throughout the journey. I try not to think about what happens when we get to the house; do we just hand him over? The thought of it upsets me, like I'm drawing a line under something I'm not ready to wrap up just yet.

The more we walk, the clumsier I get, the weight of the crate knocking my balance. At one point, my hand brushes hers, and I hear her breathe in sharply.

'Sorry, you made me jump.' A flush is creeping up her cheeks. I haven't seen her flustered before.

My heart pounds. What *is* it about her? It feels like I know everything about her, but absolutely nothing at the same time. I simultaneously want to walk in silence with her for hours and sit her down to ask her a million questions all at once.

I can feel her mind whirring beside me, like I could on the train. It feels somehow like she always knows something, has always figured something out before I've even left the starting blocks.

'Here,' she announces, and suddenly, we are standing in front of a house. There's nothing special about it; it's just another 1960s semi on another nondescript close. We could be anywhere in the country. The only thing making it stand out from the houses around it is its disrepair: weeds have over-taken the front garden, where there's an abandoned shopping trolley, and the paint on the front door is peeling. It also doesn't seem like anybody's home.

'All the lights are off,' I state.

'Yeah.'

'Should we maybe have called before we came?' I don't know why this is only occurring to me now.

'I did that,' she says. Of course she did. 'Nobody answered.'

We stand, staring at the house, for a minute or two. 'So, what should we—' I start, but she's taken off and is striding up the path to the house next door. I chase after her.

She raps loudly, and an older woman answers the door.

'Hi, I'm so sorry to bother you at this time of the evening,' Eve says smoothly, her face warm and open. What did she say she did for a living? Marketing? She's perfect. 'My friend and I are trying to return a cat to its owner, and we believe it's from the house next door. Do you know when they might be home?'

The lady looks startled and shakes her head. 'I'm sorry, love. Mr Barnes died about six months ago.'

'Oh.' Eve looks lost for a second, her face dropping, but she recovers quickly and straightens up. 'Right. Did he have a cat, do you know?'

'Oh, yes. Tabitha. Went missing just before he passed, I believe.' She nods towards a lamppost, where a water-damaged laminate is drooping sadly. I walk over. There's a picture of Old Sausage, looking decisively less weather-beaten, underneath the word MISSING.

'Well, thank you so much for your time.' Eve smiles, and the lady closes the door.

She turns to face me. 'Well, shit.'

'Shit indeed.'

She comes to join me on the pavement, the closest she's been to me yet, and we stare at the poster. 'That's really her, isn't it?'

'Turns out she was a girl after all,' I say, nudging her. I can smell her perfume, feel the warmth of her next to me.

'I know — I asked the vet. I was saving it to hold against you.' She grins at me.

'Oh, very mature.' I laugh. 'We should've bet on it.'

'That wouldn't have been very fun.' She turns to face me now, and in the dimming light her eyes gleam. 'I knew I was right.'

We stand, looking at each other, and the air feels charged. For a second, neither of us speaks, and I take her in: her small nose and mouth, the big, green eyes.

'Right.' She turns away from me, and the moment's gone. 'Let's try and get a taxi. We've got twenty minutes.'

Eve checks Uber, but it's still a ten-minute wait. We'd never make it. I put the crate down and pull out my phone, Googling Windermere taxi companies and calling the first three on the list. None can get to us in time.

'Shit, shit, shit.' Eve paces up and down the pavement, the phone pressed to her ear. 'I know it's Friday, but come *on*. It's hardly the party capital.'

I avoid pointing out that that's probably the exact reason we're struggling to get a taxi, and instead go onto the Trainline to double-check the train times. 'There's one at ten to eleven!' I cheer.

She turns to face me, cupping her hand over the receiver to block her voice. 'Isn't that the one with a four-hour change-over in Preston?'

I look again. Total journey time: five hours and fifty-eight minutes. 'Always one step ahead, aren't you?'

Time ticks on, and the numbers to call dwindle. It becomes clear that no taxi will get us to the station in time for the last train.

'Can you give me a quote for two people, going to Manchester?' Eve is saying down the phone now. 'Piccadilly.'

I grimace. There's no way.

'OK, yep, great, we'll think about it and call you back.' Eve puts the phone down and turns to me. 'Two hundred quid.'

'Shut up.'

She throws her head back and laughs loudly. 'Oh my god. What the fuck are we going to do?'

'We could go for a drink and then kip in the station?' I ask tentatively. 'Wait until the first train home?'

She shakes her head. 'Have you ever seen a cat at the pub?'

We look at each other, and there's a moment — one of those clear ones, the kind you stop having in your early twenties; the kind that people try to replicate by cliff diving and drinking too much and getting high — where everything feels so illicit in the best kind of way. We're trapped, and it's wrong, this frisson between us — but why?

Under the glow of the streetlamp, Eve's face is electric. 'Christ,' she says, pressing her lips together. 'I've never been so disorganised in my life.'

A rush of laughter erupts from me. I'm giddy, ridiculously so, because what are we *doing* here? How am I standing here, on this street, in this town, with this mystifying, incredible woman, with no way to get home?

Eve watches me, and then grins. 'Stop it.' She starts laughing too, her eyes crinkled and her mouth wide. 'No, stop it.'

'You're amazing,' I say, because although this is the least romantic place I've ever been, it's true.

She carries on laughing, but her eyes drift away from mine, and then the moment fades, like taking a filter from a photo. 'Let's go to the lake,' she says.

We walk, chuckling again every so often, sober now, until we arrive back at the cluster of buildings dotted along the edge of Lake Windermere. People weave in and out of pubs, shouting and laughing, and hotels rise proudly, overlooking the invisible blackness of the water beyond.

We stop at a bench and sit down. I turn to her, and it hits me again, that feeling I can't quite describe. 'I think we're going to have to stay over, aren't we?'

CHAPTER 43

Eve

I didn't plan for this to happen.

When I thought of coming to Windermere, when I looked at train times and invited Adam along, I really thought we could do it. Two hours up, two hours back, with an hour in the middle to drop the cat and go.

But even by my standards, I was being ambitious.

Adam sits on the bench, his head buried in his phone, searching for hotels. I have Old Sausage on a lead I bought on Amazon and am coaxing her to poo at the edge of the most famous lake in the country.

'Come on. A wee, at least,' I beg. She stares at me.

We're staying over. This isn't a huge deal — I've been to enough conferences to have lost the novelty of a night away — but something about it feels clandestine, like we're sneaking off during a school trip without the teacher's permission.

There was a moment, earlier, while we were standing outside Old Sausage's house, when something weird happened. I realised that I'd fucked up — that my timings were off, and we couldn't get home before tomorrow — and just for a moment, while we stood under the streetlamp, I felt this unfamiliar jolt of excitement about it all. My mind stopped turning, I stopped filtering for solutions, and out of nowhere I thought, *I'm glad.*

And then the weirdest thing: Adam looked at me, and said, 'You're amazing.'

You're amazing. What did he mean by that?

'Right, there's only one pet-friendly hotel with a vacancy.' Adam looks up from his phone and jolts me back to the present. 'The Palmgrove. Funny name, considering the marked absence of palm trees and groves of any kind in the area.'

'How much is it?' It's practically dark now, and I'm struggling to see Old Sausage. It looks like she might be squatting. 'I think she's doing it!' I cry.

'Hallelujah.' Adam gives me a lopsided grin. He taps at his phone again. 'It's only sixty quid a night. Looks a bit crap, but it's got a lake view.'

'If we're going to pay a hundred and twenty, why don't we just sod it and see if we can get a taxi?' I muse, but a part of me is wondering whether I really want to go home.

'No, it'd be sixty quid for the both of us,' Adam says slowly, cautiously.

'That seems cheap?' I squint into the darkness. What is Old Sausage doing?

'There's just the one room.'

It takes me a second to process what he's said. Old Sausage starts scrabbling at the grass, signalling to me that she has, in fact, done the deed.

'There can't be.' My heart is in my throat. I pull out my phone and check. He's right. One vacancy in the vicinity that allows pets. 'Right,' I say. 'I'll stay there with Old Sausage, you get another room somewhere else. We can split the cost of the total.'

Adam stands up. He walks towards me until we're almost touching. In the darkness, his eyes are black. If, later, you were to ask me what was going on around me, I wouldn't have been able to tell you. 'If you're more comfortable with that, that's OK. But just to throw it out there, we can pull the beds apart. We'll sleep for a few hours and then jump on the first train?'

I turn it over in my mind. I want to — shit, I realise I *want* to — and the strength of the feeling scares me. 'Two beds,' I say.

'Yes.' He looks at me intently.

I crouch down, running my fingers through Old Sausage's fur. Thinking. I pick her up around her middle and stand, so that we're facing again. 'Alright,' I say. 'Let's go.'

* * *

The bed doesn't pull apart.

It's one shabby-looking double, smaller than the one I have at home. On either side are two bedside tables, and there's a desk by the window. A small en suite sits next to the door to the terrace, where the lake is inky under the moon.

Adam immediately calls down for a camp-bed. 'I'll sleep on it.' He sits at the desk and twiddles the complementary pen between his fingers.

'No, it's fine, honestly,' I say. 'I barely sleep anyway, it makes sense for one of us to get a good night.'

The way I say it sounds charged, and Adam looks away, a small smile on his face. I feel myself flush.

'Shall we order a beer?' He picks up the creased room service menu and flicks through it.

'Sure.'

He calls down again, and five minutes later, two men arrive. One carries a camping cot, the other two bottles of Budweiser. They set up the bed in the corner and then leave.

'So . . .' Adam says, once they're gone.

The awkwardness is palpable. 'Shall we check out the terrace?'

We step outside onto wooden planks leading onto a pier that sits directly on top of a small outlet for the lake. The

230

overhead light doesn't work, but the temperature is nice, so we sit on the patio chairs and leave Old Sausage to explore the room.

'Well,' Adam says once we've sat down. 'Cheers to the weirdest evening of my life.'

'So far,' I say, intending for it to come out jokily, but in the darkness, with my voice lowered, it sounds like an invitation.

I clink my beer against his hurriedly, steamrolling through the moment. 'How the hell did she end up in Manchester?' I muse.

'Back of a lorry, probably.' Adam takes a swig of his drink. 'I've heard of it happening before.'

'Little road-tripper,' I say fondly. Part of me is glad she's still with us, that we haven't had to give her away.

I can feel Adam's gaze on me, and I turn to meet it. In the dark, it's easier, less exposing. 'What shall we do with her?'

I shrug. 'One of us could keep her.'

'Custody battle.'

'I've been thinking about your situation,' I say, suddenly, the cogs in the back of my mind still turning. 'Have you looked at self-employed mortgages?'

Adam laughs, and I see the sudden whiteness of his teeth in the dark. 'You're remarkable.'

I'm instantly on guard. 'How so?'

He's silent for a moment. He just looks at me. I take a sip of my beer. 'You're . . . sharp.'

'Is that a compliment?' I ask. Sharp as in with it, on the ball, or sharp as in pointy, could stab?

He smiles. 'Of course.'

We watch as the moon ripples on the water, sipping in silence. Adam wants to get to know me. I can feel him prying — no, not prying, asking questions, like any person would — and I can feel myself resisting them. He's kind. He has a brother that he cares for, and a job that makes a difference. He thinks of others before he thinks of himself. I've just failed an intense mission to destroy my best friend's career. What would he make of me if he knew that?

'There's an investigation going on at work. Into me. My behaviour,' I say, not looking away from the water.

Adam is quiet for a moment. 'I'll get us another drink.' He disappears inside, and two minutes later there's a knock, and he returns with two more beers. I thank him, keeping my eyes averted. He sits back down.

'I work for Florina.' I'm talking almost mechanically, as though this is a story I'm reading from a webpage. Or a confession, maybe. I haven't yet admitted to anyone what deep down I already know: that I did the wrong thing. 'I got put forward for a promotion. Head of Marketing for the whole company. A member of my staff, my best friend, actually, went behind my back and applied for it as well. A war sort of broke out.'

Adam doesn't say anything for a few beats, and I worry that he's judging me. 'And did you win the war?'

I laugh softly. 'No, I didn't.'

His chair creaks as he leans back. 'I used to think you could get anywhere by being kind. By having good intentions,' he says, and this time he's the one gazing at the water. 'I still think it's true, for the most part. But sometimes it doesn't work like that.'

'No.' I study him. I suddenly want him. I really, really want him. And it terrifies me, because it doesn't feel like a Graham kind of want, or a Tryst kind of want. I don't know what it feels like.

'Shall we go to bed?' He turns to me, and everything inside me liquifies. I shiver.

'Yeah, OK.'

We walk back through, but in the stark light of the bedroom everything has changed. My ease evaporates. Old Sausage is curled up on the desk chair. I sit on the edge of the camp-bed.

'Uh-uh.' Adam pushes me gently. 'Up.'

I grip the edges of the mattress. 'Honestly, I don't mind.'

'Don't make me use my brute strength.' He plonks himself onto the bed next to me and shoves me softly sideways.

232

'Oh yeah? What about mine?' I shove him back, harder.

'Can't compete with that.' His eyes burn into mine, a playful smile creeping across his lips.

'Move then.' I laugh.

'Make me,' he challenges.

A dull, longing ache thuds in my lower abdomen. 'I will.'

'Go on, then.' He leans forward, his eyes fixed on mine, daring me. I put my hands on his shoulders and push. He pushes back, and our faces inch closer, closer, until I can feel his breath on my lips.

Suddenly, he grins, and picks me up by the waist. I squeal, and he drops me on the double bed.

'That's not fair!' I scramble up again, but he's lying on the camp-bed, clutching it for dear life.

'All's fair in love and war,' he says jokingly, and our eyes lock for a second before I turn away. I'm short of breath, my head spinning, my judgment undeniably impaired by the weirdness of this situation.

Neither of us says anything for a long while.

'Well, we've no toothbrush or pyjamas,' he mumbles eventually, when I think he might have fallen asleep. 'Shall we turn off the lights?'

CHAPTER 44

Adam

This is torture.

The camp-bed is the most uncomfortable thing I've ever slept on, and I have a gold Duke of Edinburgh award. But it isn't the furniture that's rendering me unable to sleep. It's Eve, lying there, three feet away from me in the dark.

This evening . . . this evening has been like a weird, exhilarating dream. What am I doing here, in the middle of the Lake District, with a neighbour I've known for a couple of weeks and a stray cat? I almost laugh into the darkness.

I can hear her tossing and turning too, struggling to sleep. She said she was a bad sleeper — said that things plagued her at night. A busy brain, she called it.

She's a problem-solver, that much is clear. She gets things done. But there's something under that, a vulnerability that I can't seem to tap into. Her confession outside, about the war that broke out between her and her colleague, felt like the first piece of real truth I'd heard from her since we met.

I roll over in my cot and sigh. I know I won't sleep. I feel like I've been jabbed with adrenaline. I think she might be the most beautiful person I've ever seen. I banish the thought. She's a neighbour, a potential friend, and we each of us have too many problems. But the more I get to know her, the more attractive she becomes. I roll onto my other side, pulling the cover up higher. In a moment, I'll go out onto the balcony and watch the lake until the sun comes up.

'Adam?' Her whisper carries across the room, and I startle.

'Yeah?'

'Are you sleeping?'

'Obviously not.' I laugh softly.

'Is it really uncomfortable?'

'It's like sleeping on gravel.'

'Do you want to swap?'

'No.'

She's silent for a while, and I think she's fallen asleep, but then she speaks again. 'Do you want to just share? We can build a pillow wall.'

My pulse jumps. 'No, don't worry.'

'Come on. I don't mind, honestly.'

I lie on my back, staring at the ceiling. I can't. *Why not?* We can build a pillow wall, like she said. I get out of bed and stand up, feeling my way over to the double bed.

'Hang on, let me shift over,' she whispers.

'Why are we whispering?' I murmur back.

'I don't know.' She giggles — a vulnerable sound I haven't heard from her yet — and I slide under the duvet.

We lie for a second, one single pillow wedged between us. I can hear her breathing. 'This is also very uncomfortable,' I say.

'I know. Fucking Palmgroves.'

We laugh together, and in the darkness it's easy, like we're two bodiless souls, floating blindly.

'Do you think you'll sleep?' I ask.

'Probably not.'

I mull my next question over in my mind. 'What do you think about, when you can't sleep?'

She sighs. 'Friends. My parents. Myself.'

'That's quite the combo.'

'Yeah.'

I roll over so that I'm facing her, and I can see her outline as she lies on her back, staring at the ceiling.

'Do you miss your parents?' I ask.

'No,' she says, quickly. 'I mean, I don't know. They left.'

'You're not close?'

'I suppose we are, sort of.'

I sense that she's closing down again, but then she continues. 'When you saw me, the other day . . .'

'Yeah.' My voice is barely audible, I'm so desperate not to break her confidence, to hear what she has to say.

'That was the first time I've cried since I was seventeen.'

I swallow. 'That's a really long time.'

'Mmm.'

'What happened?' I ask. I don't mean the other day, I mean back then, when she decided she wouldn't cry anymore.

She understands my question. 'My grandad died, and my boyfriend left me the next day. It's a pathetic story.' She laughs sadly. 'But I feel like it might have fucked me up a bit.' She pauses. 'People leaving, depending on people, you know? That sort of thing.'

I watch her, the silhouette of her chest rising and falling as she breathes. 'My parents are dead,' I say.

She rolls over, so we're facing each other. 'Shit.'

'Yeah.' I laugh at her response: inadequate, but also perfectly fitting. 'But I have Hugh, you know? And aunties and uncles who send birthday cards and a brilliant group of friends. It's OK.'

'How did it happen?' she whispers, and I feel her breath. She's only centimetres away.

'Car crash. When I was sixteen.' I look beyond her, to the tiny slither of moonlight filtering through the curtains.

'Shit,' she says again.

We're quiet for a while.

'Don't you feel it too? That everyone's going to leave you one day?' she asks, and there's a tremor in her voice.

'No,' I say, certain. 'I know it.'

She hesitates. 'And so you hold on to what you have while it's there.' It's a statement, not a question, and it's posed as though it's just occurred to her, like she's not really talking to me at all.

A moment passes, the only noise the whir of the empty mini fridge and our breathing.

'So your ex left you,' Eve murmurs.

'She did.'

'Sorry. I imagine it's quite fresh?'

'Doesn't feel as fresh as I'd have thought,' I say truthfully. 'What about you?'

She doesn't answer, instead asking, 'Are you . . . dating?'

'No,' I laugh, remembering my terrible attempt at things with Becky. 'Absolutely not.'

We lapse into silence again. I want to repeat the question back to her, but I stop myself. Maybe I'm sure she's single, maybe I don't want to hear otherwise.

Our faces are just inches away from each other. I want to reach out, to run a finger down her bare arm, to hold the back of her head and pull her towards me, to feel her pressed against me.

She's looking at me. I can see the glint of the dim light reflecting in her eyes. I want her hands on me, my mouth on her neck, her smooth thigh looped over mine.

There's a breath, and I lift my head.

'Night, then,' she says.

I blink, and then lower my head back down and close my eyes, the image of her staring at me in the dark printed on the back of my eyelids.

Eve shuffles beside me, and I feel the pillow between us move. She reaches under and takes my hand in hers, running her fingers over my palm, and then holds it tight.

* * *

When I wake up, Eve is sitting on the edge of the bed.

'Morning.' I sit up, feeling stiff, a sharp pain in my hip where the seam of my jeans has dug into me during the night.

'Hey.' She turns around and smiles. Her face is bare — she must have washed her makeup off with the tiny bar of soap in the bathroom. 'I'm starving.'

'Me too,' I say, trying to remember the last time I ate. We skipped dinner last night, but I didn't notice at time. 'Where's Old Sausage?'

She nods to the other side of the room, where the cat is curled up on the camp-bed. 'At least someone got some use out of it.'

I stand up and go to the bathroom, running my fingers through Old Sausage's fur as I pass. 'I'll just grab a shower and then we can go and find some food?'

'Sure.' She smiles at me again.

I manage a full wash with the minuscule soap, the bathroom filling with steam so thick it dampens my clothes, which I've piled next to the sink. Out of the shower, I wipe a smear across the mirror and inspect my face in the three seconds before it clouds over again. There's a brightness to my eyes I haven't seen in months.

My mind goes back to last night, but the whole thing is dreamlike, the heightened moments fading as I inspect them in the light of day. Did she feel what I felt? Did she sense I was about to kiss her, and that's why she said good night? For her, was it just another evening — albeit a weird one — that she'll forget as soon as we're back in Manchester?

I towel dry my hair and emerge back into the bedroom accompanied by a plume of steam, wearing yesterday's clothes.

'I need to buy some deodorant,' I say, looking outside to the already high sun. 'Think there's a Boots round here?'

Eve rummages around in her backpack and pulls out a small aerosol. She tosses it to me.

'Always prepared,' I remark, ducking back into the bathroom and leaving the door open.

We take Old Sausage for a stroll around the terrace before chivvying her back into her crate, where she promptly falls asleep again. As we're closing the door, I allow myself one final glimpse of the bed. I can't be the only one feeling like something happened there last night, can I?

We emerge into Windermere, scouring for somewhere that does takeaway breakfasts. Eventually, we locate two bacon wraps, and eat them with difficulty as we walk to the train station.

Our phones are almost dead, so we buy physical tickets, and the act of it feels quaint, like it's a special occasion.

As we settle into our seats, I look out of the window. Windermere begins rolling past us, fading into the distance, and if Eve wasn't sat here, with me, I could almost believe it had never happened.

CHAPTER 45

Adam

'How did it feel?' she asks.

I think before answering. 'It was . . . scary. Completely different. But also exciting — it's something I've wanted for so long.'

She nods. 'Me too.'

I lean across the table towards her. 'Do it!'

'I don't know . . .' She looks down at her hands, biting her lip.

'What's stopping you?'

'I'd be . . . quitting. Giving up.' She shrugs. 'I've worked so hard, it almost feels like I'd be dropping out as the going gets tough.'

'It's not quitting.' I shake my head. 'It's being your own boss. I promise you, going freelance was the best thing I've ever done. I don't answer to anyone, I get to make all the decisions.'

Her eyes brighten as I speak. 'That sounds like my idea of heaven.'

'If you're passionate enough about it, you'll make it work.'

She stares out of the window. The train is nearing Manchester now, and something heavy sits in my stomach. This feels like the end of a holiday, or a first date. A return to normality, with unanswered questions. I don't want it to end.

'When do you go back to work?' I ask.

She turns back to me. 'Monday.'

'Shall I keep Old Sausage, then? For now?' I suddenly want her to say yes, to let me have this tiny link to our small adventure.

'That's probably the best way to do it.' She smiles, and I see sadness in her eyes. 'I'll be in the office all day soon.'

'You can come and visit her any time,' I say, hoping she understands that this is an invitation, not a formality.

She stands up as the train pulls into Piccadilly, and we carry Old Sausage through the station and onto the tram. The journey feels shorter than it usually does, and before I know it, we're walking up our street.

'Well,' she says, and the distanced edge has returned to her tone. 'Thanks for . . . everything. Sorry it didn't have a better outcome.'

'I had a really nice time,' I blurt. I have to say it — *have* to — I can't bear to watch her closing off again.

'Me too.' She softens for a second, her eyes meeting mine. 'Fucking Palmgroves.'

I laugh loudly. 'I had a good sleep, though.'

'Yeah,' she frowns, 'so did I. Maybe I need to invest in a gravel bed.'

'Maybe you do.'

We stand quietly, and I take her in one last time. That fringe, those big eyes, those straight, defensive shoulders.

'Well, here you go.' She passes me the crate, and I take it, my thumb brushing hers. 'I'll see you around?'

'I hope so.'

She goes to turn, but hesitates. 'I mean, unless you wanted to—'

My phone beeps loudly in my pocket, a notification tone I don't immediately recognise. 'Oh, I must have some battery left.' I smile at her.

Her face has closed off completely, her mouth turned down. Something has shifted: what have I said? What have I done?

'See you.' She turns on her heel and walks to her front door, letting herself in without looking back.

* * *

'God.' I pace around the room, infuriated. 'How could I be so stupid?'

'Mate, it's really not the end of the world.' Bil is lying prone on Hugh's bed, his socked feet up against the wall. 'You're not even seeing each other.'

'Plus, you don't know if she even heard it.' Ferg pipes up from his position on the floor. 'She could have been thinking about something else.'

'Oh, she heard it.' I squirm as the memory resurfaces. 'And she knew what it was as well.'

The tone of the notification I received when I was saying goodbye to Eve yesterday was unfamiliar to me for a reason. It was a Tryst message, from a girl I matched with weeks ago, the last time I was on the app. I also had a text from Chloe, but somehow my situation with her has paled into insignificance in comparison.

'It's not like you did it on purpose?' Piotr ponders, leaning against the wardrobe. 'Hasn't everyone got Tryst?'

Hugh shrieks at the perfect time, and we laugh. 'No, we know *you* haven't, Hugh,' Bil says. 'You've got all the nurses here wrapped around your little finger, you don't need it.'

'Why don't you just text her?' Ferg asks. 'Or knock on her door, see how she is?'

'Yeah, OK.' I nod. 'I'll drop her a message this evening.'

We spend the next half an hour going through Disney+, which Piotr has set up for Hugh, trying to find a film that he can get obsessed with again. As we pass *Moana*, Hugh shakes his head vigorously.

'Nope, I know,' I laugh. 'No more *Moana* — it's time for a change.'

We put *Frozen* on, and Hugh watches intently, while Bil and Ferg sing along mockingly to the better-known parts.

'What's going on with your student, then?' Piotr asks, during one of the more boring moments in the film.

'Okie?' I ask, and he nods. 'Nothing. Still nothing.'

Ferg sighs. 'Is there really no way of getting the money together?'

'There has to be,' Bil urges.

'I thought you were all for me backing off?' I challenge.

He shakes his head and laughs. 'You are what you are, Adam.'

'I might contact some autism charities,' I muse. 'Eve suggested it.' Saying her name gives me a thrill, like I'm fifteen again and bringing my crush up in every conversation.

Bil winks. '*Did* she.'

'That's helpful of her,' Ferg says genuinely.

'And did you help each other in . . . *other* ways?' Bil drawls, his eyes mischievous. 'In Windermere?'

'No.' I laugh, leaning over to thump him on the arm. 'We slept. That was it.'

'I believe you.' He raises his eyebrows, indicating that he really doesn't.

Talking about her feels addictive: I want to tell them how we spoke into the darkness, how she curled her hand around mine, how we fell asleep attached to each other, holding on. But the boys are now arguing about the best way to cut a watermelon, so I can't interject without looking obsessed.

I think that maybe I *am* a little bit obsessed. It's all I can think about; remembering things she said or the way she looked at me makes me giddy, remembering the Tryst notification sound makes me feel helpless, like I've ruined it all. When I'm in bed at night, I know that she's only a few metres away, lying just like I am, and I wonder if she's running through it all in her mind, too.

As we're leaving the home, ruffling Hugh's hair and tidying his bed again, my phone beeps in my pocket.

My heart somersaults. It's Eve. She's sent a single link.

I click through, and there's a list of charities offering financial grants to students with autism pursuing higher education. I grin.

'What's that?' Piotr peers over my shoulder.

'A link to some charities that might be able to help Okie,' I answer absentmindedly, tapping back a reply.

Me: *You're amazing. Thank you.*

We emerge into the corridor, passing Becky and saying hi, and out into the car park. The boys get into their cars and drive away, and I walk over to my bike, checking my phone again.

My message has been read, but there's no reply.

244

CHAPTER 46

Eve

The studio space Jess rents is advertised as being calm and tranquil, an oasis for the mind, but in reality it looks like a bomb's hit it.

There are half-full cups of tea everywhere, and patches of mud by the door where people have wiped their feet. Yoga mats are crumpled in the corner, and books and papers are scattered across the table by the window.

I tread softly across the small room, conscious of the sessions going on downstairs, and perch on the edge of the desk. I should clean this for her. I don't visit enough, really — she always comes to me. I stand up again and start collecting the cups, placing them in neat stacks on the windowsill. She's doing her Sunday sessions this afternoon, so I know she'll be here soon. I'm shuffling the papers into some kind of order when the door opens and she walks in.

She blinks at me. 'Hi?'

'Hey.' I smile sheepishly. 'Sorry, I couldn't help myself.'

She walks over to the corner of the room and bundles two mats into her arms. 'You can clean any time you want to.' She smiles and lays the mats down in the middle of the floor. 'Sit.'

I push down the urge to say no, and join her on the floor. 'How are you?'

'Good.' She leans on her elbows, arching her back. 'I'm good.'

'You feeling OK about . . . you know?'

'I have my days.' She sighs and sits upright. 'But distance and hindsight are great healers.'

'Yeah.' I look down at my feet. I want to be there for her, but I missed the moment I was needed.

'So what's up?' She wraps her arms around her knees. 'Have you seen Will?'

'No, not yet.' I swallow. 'I've messaged him a few times, but I think he needs space. From me.'

Jess leans forward and wraps me in a hug, burying me into her shoulder. 'It's all going to be OK, Eve.'

I squeeze her back and then pull away, tears gathering in my eyes. I was right: now that I've started, I don't seem to be able to stop. 'I don't want to make this all about me.'

'No.' She studies me. 'But sometimes it's OK for it to be about you.'

'But just sometimes.' I smile.

She lies down on her mat, her knees bent, and I join her. Together, we stare at the flaking plaster on the ceiling.

'I rewrote my manifestation thingies for you,' I say.

She slaps her hands to her chest dramatically. 'You *did*? Read them to me!'

I laugh. 'OK.' I find the piece of paper in my pocket and hold it above my face.

'Number one: Stop thinking so much about work.'

'Good!'

'Number two: Go freelance.'

'Sort of contradicts the first one, but—'

'Hey!' I interrupt. 'Can I finish?'

'Sorry, go on.'

'Number three: Be a better friend,' I say, my voice less confident now.

Jess reaches over and squeezes my hand.

'Number four . . .' I trail off, feeling self-conscious.

'Number four?' she asks.

I clear my throat. 'Number four: Meet a guy.'

Jess sits up so quickly one of her dreadlocks whips her across the face. 'Come again?'

'Don't make me say it twice!'

'Who is he?' She hones in on me like an aged detective in an ITV drama. 'Who? Where did you meet him?'

'There's no one!' I protest, my face flushing. 'I just want to . . . give it a go. Be more open to it.'

She narrows her eyes at me. 'Liar.'

I look back at her. It's on the tip of my tongue. *Adam*. I haven't done this before, haven't discussed love interests with friends. There have *been* no love interests. The way Adam makes me feel is confusing and terrifying. The way I slept when I lay next to him, the safety he radiates, petrifies me. For less than a day, in Windermere, I felt like I'd come home to myself.

When I saw the text come through on his phone when he was in the shower, the message hidden behind the lock screen, I brushed it away. Chloe. A friend, a student, none of my business.

And then, later, his phone went off again.

Are you . . . dating?

Absolutely not.

Adam is the antithesis of anyone I have been with before. He has none of Graham's arrogance and bravado, and none of the vacuous self-interest of my Tryst conquests. He's the type of man I've never met — never allowed myself to meet — because he's kind, and interesting, and human.

But that notification sound; that soundtrack to my entire dating history. Hearing it come from him, when that section of my life was so firmly *separate* from everything I felt in

247

Windermere, has sent doubts rippling through my mind. He lied to me. He'll leave me. And even if he wouldn't, it couldn't work — it *wouldn't* work. I am not made for people like him.

Jess is still looking at me.

'No one,' I say. 'There's no one.'

* * *

I am pacing my living room, allowing myself a small relapse into my old habits while I figure out what I'm going to say.

Will won't tell me what's wrong, but it doesn't take a genius. When I went round to his house, Nina was nowhere to be seen, and he was asleep in the middle of the day. Either she's gone, or he's turfed her out — and she's taken the baby.

I have to *listen*. My mind pushes me to find solutions: can they try couples therapy, could they get a babysitter, are there any apps they can try? But I force myself to sweep them to one side. Will doesn't need my solutions, he needs to know that I'm here for him.

I'm still mulling things over when there's a knock at the door. My heart jumps. Is it Will? Or Adam? I sent him that text with links to the autism charities because I physically couldn't stop myself, but I haven't responded to his thank you message. Has he come round to see me?

I pull the door open quickly, my breath caught in my throat.

It's Graham.

'Hey.' He's wearing a tailored blazer and nice jeans.

It takes me a moment to gather my thoughts, and then I step back to let him in.

He stands in the middle of the living room.

'Coffee?' I ask.

'No, thanks.' He buries his hands in his pockets. His hair is cast back again, neatly coiffed against his head.

'What's up?' I run my fingers through my fringe. He's surprised me, turning up like this.

248

'I want to talk to you.' He sounds serious.

'Oh? Is it about work?'

He shakes his head, smiling. 'No, Eve. It's not about work.'

'OK . . .'

'We've got to stop doing this,' he says quickly, as if he's forcing it out.

'Doing what?'

'*This.*' He gestures to the space between us.

'Sleeping together?' I frown at him. We haven't spoken since Dublin.

'Messing with each other's heads,' he says plainly. 'I can't take it anymore.'

'Alright.' I nod, surprised at how easily I'm willing to put this behind me. 'OK, I get it.'

He takes a step towards me, and a breeze from the open back door makes me shiver. The heatwave is winding down.

'You . . . get it?'

'Yeah.' I look up at him. 'I'm sorry.'

He pauses. 'About what?'

'About . . . using you. To get at Kirsty.' I shake my head. 'It was really shitty. I've been unbelievably selfish, and I didn't look beyond my own end goals.'

He closes his eyes for a second. When he opens them, he's looking at me differently. 'It's OK.'

He takes another step toward me and reaches out his hand, tucking a stray hair behind my ear. He's so close now I can feel the heat of him. He leans down to me, brushing his lips against my cheek.

For a moment, I'm consumed by it. It would be so easy, so familiar. The smell of him, the feel of him, every tiny part of him: I know it like the back of my hand. I tip my head back, and he grazes my neck with his mouth.

'I think I love you, Eve,' he murmurs.

I step back quickly, my heart pounding. 'What?'

His eyes are wide, shocked. 'I—'

'You think you *what?*'

His mouth moves, trying to form words. 'I thought we just agreed — we—'

I take a deep breath. 'We agreed to stop messing with each other. We agreed to end this.'

'No.' He shakes his head. 'I meant — I meant that I wanted this. All of it. I meant that I wanted us to stop treating each other so casually.'

I take another step backwards. 'Graham, no. We're fucking terrible for each other. *I'm* terrible for *you*.'

'Only because that's how we've always been.' He holds his hands out now, pleading. 'Eve, just listen to me—'

'I can't,' I say, resolute now. 'I agree with you, it's got to stop.'

He looks at me, and I know he knows that there's no changing my mind. His arms drop to his sides.

I feel it inside me like a warm, solid stone: there won't be a next time, not with Graham. That story has ended, and it's time to move on.

CHAPTER 47

Adam

I am on the phone to Autisome, a charity that specialises in educational grants for autistic children. Any doubt I had about getting too involved with Okie's situation has now completely evaporated; even if it's pushy, even if it's not my place, how can I sit by and do nothing, when there might be something — just *something* — that might help? What I've heard so far sounds promising, but I'm not holding my breath. Even if it's good news, I'll still have to convince Okie's dad that it's an avenue worth pursuing.

Pan flute hold music drifts into my ear as I sit on the sofa, stroking Old Sausage and chewing the end of my pen. Eve still hasn't messaged me. It's Sunday afternoon now, more than a day since we got back from Windermere. I wonder what she's doing, what she's thinking, what problems she's solving.

Eventually, someone comes back on the line. I re-explain Okie's situation and then listen as he speaks, my heart thumping, my pen struggling to note down everything he's saying quickly enough.

I quickly end the call, jumping up from the sofa.

I dial Mr Adeyemi's number immediately.

'Hello?'

'Hi, Mr Adeyemi, it's Adam. Okie's maths tutor.'

There's a pause. 'The situation hasn't changed, Adam. I'm sorry, but—'

'Wait, it's not about that,' I gabble, desperate for him to listen to me. 'Well, it is, but I'm not offering anything, I promise. I've just spoken to a charity called Autisome, and they've got educational grants that cover exam fees for students in Okie's *exact* position. The money is literally sitting there, waiting for you to claim it. It'd cover his fees, and—'

'Hold on.' I hear Mr Adeyemi close a door. My heart is pounding. 'You contacted who?'

'A charity called Autisome, they're—'

'Why did you do that?'

I flounder; I didn't think he'd ask. 'I just — I felt like I couldn't leave things as they were. It would be such a shame.' Words are tumbling out of my mouth. 'I'm sorry if I've crossed a line. I thought it was worth checking what was out there, what Okie might be entitled to.'

'What's the charity called?' His voice is level, clipped.

'Autisome,' I say, pronouncing it the way the man on the phone did: like 'autism' and 'comb' mixed together. I spell it for him. 'I think it's worth looking into. It's called the Brighter Futures grant.'

Mr Adeyemi is silent for a second. He sighs. 'Adam, I appreciate your efforts. I'll think about it, but I really don't know if now is the right time.'

'But you will think about it?' I hold my breath.

I hear him smile down the phone. 'I will think about it.'

I ring off and punch the air, letting out a cheer that sends Old Sausage flying off the sofa and under the TV stand.

Yes! *Yes*. OK, so it's not a definitive answer, but it's one step closer than we've ever been. I pace through to the kitchen and back again. This is all thanks to Eve. I feel like a part of her has rubbed off on me: look at me, getting things done!

I pour myself a glass of water and stand at the back door. The heat is waning slightly: it's cooler than it has been in weeks. I pull out my phone, I have to message her. I have to tell her the news.

The latest message on our WhatsApp chat is mine, from yesterday. Two blue ticks. I lock my phone and pass it from hand to hand. I should go and speak to her face-to-face. I *want* to speak to her face-to-face.

I step out into the garden and peer over the fences. Her back door is open. I remember what happened last time I went over there. What if she doesn't want to see me? What if the Tryst notification made her think I was seeing someone, or multiple people?

I go back into the kitchen and lean against the counter. As I'm thinking, Old Sausage emerges from under the TV stand and pads towards me.

'Hello, lovely girl,' I say, scratching her behind the ears. An idea forms. 'Shall we go and see Eve? I'm sure she's got some leftover takeaway she'd like to give you.'

Old Sausage meows, and before I can think, I pick her up and walk down the garden and through the gate. She bobs in my arms as we go, her head turning this way and that, taking in the peeling wood on the backs of the fences and the bushes hanging over the alleyway.

We arrive at Eve's gate. I hold the handle for a moment. I'm going to ask if she wants to go for a drink. I'll swallow my pride and just *ask* her. That way she'll know I'm not seeing anybody else.

Before I can chicken out, I pull the handle down and carefully push the gate open. I take a step into the garden and immediately I can see her through the open back door, standing in the living room beyond the kitchen.

I open my mouth to call her — I want to announce my presence as soon as possible to avoid a repeat of last time — but someone steps out from behind the wall that partially divides the two rooms. A man, in a jacket and jeans. He's good-looking, in a polished kind of way. An uneasy feeling washes over me.

I go to turn around, but he takes another step towards her and I can't look away. He brushes a hair behind her ear and then leans down, bringing his lips to her cheek before running them down her neck.

I back quickly out of the garden, feeling sick, knocking my shoulder on the fence. I move fast, striding down the alleyway, stopping only to put Old Sausage down when she protests against my speed by digging her claws into my arm.

By the time I get back inside I'm panting, and my stomach is twisting in on itself.

I never asked her if she was single, did I? I didn't have the balls.

How could I have been so stupid?

CHAPTER 48

Eve

The Florina offices feel different. I am used to striding in here with purpose, confident in my position and abilities, but now I feel like a visitor — a shamed visitor who has brought the company into disrepute.

Heads swivel as I weave between the desks. I naturally head for my office, but the door is closed, and behind it I see Kirsty, silhouetted, sitting at my desk.

Where do *I* sit? I hover for a moment, unwilling to knock on her door and ask why she isn't in Dev's office.

'Hello, Eve.' Brenda emerges from the staff kitchen, her eyes boggling.

'Hi, Brenda,' I say, hesitant, wondering what she's going to say. Her comments at Dev's leaving party, about me climbing to the top, make me think she'll be happy that I've so royally fucked things up.

She keeps walking until she reaches an empty desk. Meeting my eye briefly, she pulls out the chair. 'I think this is your seat.'

I move to where she is and sit down. 'Thank you.'

She hovers for a second, her mouth puckered. 'It was very unfortunate, what happened.'

'It was.' I pull at my fringe.

'I'm sure you didn't do it on purpose.'

I look up at her, and she gives me a small smile. 'No. But I did sort of deserve it,' I say, honestly.

She stares at my shoulder for a second, and then reaches out and gives my hand a pat. 'That's OK,' she says, and walks away, back over to her desk.

I log into my computer, my eyes stinging, and check my emails.

At the top, timestamped just two minutes ago, is one from Dev.

Subject: Welcome back, Eve
From: Dev.kalhora@florina.co.uk
To: Eve.slater@florina.co.uk
Cc: Kirsty.McClure@florina.co.uk
08:12:24 — 25 July 2022

Hi Eve,

Welcome back. I hope you had a nice break. Taking a brief hiatus from my baby-induced work ban to give you an update on our situation. Thought it might be best if this came from me.

As you know, we've conducted an internal investigation into the events at the expo in Dublin. Interviews with other members of staff have suggested that there was some interpersonal confrontation surrounding my paternity leave cover, but it has been almost impossible to find any physical evidence against you to support these claims. We are preparing to close the investigation now, but there are still some outstanding pieces of information that we are waiting for before we do so.

I have cc'd in your new manager, Kirsty, so that she is aware of the preliminary outcome. I am sure she has already filled you in, but she will be using your office for the time being, and you should take a free seat in the hot-desking area. For

now, please leave the two campaigns you were working on before
your holiday and liaise with Kirsty regarding your task list.
    Best,
    Dev

I stand up slowly and tuck my chair under my desk. I walk across the office floor, keeping my eyes level, my head up. When I get to Kirsty's door, I knock.

'Come in.'

I open the door. She's brought her chair in here, and has put her photos up on the desk. She looks up at me and smiles politely.

'Eve. Nice break?'

I stand in the doorway, just watching her. She meets my gaze. 'Come in. Sit down.'

I leave the door open and move towards her. I reach my hand across the desk, offering it. 'Congratulations.'

She blinks, her eyes moving from my hand to my face. And then she takes it.

'Thank you.'

The moment our hands meet, and our eyes lock, hurt radiates through my chest. My friend, why did we do this?

'I hope you fucking smash it,' I say.

She looks at me. Her eyes fill with tears. When she speaks, it's a whisper. 'Me too.'

I nod and drop her hand.

'I'm leaving,' I say, simply.

She smiles sadly. 'I thought you might be.'

There's a brief beat of silence, and the normalcy of ringing phones and muted chatter drifts through the door. 'Can I say one more thing?'

She raises an eyebrow. 'One last piece of advice from the boss?'

'Sort of.' I hesitate. 'Don't . . . don't do it again, will you?' I sweep my arm behind me, towards the desks through the glass wall. 'There are better ways to do it. Better ways to . . . to win.'

Kirsty smiles at me and then shakes her head, looking down at the desk. *Her* desk. 'No.' She raises her eyes to meet mine and draws a long breath. 'No, I won't.'

I know she means it. I push my bag up onto my shoulder. 'Yeah, me neither.'

* * *

'No, I *quit*,' I say loudly, pushing my headphone deeper into my ear. Someone barges past me, running for the tram, and I swear under my breath.

'Can you hear what she's saying, Mike?' Mum looms her face closer to the camera.

'No, it's all muffled.' Dad taps at the phone screen. 'Have you got your finger over the sound thingy again?'

'Oh.' The phone jiggles, and Mum's finger appears in the top corner of the camera, where it usually is. 'Say something, Evie.'

'Hello,' I say.

'Oh, *that's* better.' She beams.

'What were you saying, love?' Dad leans forward, his tanned face creased in concentration.

'I quit my job,' I say for the eighth time.

'Goodness!' Mum peers at me. 'And are you . . . OK about that?'

I smile. 'Yeah, I'm OK about it.'

'Well good for you, love.' Dad folds his arms across his chest. 'You know, I've been reading on Facebook that Aldi are hiring managers. Maybe you could look there.'

'Maybe,' I say. 'I think I'm going to work for myself, though.'

'Like a builder?' Mum asks, her head cocked.

'Exactly like a builder, but without any building.'

Dad nods. 'That sounds lovely.'

I laugh, suddenly appreciating their unconditional, if uncomprehending, support. 'Yeah. Anyway, how are you guys?'

Dad rattles on for ten minutes about an acquaintance of his, who got swept out to sea and drowned after eating three bowls of calamari. I listen, trying to picture their life out there.

'So I was thinking I might come and visit,' I say, once he's finished.

'Oh, wonderful!' Mum beams again and looks to my dad. 'Isn't that lovely, Mike?'

'I'll take you to meet the boys at the pub!' Dad says. 'One of them used to work in telesales, you'll have loads to talk about.'

'Can't wait,' I say.

I tell them I'll look at flights, and they give me a video tour of the spare bedroom, which I've seen approximately sixty-four times on all the other video tours we've done.

'Plenty of room for a boyfriend, too.' Mum winks.

'Got one lined up for me, have you?'

Dad tuts. 'Don't pry, Carrie.'

'I'd just like to see her settled, that's all.' She looks at me sadly. 'Is there really nobody?'

I open my mouth to speak, but my usual retort gets stuck in my throat. For so long, my mantra has been *don't need it, don't want it* when it comes to relationships. But now . . .

From across the tram station, I spot a familiar figure. It's Graham, striding purposefully towards the office. Somehow, I know I won't see him again.

I close my mouth and shrug, trying to look nonchalant. My pulse quickens at the thought of someone else. 'We'll see.'

CHAPTER 49

Eve

I take a deep breath before knocking.

I hear his footsteps coming through from the kitchen, and then he opens the door, and he's standing there.

'Hey,' I say. 'Can I come in?'

He hesitates. 'Yeah.' He walks up the hallway and into the kitchen, and I shut the door behind us.

The kitchen is markedly devoid of baby things. Benny's bottles are gone from the countertop, his carrier isn't in the corner. If you didn't know, you'd think Will lived alone.

He turns around and leans against the sink.

'I'm here to apologise,' I say, not sitting down. 'I've been selfish, and distracted, and my priorities have been really, really out of whack.'

Will doesn't respond.

I swallow before continuing. 'I've been so caught up in getting to the top and making myself untouchable . . . but I'm not untouchable. Losing you, like this, has hurt so much. And I did it to myself. I deserved it.'

Will shakes his head. He speaks quietly. 'It wasn't a punishment. This distance was what I needed, not what you deserved.'

'I needed it too,' I say. 'I might not have wanted it, but I needed it.'

We stand in silence for a moment, the ticking of the kitchen clock the only sound. A picture of Nina and Benny is pinned to the fridge, and I study it, wondering how it makes Will feel, seeing that every time he makes his breakfast.

Will follows my gaze and breathes out, his breath juddering. 'It's all such a mess.'

I walk towards him and hold out my arms. He hesitates, and then lets me hold him for a moment.

'Where are they?' I ask, when he pulls away.

He swipes at his eyes. 'At Nina's mum's.'

I nod. 'What happened?'

'I think she's got postnatal depression.' The bags under his eyes are so pronounced, he looks like a different person. 'She just drinks and cries.'

Solutions clamour around in my head. Go and speak to her, book a therapist, call the GP, get community support, hire a childminder, take some time off work.

'I'm really sorry, Will,' is what I actually say.

'I miss them.' His eyes pool with tears again. 'I really miss them.'

My heart twists as I think how lonely he must be. His wife — his best friend — and his son, leaving him here alone. And me, too.

'I know,' I say.

I pull out a bar stool and sit down. For a long while, I ask questions and Will answers them. He tells me how Nina stopped getting out of bed, how she lay there while the baby cried, how he couldn't bear to come home from work but spent every hour he wasn't home worried about what was going on. He explains how they fought, how lost sleep made him irritable and irrational. When he talks about the day she left, his eyes fill again.

'She wasn't the same person,' he chokes. 'She just wasn't, Eve. I know mental illness, it's my fucking job. But Jesus . . .' He shakes his head, as if he wants to expel the memory from his mind. 'I can't fix this one.'

'I can't even imagine.'

Will looks at me for a second, and then raises his eyes to the ceiling, chuckling.

'What?'

'Go on.' He raises an eyebrow.

'I don't know what you mean.'

'Give me your gold. Solve my problems.'

I shake my head. 'I'm not here to do that.'

'No.' He hoists himself up onto the counter and runs a hand through his hair. 'I know you're not.' He looks at me seriously. 'Thank you.'

'Any time. I mean it.'

Will picks up a pen that's lying by the toaster and starts twiddling it between his fingers. The gesture reminds me of Adam, and I look away.

'You know what's annoying?' he says.

'What?'

'Now that you're here, I really do want your advice.' He glances at me hopefully, a lopsided smile on his face.

'Tough shit.' I grin.

'Wow.' He widens his eyes. 'Where is Eve and what have you done with her?'

'It's taking every last drop of my resolve,' I say. 'Trust me.'

'Hmm.'

I sit, biting my tongue. It's hard. 'I've got an idea,' I say.

'Good. Give it to me.'

'Well, I promised myself that when I came here I'd just listen,' I explain. 'I'd give you the floor.'

'I appreciate it.'

'Yeah.' I hesitate. 'But also, I've got so much stuff in my head that I want to give you and I feel like I might not sleep if I don't tell you what I think.'

Will laughs loudly. '*There* she is.'

'But,' I hold up my hand, 'I want you to take it or leave it. I don't just want to . . . push it on you. So could you give me half an hour in your office?'

He narrows his eyes. 'Sounds suspish.'

It's my turn to laugh. 'I promise I won't mess with your work and get you sacked.'

'I know it's your specialist skill.'

I stick my finger up at him.

'Go ahead.' He nods towards the stairs.

In Will's attic-cum-office, I sit at the desk. His laptop is open, and I start a new Word document and open the internet browser.

I do my research: support for new mothers, postnatal depression therapy groups, couples communication tips, workplace rules for those supporting someone with a mental illness. I write out the names and numbers and websites, listing them in order of helpfulness. It takes me almost forty-five minutes, but Will doesn't interrupt me. When I'm done, I print what I've collected and fold the pages in half.

When I get back down to the kitchen, Will has put the kettle on.

'Here you go.' I hand him the paper.

He goes to open it, but I put my hand on his arm. 'Not now. Save it for when you feel like you want my advice.'

He smiles at me. 'I could just call you.'

'I can't leave this house without offloading.' I shrug. 'What's your diagnosis for that?'

He shakes his head, laughing. 'I don't think the world has quite got words for you yet, mate.'

I take over the tea-making duties and Will goes through to the living room. I bring our cups through and sit next to him on the sofa.

'I missed you,' I say. 'Like, a lot.'

'I missed you, too,' he says, and I can see that he means it.

* * *

263

It's still morning, so I decide to walk home, moving slowly along the streets in the last remnants of the heatwave. People are milling everywhere; the upcoming weather forecast has reminded them that the sun isn't to be taken for granted. It'll disappear again soon enough.

I am filled with a strange sense of calm, like the feeling I get when I finish on the exercise bike and my heart rate slows as the endorphins kick in. I reflect on what I've gained and what I've lost. I feel like I've been recalibrated, like my vision has been adjusted. Jess and Will are what's important. *People* are what's important. Kirsty is heart-breaking collateral damage from my own inability to see that.

I pass by a pet shop window. Inside are rows of tiny collars, some with bells, some patterned, some plain. I step inside without thinking, drawn to one at the back of the display: a bright orange tweed band with tiny palm trees all over it.

Palmgroves.

I take it to the till and pay, my mind somewhere else. I reject a carrier bag, and step out onto the street with the collar threaded through my hands. I bend it between my fingers as I keep walking, my pace getting faster now. This is important. *This* is important.

I don't know how I didn't see it before.

CHAPTER 50

Adam

The leather of the chair squeaks loudly as I shuffle in my seat. The room is big and airy, and I feel shrunken in the middle of it, like someone could overlook me if they came in.

A bead of sweat rolls down my back. Please, please, please . . .

The door opens, and Janet, the bank manager, comes back in.

'Right, Mr Parks.' She sits down opposite me and taps at her computer. 'I'll run the checks before I give you a definitive answer, but . . .' She hits enter and waits a moment, and then sits back in her chair. 'Right, yes, OK. Your earnings qualify you for the mortgage and the loan. Do you want to proceed?'

I have to stop myself from jumping up from my chair and cheering. Mine! The house is going to be *mine*. Granted, the interest I'll be paying is obscene, but god, it feels good. I want to tell Janet I love her.

'Yes, please,' I say.

She prints off some forms, which I sign, and runs through a list of questions and some legal stuff with me. The whole process takes less than an hour, and then I'm out on the street, clutching a plastic wallet in my hand and feeling like I've just had my entire life fixed.

I call Katie.

'Hi, Adam,' she answers on the third ring. She must have re-added my number.

'Hey, how are you?'

'Good, thanks. I'm glad you called, actually. I've spoken to an estate agent and the houses on our street are generally worth at least fifteen percent more than ours was when we bought it. He thinks he can get it on the market for—'

'I know,' I interrupt.

'Oh? Have you spoken to someone?'

'I've had it valued,' I say, unable to stop the satisfaction from seeping into my voice.

'That's great!' She sounds happy. 'Brilliant. How much was it worth? I'm happy to go with whichever estate agent you think is best. I think Stanley and Robson—'

I interrupt her again. 'We're not selling it, Katie. I'm buying it. I'll have it all sorted by the end of the week, and you'll have your equity by the start of next month.'

'You're—' She hesitates. 'Adam, no offence, but are you sure you can afford this?'

'I can afford it,' I say tersely, and then take a deep breath. 'I've sorted it.'

She's silent for a moment. I meander down a side-street and sit down on a bench.

'Well, that's good,' she says eventually. 'I'm happy for you.'

'Yeah. Me too.'

'Thanks,' she says, misinterpreting. I meant that I was happy for myself.

'I meant . . .' I stop myself. 'Yeah. Good luck with everything, Katie.'

'You too,' she says, and there's a hint of sadness in her voice. 'It was a great six years.'

'For the most part.'

When she speaks again, it's the first time I've heard regret from her since everything happened. 'I'm sorry it ended the way it did.'

I shrug, even though she can't see me. 'Shit happens, doesn't it?'

* * *

Old Sausage and I decide to treat ourselves to a takeaway and a movie night.

'I shouldn't be doing this,' I say to her as I tear a piece of pepperoni pizza from its box. 'My mortgage payments have just doubled.'

I pick up the remote and start flicking through the library of films on the TV.

'What shall we watch, then?' I ask her. '*Aristocats*?'

She looks at me scathingly.

'Sorry. OK, what about . . .' I keep flicking, and somehow end up on the Romance section. One of the thumbnails features a woman who looks a bit like Eve. I hit play and sink back into the sofa.

'Am I obsessed?' I ask Old Sausage through a mouthful of pizza. 'It's not normal this, is it?'

The film begins, but I can't really concentrate. I know she's there, or somewhere near here, being funny and serious and fierce and soft. With her boyfriend and his tailored jackets and smart shoes and slicked-back hair.

But I *felt* something that night, I know I did. And I know she did too.

I pull out my phone, and then drop it back down on the sofa. I just got out of a long-term relationship. I'm independent for the first time in over half a decade. Why am I pining over a girl I barely know who clearly has a boyfriend? Do I enjoy embarrassing myself?

No, I decide, but my hand is reaching for my phone. Old Sausage eyes me warningly. *Don't do it, idiot*, she seems to be saying.

I tap onto the boys' group chat.

Me: *What you all up to?*

Piotr: *Have you text her?*

Bil: *Yes, have you???*

Me: *Obviously not!*

Piotr: *Why?*

Ferg: *How come?*

Me: *Guys*

Me: *Can I remind you*

Me: *She was literally necking someone else in her kitchen*

Piotr: *Why are you messaging in tiny chunks like that?*

Piotr: *How do you know you've not got the wrong end of the stick? He might have been getting something out of her eye.*

Me: *He was *not* getting something out of her eye. There's no way I got the wrong end of the stick.*

Fergus: *You won't know if you've got the wrong end of the stick unless you *look* at the stick.*

Bil: *Deep, Ferg*

Me: *I'm not messaging her. It's invasive and rude and inappropriate.*

Bil: *Anything else? You sure it's not intrusive, too?*

Fergus: *Intrusive is a synonym of invasive.*

Bil: *Shut up, Ferg. Whose side are you on?*

Fergus: *Sorry.*

Fergus: *MESSAGE HER.*

I lock my phone and look back to the TV. The actress I thought looked a bit like Eve doesn't really; her fringe is less unruly, and her eyes are brown. She's sitting in an American diner, and the man sitting opposite her is shouting. 'Why couldn't you have just been honest with me?'

Yes, I think, remembering how her hand felt in mine as we lay in bed. *Why couldn't you?*

Suddenly, there's a knock at the door.

I drop the pizza crust I'm holding back into the box and stand up, brushing crumbs off myself, before walking over to see who it is.

CHAPTER 51

Adam

I open the door and my breath catches in my throat. She looks different; her hair is shorter, her eyes lined differently. She's wearing jeans that are worn at the knee and a pair of fashionably-greying white shoes.

For a moment, I can't speak. I don't know what to say. It seems like she doesn't, either — she just stares at me, her mouth partly open.

Eventually, I find my words. 'Chloe.'

'Hey.' She cocks her head to one side and smiles. 'Long time no see.'

The phrase is so vastly out of proportion with everything that has transpired that I don't know how to respond. I step back and she walks into the hallway.

'Let's go out into the garden.' It's just before sunset, and the house is making me feel claustrophobic. Big conversations, if possible, should always happen outdoors.

I pull a spare chair from the kitchen and heave it onto the patio, positioning it next to mine. I sit down heavily, and she perches on the edge of her seat.

'So.' She shrugs in a playful way. 'You've been ignoring me.'

'If you're here to rub it in, don't bother. I got what was coming to me.'

Her face drops and she leans forward. 'Jesus, Adam, no. You didn't.'

I laugh, tipping my head up towards the sky. 'OK. Sure.' I let my gaze land on her again. 'So why are you here?'

'You've moved Hugh,' she says simply. 'Fair enough if you don't want to see me, but at least give him the opportunity.'

My pulse slows. Of course. 'Shit. I'm sorry. I didn't think.'

'That's OK.' She smiles. 'You've had a lot going on, by the sounds of things.'

'Yeah.'

We lapse into silence. The sun shines lazily just above the horizon, casting long shadows across the garden.

'I've really fucking missed you, Ad,' Chloe says suddenly, her eyes welling.

I shake my head. Renewed sadness pools in my stomach. What is there to be angry about anymore? Katie's gone. 'Holding a grudge is really exhausting, you know,' I say, flashing her a smile.

She kicks me under the table. 'You're not made for it. You're too nice.' She looks over across the fences, and then leans forward and takes my hand. 'I'm sorry. I'm really, really sorry.'

I squeeze her hand. 'Don't be. You were right.'

'Fuck being right.' She pulls away. 'It's not about being right. It's about being there for your best friend in whatever capacity they need you. You didn't *need* me to do what I did. You needed me to support you. You could figure everything else out on your own.'

I feel tears welling at the back of my nose and I cough. 'I really couldn't see it. I couldn't.'

I'm transported back six months, to the last time I saw her. A dark, wintery evening at Piotr's house; me and Katie, the boys, Bil's girlfriend at the time, and Chloe. We were playing Cards Against Humanity and Katie wasn't concentrating; she was on her phone, haphazardly throwing random cards into the middle without looking whenever she was told to.

'Batman?' It was my turn to judge, and I looked around the table, laughing. 'Who put Batman? It doesn't even make sense.'

Nobody answered. Katie, noticing the silence, looked up from her phone. 'Hm? Oh, it was probably me.'

'Aw, come on.' I nudged her. 'At least play properly.'

She didn't say anything. She just fixed me with a look that told me to shut up.

Piotr coughed awkwardly. Chloe stood up. 'I'm getting another beer. Adam, you want to come?'

I stood up and put my cards down, and we moved into the kitchen as the next round of the game continued without us. I went straight for the fridge, but Chloe blocked my path.

'When are you going to say something?' Her eyes were slightly unfocused, and she gripped the counter for balance.

'What?'

'Well, the way I see it, you've got two choices.' She held up her fingers. 'One, tell her she's got to stop being such a moody cow all the time, or two, drop her and find someone who actually respects you.'

It took me a moment to catch up. 'Are you talking about Katie?'

Chloe rolled her eyes. 'Yes, I'm talking about Katie. She's a really crappy person.'

Anger flared through me immediately, and I straightened up defensively. 'Where the fuck has this come from?'

She laughed. 'Adam! Jesus Christ.'

'What?'

'Open your eyes. She treats you like shit.'

I shook my head. 'We've been together nearly six years, Chloe. You've never said anything like this before. Why now? You're just drunk. Leave it.'

'No. I mean, yes, I am drunk. I am. But I can't keep quiet anymore. I'm sick of watching her walk all over you.'

I stepped backwards, moving towards the door. Before I got there, I turned back around. 'We're really happy, thanks so much for checking. We've got a beautiful house, we're in a really good place in our careers, our lives. Don't project your insecurities onto me.'

Chloe stumbled sideways as though she'd been slapped. 'You're so bloody *careful*, Adam. You know the sensible choice isn't always the right choice, don't you?'

I turned around again and left, walking through the living room and slamming the front door behind me.

Katie hadn't asked what had happened, and I hadn't brought it up. She'd come home a couple of hours later while I was staring at the wall and had slid into bed next to me. We'd woken up the next day, gone to work, and life had continued.

I'd never thought to wonder why she hadn't brought it up. At the time, I'd just been angry at Chloe and glad I wouldn't have to repeat her words to the woman I loved. Now I wonder if she didn't ask because she knew what she might hear.

Now, Chloe sits in front of me, her face sober and sad. 'I'm not glad that I was right, you know. I'm glad she's gone, but I'm not glad I was right.'

'I know.'

'And anyway.' She sits up and her voice lifts. I notice her change in tone and immediately smile; everything becomes a joke with Chloe, nothing is ever serious for long. 'I'm not here for you, am I? I'm here because you're hiding your brother from me.'

'He has missed you.' I grin.

'Of course he has. But not as much as I've missed him.'

Chloe visited Hugh at least once a week up until our argument. When I moved him, it hadn't even occurred to me that I hadn't told her the new address. I assumed she was staying away because our friendship had fallen apart.

'Why didn't you just ask the boys?' I ask.

'I did! They said it would have to come from you.'

I smile. 'Fair enough. I'm not his gatekeeper, though. You can go whenever you want.' I pull out my phone and send her the address. 'There. Rosewood Residential.'

She stands up and holds her arms out, and I wrap her in a hug. 'I'm sorry, Chloe.'

She pulls back, confused. 'What for?'

'For choosing her over you. Bros before hoes, or hoes before . . . oh, god, nobody's a hoe, I don't know. Whatever. I'm sorry.'

She throws her head back and laughs. 'Shut up. Now, are you going to offer me a drink, or what?'

CHAPTER 52

Eve

I'm still clutching the collar in my fist as I slide my key into the door, trying to catch my breath. I dump my bag in the hallway and hurry through to the kitchen, yanking the window open to cool the air before rummaging in the cupboard for the wrapping paper.

I'm measuring a sheet on the dining table when I hear the noise through the window. I move over to the back door and open it wide, and there she is. Sitting on the patio and staring at me.

'Hey.' I stand back and she pads softly inside, already purring before my hand makes contact with her back. 'I got something for you.'

I look at the collar on the table, still unwrapped. All the way home, I planned how this would go: I'd give the present to Adam, let him see that I cared, that I could open myself up to something. Now that I've thought it over, the Tryst sounds are a sign of nothing, the text message more than likely a check-in from a friend. If I don't do this — if I don't let him see what I want, how I'm feeling — how will he know?

But as I look at Old Sausage, her scabby ears and her matted fur, I waver. I want to give it to *her*. I want to show her that she's loved.

I unclip the collar and slip it around her neck. Immediately, she looks brighter. She looks like she has a place to call home.

'Come on then.' I tickle her gently under the chin. 'Shall we go and see what Adam thinks?'

I pick her up, my heart hammering, and step out onto the patio. Three gardens down, I can see him, sitting under an umbrella. I pause for a moment and take in the sight of him: soft, curly hair, out-of-control stubble. That gigantic smile. Is he smiling at me?

I take another step forward, heading towards the back gate, but I freeze. There's someone else — a girl — she's standing up and stretching her arms out towards him.

He buries his face into her shoulder. Their voices carry over the fences.

'I'm sorry, Chloe.'

'What for?'

'For choosing her over you.'

I clutch Old Sausage closer to me and stumble backwards, my chest tight, until I'm back inside the house.

* * *

For choosing her over you.

I am on the sofa again, holding an unwilling Old Sausage to my chest. So Chloe is his ex-girlfriend. The woman who broke his heart. I didn't see her face, she had her back to me, but I'm sure it's the woman I saw in his hallway the first time we met. And now she's back. He's apologising. They're making up. *Choosing.* Who did he choose? Me? No, that's ridiculous. We held hands through a pillow wall, worse things have happened to relationships.

But what else could he mean? Was he supposed to see her, the night we went to Windermere? Has he confessed that he felt something between us, but that he doesn't want to pursue it?

I shake my head. Stupid, this is all stupid. He's a player, that's all, just like the rest of them. He'll have cheated on her, she'll have left, and now he's grovelling to get her back.

It's so obvious I want to scream. How could I be so gullible? *Lovely* Adam, *kind* Adam. Of course it was all a game. It always is.

Tears are tickling at the back of my nose, and I swallow them down. I will *not* cry about this. I promised I'd never let another man do this to me. I promised I'd never let another man fuck me over, and I haven't. It was a near miss, but I've done it. I've protected myself again, guarded against all the unpleasant possibilities. I've been proven right.

So why doesn't it feel good?

There's a knock at the door. I stand up and peer through the peephole. It's him. He's here.

I rearrange my face, pulling my shoulders back, and swing the door open.

'Eve.' He looks breathless, his eyebrows raised. 'Hi. Sorry, I—'

'What's up?' I cut in, blocking the doorway.

'I have to say something.' He coughs, as though he's rehearsed this. 'I–I've been in relationships where there's been cheating before. My ex . . . I'm familiar with it, I mean. There's—'

'I'm sorry, I'm not following you,' I say, raising my eyebrows. My blood is thundering in my ears.

He takes a deep breath. 'I can't do it. I can't let someone else get hurt.'

Something inside me sags. It's true, then. They're back together. I feign a look of confusion. 'I have no idea what you're talking about.'

He looks at me then, his eyes dark and vulnerable. 'You and me. I mean, what I felt in Windermere—'

I launch my final blow with everything I have, watching as my words slice through the air. 'There is no you and me, Adam. Whatever you thought you felt, you were on your own.' I go to push the door closed, but my thoughts are still bubbling to the surface, my defences fully engaged. The me I try to rein in, the one who stands between my softest parts and the outside world, is running ship again. 'But you're right,' I spit. 'There's nothing worse than a cheat.'

CHAPTER 53

Adam

Whatever you felt, you were on your own.

The words thunder around my head like boulders, knocking everything I thought off balance. I sit outside under the umbrella and stare at the chair where Chloe sat yesterday.

'So, any danger of moving on any time soon?' she'd asked, before shaking her head. She'd placed her beer on the table. 'Sorry, I know you don't take these things lightly.'

'No, it's OK.' I'd surprised myself with how relaxed I was talking about it, how quickly I felt able to discuss a future without Katie. 'I thought there was someone, but I think she's got a boyfriend.'

Chloe had leaned forward in her seat. 'Who?'

'A girl two doors down.' I'd nodded over the fences. 'We . . . well, I certainly feel something, and I'm pretty sure she does too. But the other day I went over and she was . . . she was kissing someone. In her kitchen.'

Chloe had leaned back, letting a thin stream of air out through her teeth. 'Are you sure?'

'Unless he was sucking snake poison out of her neck, I'm sure.'

'Might it have been a fling? You two weren't serious, were you?'

'God, no. We've never even kissed. Never . . . I don't know, I just felt it. But maybe I was wrong.'

She'd shaken her head. 'What if, though? What if it was just some one-night thing? Or some guy she was casually sleeping with?'

The thought hadn't occurred to me. 'What if it was?'

'Well, wouldn't it be a waste to chuck what you're feeling away on a presumption?'

I'd thought about it for a moment.

'Come on. At least ask her.' Chloe had smiled mischievously. 'What do you have to lose?'

* * *

And then I'd gone over there, and I'd said all those things about hating cheating, hoping that she'd say she was single, there was no one.

But she hadn't.

She'd told me, in a voice that sliced right through me, that she felt nothing for me. She'd told me that she hated cheaters.

So I was right. She isn't single, and I've misread everything.

Old Sausage appears over the fence and leaps onto the patio. At first, I don't recognise her, but the matted ears give her away.

'Come here,' I say, reaching out my hand. 'What's this?'

I feel the collar around her neck. Orange, with tiny palm trees. My heart rate quickens. *Fucking Palmgroves*.

It's nothing, I think as I run my fingers along the tweed fabric. She felt nothing, and this is nothing, too. A quirky collar. She probably didn't even think about it.

My heart feels so heavy, I can't focus on the marking that's in front of me. Okie's paper: it's probably all correct anyway. What's the point?

I sit back in my chair, surprised at myself. When have I been like this? I've never brushed the importance of a student's work off like this before. Never been so readily careless.

I lean forward again, forcing my eyes to read through the questions and answers. But it's no use. I pull out my phone and pull up the Florina website. She said she was having problems at work, her name might not even be on here. I scroll through until I find 'Our Manchester Team'.

I spot her immediately: dark hair, bright eyes, straight shoulders. A fierce, defiant look on her black-and-white face.

Eve Slater — Head of Digital Marketing

I tap into Instagram.

I type *Eve Slater*.

There are so many of them, and I almost give up. What am I doing? This is over; it never was anything in the first place. I go to close the app, but my eyes land on her face, a few names down, past the blue ticks and bots. *Manchester, UK.*

I tap into her profile, keeping my thumb steady to avoid pressing anything I shouldn't. The majority of her feed is work stuff: campaigns, pictures of flowers, edited posters of inspirational marketing advertisements. But there, a bit further down, is a selfie with three people in it. Eve's in the middle, the girl on the right holding the phone to take the picture. To her left is a man. *Him.*

He's been tagged: *Graham Holden.*

The image of him kissing her in the kitchen the other day, the way she'd tilted her head back, flashes in my mind. I tap into his profile automatically.

He posts much more regularly than her; almost daily pictures of nights out and Manchester scenery. I can't see Eve in any of the pictures, but the most recent post, dated just two days ago, is of him with a tall, red-haired woman. He has his arm around her waist, and she's kissing his cheek.

The caption reads: *Out with the old, in with the new . . . time to move on to pastures greener ;)*

I drop my phone onto the table. It's him. It's definitely him; I'd recognise that slicked-back hair and tailored blazer anywhere. But what does this mean? This was two days ago, posted shortly after I'd seen them in the kitchen. Had they broken up? Oh, god. This throws my conversation with her last night into a whole new light. She's mourning a breakup, and I'm blathering on to her about cheating.

I run my hands through my hair. But she still said it, didn't she? She felt nothing. I'm on my own with my feelings.

I pick up my phone again. Even if she feels nothing, she deserves an apology. Shakily, I tap out a message.

> *Hey. I'm so sorry about last night. It was wrong of me to assume and accuse you. I get it if you don't want to speak to me anymore. X*

I wait a few moments and watch as the message is delivered, and then read.

She doesn't reply.

CHAPTER 54

Adam

I wake up the next morning to Old Sausage pawing at my chest. It's early; the light is just beginning to filter through the curtains.

I make a coffee, and then another coffee, and then another. I watch the clock until nine, and then get on my bike and pedal over to Hugh's, purposefully going the long way so I don't have to cycle past Eve's house.

Hugh is having a wash when I arrive, so I wait outside until he's done. It's cooler today, so once he's ready, I take him outside for a walk around the garden.

'Have I got an update and a half for you, pal,' I say as I push him down the ramp into the shaded woodland area. I park him up next to a bench under a large oak tree and sit down heavily next to him. He looks around happily, and I feel a sudden urge to hold him tight, squeeze him to me and never let him go.

I focus on my story.

'Right, so there's this girl, called Eve. I think I've mentioned her.' I tell him everything, about how Old Sausage came to visit us both, and how we united to try and get her home. How we went on an adventure to the Lake District, and spent the night together, and how she spoke to me and shared herself, even though I could tell it was hard. I tell him about how I liked her, but she never felt anything for me at all. 'I told her about Mum and Dad,' I say. 'Do you know what she said?'

Hugh doesn't answer; he's mesmerised by the dancing light on the floor as the sun filters through the leaves.

'She said, "shit".' I laugh.

Hugh laughs too, and I ruffle his hair. 'Shit indeed, eh? But we've got each other, haven't we? I'll get over it.'

We set off again, walking around the flowerbeds and enjoying the fresh air until the sky begins to darken and foreign-looking clouds mill above our heads. The temperature drops, and I wrap my coat around Hugh's shoulders as the wind picks up. As we turn out of the gardens, I am conscious of the weight of my phone in my pocket, of wanting it to vibrate. I have to keep reminding myself that she doesn't want me. That even if she does respond to my message, it doesn't mean anything.

We pass Hugh's window, and Becky waves from where she's changing the beds. Hugh shrieks delightedly, and she laughs.

Back inside, we get Hugh set up in the day room, where they're doing a sensory stimulation session. Freshly cut flowers, trays of paint and twinkling lights are dotted around the space, and Hugh is instantly delighted. I intend to stay and join in, but Becky asks if she can have a word, so we go into Hugh's room, a familiar panic washing over me.

'Nothing to worry about,' she says, catching sight of my face. 'I just wanted to show you something.'

She reaches up to the top of the wardrobe, and my heart sinks.

'Any idea where this has come from?' She holds up the camera.

'I'm really sorry,' I say, but then I stop myself. Why am I sorry? What have I done wrong? I'm looking out for my brother; it's the one thing I should never apologise for. 'I had to.'

A half-smile tugs at Becky's lips. 'Adam, I get it. Hugh's a very lucky man.'

I look at her. 'Thanks. He's really lucky to have you, too. Until you jet off to Dubai.'

She shakes her head. 'I think I've changed my mind. Doing this . . . it's different to regular nursing. I'm thinking of specialising in brain injury care, working my way up to sister.'

'I can't imagine anyone better for the job,' I say, nudging her. 'Look at how Hugh is with you. I think he loves you more than he loves me.'

Her cheeks redden, and she looks away, her eyes landing on Hugh's bed. Hei Hei lies abandoned on his pillow, all but forgotten. 'It's funny,' Becky says, 'we all need change sometimes, don't we?'

I stare at the TV, where *Frozen* is paused, *Moana* a distant memory.

'Yeah,' I agree, a thought forming in my mind. 'Yeah, I think we do.'

My phone buzzes in my pocket and my hand flies for it. Becky raises her eyebrows.

'I'm sorry,' I say, my eyes searching the screen. *1 new message from Eve Cat Neighbour.* It vibrates again, and the number of messages grows. Dopamine floods my brain at the familiarity of it. 'I have to get this.'

She smiles. 'No worries. See you later?'

'Yes, sorry, thanks, Becky. Sorry,' I blather, my head spinning. As soon as she's gone, I unlock my phone.

No need to apologise

I'm sorry I was so rude

I know what you meant, if it's worth anything

About Windermere

But you're right, it's best we don't pursue it

*I'm not right for you, and I'm happy you're making a
go of things with Chloe again*

See you around for cat chats hopefully

The pieces fall into my brain slowly at first, and then in a
sudden rush. Oh, god. Oh god, oh god, oh god. Me and Chloe,
in the garden. She must have seen. She must have assumed . . .

The Tryst notification. I never told her Katie's name. I
went to her house and told her I didn't want to be involved in
another relationship that involved cheating. She'll have put it
all together and come up with . . .

Oh *god.*

* * *

As I cycle home, the sky breaks in two.

A fork of lightning illuminates the path in front of me,
bleaching everything white for the tiniest instant. And then,
just moments later, an ear-splitting crack vibrates the air
around me, and the heavens open.

I am drenched within seconds, my shirt stuck to my back
and my shoes full of water, and the path through the park
becomes a grey sludge of weeks of uninterrupted, sun-baked
dust. I wipe my eyes with one hand, my feet slipping on the
pedals, and almost fall, righting myself at the last second.

The smell of first rain is everywhere: that musky, clarify-
ing freshness. I feel suddenly like I've just woken up, like the
water has washed something from my eyes.

I emerge from the park onto the street — I should slow
down, there are sun-dress-clad pedestrians running in every
direction, their sandals slapping — and push down harder,
skidding round corners. I can't stop; this is important, I have
somewhere to be.

As the rain chills my skin, a fire burns in my chest.

We all need change sometimes, don't we?

By the time I arrive, my heart is pounding. I sling my bike
against the railings, clumsily fastening it with the lock, and
then run up the path and hammer on the door.

CHAPTER 55

Eve

That's it.

    That's where I've seen him before.

    I'm on Tryst, scrolling miserably through the gym photos and drooling emojis in my inbox, when I see his face again.

> *Adam. 34. Maths tutor; less than one mile away. AreyOu*
> *the x axis to my Y? I can be you're triangle dadddy.*
>   *Last active: two weeks ago.*

    I feel better about the WhatsApp I sent. He's obviously trying; he ignored the Tryst message he got when he was with me. This is obviously his attempt at reforming himself, getting rid of his player tendencies. Coming over here, explicitly stating that he didn't want to cheat . . . that was a brave move. He'll carry on with Chloe, and everything will go back to normal.

    What I felt in Windermere . . .

    Why does it still hurt? Why do I still feel like my heart has been ripped out of my chest? Why can't I forget the things he said, the way he made me feel? And I know I made him feel that way, too.

Even if he is a player, it changes nothing. I can slag him off in my head all I want, but he is kind. He's selfless, and caring, and — aside from the cheating — would never do anything to hurt someone. Those are the kinds of attributes you can't fake or cover up.

But me? I'm trying, but I am not selfless. I am not caring. I am driven, and pushy, and self-centred.

It's incompatibility, pure and simple.

The living room has grown dark over the past hour, and as I move to switch on the lamp, a flash of lightning startles me. The thunder follows, rumbling across the sky, and then the rain comes thick and heavy, smacking against the windows.

I close the back door and my heart feels heavy. The end of the heatwave, and the end of a journey.

I glance at the tiny window above the sink, Old Sausage's entryway when I'd closed the back door. I smile at the memories; that bloody cat. Something tells me that I could have closed every access point and she'd still have found a way inside. She knew what she wanted and she went for it. She's my kind of girl.

I pour a cup of tea and take it through to the living room. I am booting up my laptop, ready to pass the afternoon buried in self-assessment registration, when there's a frantic banging on the front door.

I rush through, my bare feet slipping on the wood. I pull open the front door, my mind full of potentials: someone has died, it's the police, something terrible has happened, maybe it's Adam . . .

And it is.

It's him.

He's standing on the doorstep, the rain falling in sheets around him. His hair drips, spiking his dark eyelashes and trickling down his neck. His shirt sleeves are rolled up, and the hair on his forearms is slicked against his skin.

I open my mouth to speak.

'You don't get to tell me what's good for me,' he says. He's panting, his mouth open slightly.

'What?'

'You can tell me to fuck off, but you don't get to tell me what's good for me.'

I stare at him, my heart fluttering in my chest. For a moment, I still can't get my words out. 'Will you come inside?'

He shakes his head, and a droplet of water lands on my arm. He runs his hand through his hair and it tangles wetly on top of his head. 'Not until you listen to me.'

I look at the rain around him, at the beads of water rolling down his forearms. 'Adam—'

'Just hear me out.' Beyond him I can see his bike, abandoned by the front fence.

'OK, I'm listening.'

'There is no Chloe.' He breathes heavily. 'I mean, no, there is, but it's not what you think. She's an old friend. I thought — I thought you and Graham—'

'*Graham*?' My head is spinning. What does he know about Graham?

'Your ex?' He blinks at me. Water puddles at his feet. 'I saw you both—'

A laugh starts in my tummy and bubbles upwards out of my throat. 'My ex? Oh, god. No.'

Adam looks confused. 'I saw you.'

My mind runs frantically backwards. He saw us? Where? I put myself in bed with Graham, the last time, what feels like forever ago. There's no way. More recently, then.

The kitchen.

'Please,' I ask again as the rain gets heavier, 'come inside. You're dripping wet.'

He looks like he's about to refuse again, but then he looks down at his hands, hanging by his sides, and at the individual droplets plinking steadily from each fingertip. 'OK, fine,' he says eventually, in a tone of voice that suggests he's desperately trying to stay on point and be assertive, but that it really isn't coming naturally to him.

He steps inside, and I step back to accommodate him. Immediately, a dark patch begins forming on the rug beneath his feet. He looks down again. A smile tugs at the corner of his mouth. 'Jesus Christ, what a state.'

'Who do you think you are?' I joke. 'Mr Darcy?'

'See-through shirt included,' he retorts, and my eyes drop instinctively to his torso — he's not wrong. His shirt is plastered to him, displaying the outline of his chest, allowing me to follow the trail of dark hair creeping over his collar right down to where it meets his bellybutton. And a little bit beyond that, too.

He coughs, and I tear my gaze away, feeling myself flush. I force myself back on track — Graham. We were talking about Graham.

'You saw him trying to make us more than it was.' I realise. His words come back to me: *I can't let someone else get hurt.* I spell it out, speaking slowly as I assemble my thoughts. 'You saw me and Graham . . . and you assumed . . .'

'That you were with him,' he states. 'That everything I thought had been a big misunderstanding.'

I stare beyond him to the rain sheeting down, bouncing off the pavement. He's soaked to the skin. God, what a mess. Not him — he is categorically *not* a mess, from what I can see. And I can see a lot. 'Adam . . .'

'Wait. Wait, I have more to say.' He swipes at the rivers of water trickling down his forehead. 'Now that we've cleared things up, can I just . . .' For a moment he looks unsure, but then his brow hardens. 'I have something to say,' he repeats.

'Adam, I'm—'

'You can be kind,' he interrupts, looking for the first time like he's certain of what's coming out of his mouth, 'or you can be ruthless, but shit will still happen to you.' He wipes his eyes with the back of his hand, still catching his breath. 'But what you can't ever do, is let someone else walk all over you.'

I frown. 'What has this got to do—'

'All you can't tell yourself stories, either,' he continues, 'about who you deserve, and who deserves you. All you can do,' he takes a small step towards me, 'is choose your people, and hold on for dear fucking life.'

All the breath seems to have left my body; my heart is in my throat.

'So again,' he's so close now, we're only centimetres apart. Droplets of water continue to drip slowly onto the carpet, and the pattering of it is suddenly louder than the rain outside. 'You can tell me to fuck off if you want to. It's your choice, Eve.' His breathing is heavy. 'We fit. It's early days, but we *fit*. I see it, and something tells me you see it, too.'

I can't speak.

He steps closer, so close, the wetness of his shirt brushes against my arm. 'I choose to stand right here. I choose this. I choose you, us, what I felt between us, whatever that was. I choose to explore it. What do you choose?'

My mouth is on his before I can think. I collide with him, pushing up against him, my hands on his back, in his hair, his hands on my waist, the back of my neck. I give in to it, the pull I've felt since the moment I saw his face, feeling the full dampness of him seep through my clothes.

He kicks the door closed with one foot, not removing his mouth from mine for a second. His shirt comes off, then mine, then everything else, and I feel the strength of him; the power, the urgency.

We go upstairs, him leading, in my house, the carbon copy of his own, as if he knew exactly where to go all along.

CHAPTER 56

Eve

'Ladies and gentlemen,' I scan the audience, my voice level, '*this* is how you start a Twitter frenzy.'

I click onto the next slide, and laughter ripples around the room.

'Some of you might have seen this doing the rounds a few months back.' I walk slowly across the stage, tapping my clicker against my hand. 'Hands up, who did?'

A few hands shoot up in the audience.

'Well, for those of you who didn't, let me enlighten you.'

I click again, and a video begins playing. It's me, on the stage at the Floristry expo, the moment my slides changed. I watch myself talking for the hundredth time, noting the precise moment my face falls as I realise what has happened.

I pause the clip.

'Hashtag flower fail was trending for three hours on Twitter that day,' I say, gazing back out to the auditorium. I hold my hands up. 'I might have fucked up, but sales of orchids went through the roof.'

Laughter rings around the room.

'My point is,' I say, my eyes landing on him, sitting on the back row, a grin plastered across his face. 'No publicity is bad publicity, and it's what we choose to do with the shit life throws at us that really counts.'

* * *

'*Incredible.*' Adam holds my face and plants a kiss on my lips. 'Honestly, feel my hands — feel them! — I'm shaking.'

'Stop it.' I slap him lightly on the arm, my nerves higher now than they were before my talk. 'Do you think it was alright, though?'

'What do you think?' He nods towards reception, where people are lining up to write their email addresses on my *Introduction to Small Business Marketing* sign-up forms.

'Shit,' I say.

Adam laughs and takes my hand. 'Come on, we'll be late.'

We wander out into the car park, where the trees are bare and the brown leaves are almost reduced to mush. Adam checks his phone.

'Are you nervous?' I ask.

'A bit.' He frowns. 'He should be out by now.'

I reach up and kiss him, hard, on the lips. He looks into my eyes, and his shoulders drop, the tension seeming to leave him. 'OK,' he says, 'let's go.'

We mount Adam's new two-seater electric bike and set off, weaving through town towards Didsbury. Adam's push-bike was confined to the shed the second time we met in town for drinks, when he had to cycle home and I got a taxi. It sort of ruined the moment, having to wait for him in the living room for half an hour.

'Here we are.' We pull up outside a breeze-block building, its facade at odds with its beautiful gardens and bright windows.

As we get to the entrance, I stop. 'What if he doesn't like me?'

Adam turns to me. 'Since when has Eve Slater ever doubted herself?' I straighten my shoulders and he grins. 'There's my girl.'

We go past reception and down a brightly papered corridor. Three doors down, on the left, I spot a familiar name. Adam pushes open the door and steps inside.

'Hugh,' he says, walking over to a man sitting in the corner who looks eerily like him. 'I have someone I want you to meet. This is Eve.'

I take a step forward. Hugh regards me steadily, one arm bouncing up and down on the arm of his chair. 'Hi, Hugh.' I sit on the end of the bed opposite him. 'It's really nice to meet you.'

As if from nowhere, Hugh's face splits open and he grins, that same wide smile I love on Adam. I laugh. 'Are you *sure* you two aren't twins?'

Hugh shrieks delightedly, and Adam sits next to me, wrapping his arms around my shoulders. 'He only ruins the eardrums of people he likes; consider yourself accepted.'

'Well,' I say, reaching into my bag, 'as a rule, I only buy gifts for people I like, too.'

I pull out what I've bought, my stomach in knots, hoping against hope that I got it right. I hold the plush Olaf toy out to Hugh, and he takes it, his eyes widening.

Adam throws his head back and laughs. 'Oh, god.'

Hugh inspects the toy for a moment, turning it this way and that, and then squeals and bashes it down onto his lap.

'Oh no, does he not—'

'He *loves* it.' Adam is looking at me in that way again, like I'm fascinating and amusing, and I feel like my heart might explode out of my chest.

* * *

'He's done it!' Adam screams as I run around the living room, plucking at pieces of stray fluff and cat hairs.

'He's . . . he's done it?' I say, excitement bubbling in my throat. 'He's done it?!'

'Yes!' He pockets his phone, picks me up and spins me around. When he puts me down, he kisses me for a long moment. 'He's out, the exams are done.'

'Oh my god!' I cheer. 'That's amazing!'

Adam runs his hand through his hair, the biggest grin spread across his face. 'I can't believe it.'

'Of course you can!' I say, pulling a bottle of wine out of the fridge when I see that he's too distracted to focus on the task at hand. 'He's brilliant, you're brilliant, it was inevitable.'

He paces the room, his hands on his head. 'Just got to wait for results day now.'

'Are you worried?'

'Nope.' He comes up behind me and wraps his arms around my waist. 'I'm not worried at all.' He sighs, 'God, to think things could have been this good after everything that happened in Dublin.'

'Dublin?' I turn around and look at him. 'When were you in Dublin?'

The doorbell rings before he can answer and he walks over, pulling open the door to let everybody tumble in: Piotr, Bil, Ferg and a blonde girl, followed by Will and Benny, and then Jess.

'We found these four on the street outside,' Jess says, shaking her coat out all over the hallway.

'Couldn't remember if it was forty-three or forty-five . . .' Piotr says, and then holds his arms out to me and hugs me tight. 'Good to see you again, Eve,' he extracts himself. 'Feel like I know you better than I know my *own* girlfriend, the amount he goes on about you.'

Adam looks at me and shrugs. 'It's probably true.'

'He's like a broken record.' Bil says. 'Ferg's bought a pair of noise-cancelling headphones.'

'Those are for my tomatoes,' Ferg clarified. 'Studies have shown that horticulturists who listen to music while tending to their—'

'I'm Chloe,' the blonde girl says, stepping in front of Ferg and rolling her eyes exasperatedly at me.

Ferg begins to protest but Piotr throws his arm round his shoulder and says, 'We can discuss the tomatoes *after* dinner, Ferg. When everyone's exhausted all other possible subjects of conversation,' before leading him away.

'Lovely to meet you,' I laugh and give Chloe a hug. 'I've heard lots of great things.'

'All of them true, of course,' she winks. 'Sorry it's taken this long to get us in a room together! I swear life just gets busier and faster every single day.'

'God, tell me about it.' I get the nice, unfamiliar rush of remembering that I have the next two days off — my first since starting my marketing consultancy. A few months ago, the thought of all that free time would have panicked me, but now I'm looking forward to putting my laptop in a drawer, turning off my alarms and seeing where the days take us.

Drinks are passed around, and soon we're all settled in, sitting on the sofas, the floor, the footstools.

I'm sitting next to Will, and I turn to him while the boys are fawning over Old Sausage. 'How are things?'

'Good.' He bounces Benny on his lap. 'Nina's out with friends tonight.'

'Is she doing better?'

'Every day.' He smiles. 'Baby steps.'

'What's for tea then?' Bil asks. 'Need a hand?'

'It's a surprise,' Adam says, raising an eyebrow at me. 'I'm under strict instructions not to interfere in the kitchen.'

'Yes, you stay put,' I instruct, sliding onto the floor next to him and looping my arm through his.

Bil mimes putting his fingers down his throat, and everyone laughs. He turns to me. 'Only joking. You've done him the world of good.'

My eyes land on Chloe, who's sitting on the sofa. She's watching us, a small smile playing on her lips.

'And word on the street is there's a holiday on the cards?' Jess strokes Old Sausage on her lap.

'Yeah.' Adam grins. 'Costa del Sol.'

'Twenty quid says Eve's got a full itinerary planned,' Will pipes up.

'6.20 a.m. Watch sunrise over ancient ruins,' Jess says. '7.13 a.m. Climb local mountain to see views—'

'Alright,' I laugh. 'You can shut up now.'

'Wouldn't have her any other way.' Adam grins at me. He doesn't yet know about my Excel spreadsheet timetable, which documents every hour of our trip, including rest time. I've promised myself that by the end of the week, I'll have reduced it by a third — leaving a bit more room for spontaneity. I've seen the weight lift from Adam's shoulders the past few weeks, and I want to make sure this holiday is perfect for him, too.

I suddenly remember the food and scramble to my feet. I go into the kitchen and pull the oven door open, where a blackened beef wellington is smoking on its tray.

I walk back into the living room and hold my hands up. 'Pizza or Chinese?' I ask.

Laughter and arguments break out over food choices and the stench of the wellington, and as everyone scrabbles to check local takeaways on their phones, Adam sidles over to me and wraps his arm around my shoulder.

I lean my head against his chest, feeling his solid warmth, and listen to his heart beat steadily. I survey the room. Our people, our cat — but soon to be someone else's home. Boxes are already being filled upstairs, ready for the big move two doors down.

I'm attached now, I think. There's no hiding from this. No games, no defences, no running away.

This is home.

THE END

ACKNOWLEDGEMENTS

If you've made it this far, yay! That means you finished the book (unless you skipped straight to the acknowledgements, in which case, you do you) and saw it through to its happy ending. So obviously, firstly, I'd like to thank you. Without you, I'd be writing into a void, giggling to myself, intermittently weeping and wondering what it's all for. Thank you for saving me from that fate. You taking a chance on me and using your time to let something that came from my brain filter into yours is truly a pinch-me concept. I am so grateful for you, and I hope more than anything that Adam and Eve's story (this one, not that other one) left you with something, whatever that may be.

An eternal thank you to Tanera, Rebeka and the Darley Anderson team, for believing in this book and getting it into Joffe's hands. Speaking of Joffe, a big whopper of a thanks to Emma, Becky, Kate and the rest of the team for their passion for this story and hard work in getting to where it is today. I'm so glad you fell in love with Adam as much as Eve did.

Thank you to my amazing, wonderful, vibrant, hilarious friends, without whom life would be unbearably dull. Zara, thank you for being even more interested in my career than I am, and for the prize-winning tarka dhal that sustains my very soul. Holly, thank you for being my unpaid therapist and receptacle for my every weird waking thought. Alex and Lauren, thanks for the gossip-swapping marg nights that keep me sane. Amie, thanks for abandoning me for Australia, you cow.

Mum, Dad, Patrick and George — thank you for being the most bonkers group of people anyone has ever met. Life would be quite boring without you in it, and I will always be grateful that I don't have a normal family. To my extended, but equally unhinged, family, thank you for reading, sharing, championing and supporting. You're all top-tier human beings.

Finally, thank you to Stef. I could run with the cliches and harp on about your unwavering support, huge heart and readiness to catch me whenever I falter, but instead I'll just say it simply: thank you so much for being you.

All best,
Mary

THE JOFFE BOOKS STORY

We began in 2014 when Jasper agreed to publish his mum's much-rejected romance novel and it became a bestseller.

Since then we've grown into the largest independent publisher in the UK. We're extremely proud to publish some of the very best writers in the world, including Joy Ellis, Faith Martin, Caro Ramsay, Helen Forrester, Simon Brett and Robert Goddard. Everyone at Joffe Books loves reading and we never forget that it all begins with the magic of an author telling a story.

We are proud to publish talented first-time authors, as well as established writers whose books we love introducing to a new generation of readers.

We won Trade Publisher of the Year at the Independent Publishing Awards in 2023. We have been shortlisted for Independent Publisher of the Year at the British Book Awards for the last four years, and were shortlisted for the Diversity and Inclusivity Award at the 2022 Independent Publishing Awards. In 2023 we were shortlisted for Publisher of the Year at the RNA Industry Awards.

We built this company with your help, and we love to hear from you, so please email us about absolutely anything bookish at feedback@joffebooks.com

If you want to receive free books every Friday and hear about all our new releases, join our mailing list: www.joffebooks.com/contact

And when you tell your friends about us, just remember: it's pronounced Joffe as in coffee or toffee